ESP✝NAS

HISTORICAL
NOVEL

ESP✝NAS

THE EXTRAORDINARY LIFE OF
VENERABLE FATHER ANTONIO MARGIL DE JESÚS
THE APOSTLE OF THE AMERICAS

FERNANDO PÉREZ VALDEZ

In Collaboration With
Peggy Arriola Jasso and Linda Arriola Austin

STEPHEN F. AUSTIN STATE UNIVERSITY PRESS
NACOGDOCHES ★ TEXAS

For more informaion:
Stephen F. Austin State University Press
P.O. Box 13007 SFA Station
Nacogdoches, Texas 75962
sfapress@sfasu.edu
www.sfasu.edu/sfapress

Distributed by Texas A&M Consortium
www.tamupress.com

LIBRARY OF CONGRESS CATALOGING-IN-PUBLICATION DATA

Valdez, Fernando Pérez
Espinas / Fernando Pérez Valdez - 1st ed.

p.cm.

ISBN-13: 978-1-62288-016-4

1. Title

*If Your Father were to see a ball of gold, which is such a heavy metal,
suspended in the air, would you not be persuaded that it maintained itself
there alone? No, but rather that some invisible hand had sustained it. In
this way, I have been a brute, and if God had not had me in his hand, I do
not know what would have become of me.*

Venerable Father Antonio Margil de Jesús
At his last confession to Friar Manuel de las Heras

*He had been the voice that rang out in the cities, towns, and country sides,
in the mountains, and in the deserts, even in the most distant nations.
He was the lion's voice for idolatries, the law's voice for penitent ones, and
the angel's voice for virtuous ones, lightening voice for perverse ones, the
father's voice for distressed ones, and the Shepard's voice for lost sheep. A
voice that, while he now rests in the grave, will remain echoing in the entire
sacred religion, in all this New World and it will deserve resonating to
the Roman Curia. A voice that, although dead, preaches to all of us, and
undeceiving us, gives us breath and fervor, and I hope to carry his untiring
zeal for the salvation of souls his apostolic works, and his holy examples
very much in my memory on my next trip.*

The Very Reverend Doctor
Don Carlos de Bermudez y Castro
Archbishop of Manila
1669-1729

Venerable Anthony Margil de
Jesus - Founder of Missions in Texas
from 1715 to 1726.

PROLOGUE

The 300th anniversary of the founding of the East Texas missions by Father Antonio Margil de Jesús and his fellow Franciscan priests will be celebrated in 2016. It will be a celebration honoring the life and enduring legacy of a most remarkable man who with a peaceful and gentle demeanor brought Christianity to thousands of indigenous during the early settlement of New Spain.

His life began in 1657 when he was born to poor, but respectable parents in the city of Valencia, Spain. He entered the Order of the Friars Minor (O.F.M.), at the age of fifteen and was ordained to the priesthood at the age of twenty-four. The majority of his life was devoted to delivering the word of God to far-reaching and uncharted territories in New Spain. In 1683, he volunteered for the American missions and when he left his homeland for the unknown New World, his recruiter and mentor Father Linaz de Jesús Maria told him: *what I offer is thorns, no conveniences, as you could face death, torture, persecution, hardship, starvation, and illness during your travels.* The young friar humbly accepted the role of adventurer for God and did not hesitate to accept the thorns of Jesus Christ with love and affection. It was from these thorns, *espinas* in Spanish, from which this book drew its name.

Father Margil arrived in New Spain in 1683 and for the next 43 years he served as a missionary in North and Central America. He gave up all personal belongings and walked in his meager habit in crude leather sandals, aided only by a wooden staff, a crucifix and his sacred vessels. He fasted every day of the year, never eating meat or fish, slept little and passed his days in prayer. During this time, he established countless new missions in remote territories and converted thousands of indigenous from the jungles of Costa Rica to the borderlands of Louisiana. All the while, he titled himself and signed every letter as *la misma nada* – nothingness itself.

One of his journeys in 1716, when he was nearly sixty years old, was the Domingo Ramon *entrada* into the land of the Tejas Indians in the eastern most regions of the Spanish borderlands. Due to illness, he was unable to leave with the original band of soldiers, priest and families. They left him at the *Mission San Juan Bautista* on the verge of death, but soon he made a miraculous recovery. Days later, with the aid of two guides, he traveled at a record pace the harsh 500 miles to rejoin the Ramon party. For the next six years, except for a short period of abandonment, he labored among the *Caddos* and indigenous in the area.

His epoch adventure included the founding of three Franciscan colleges whose aim was to train monks in the evangelization of infidels in New Spain: two were in México and one was in Guatemala. The hundreds of Franciscan missionaries trained in these colleges were bearers of Christianity throughout Spanish Americas. In addition to the six Texas missions, he is noted for founding of the *Mission of San José and San Miguel de Aguayo* in San Antonio. It is known as the *Queen of the Missions* because of its imposing complex of stone walls, bastions, granary, and magnificent church.

As a messenger of God, historians believe he walked over 2,000 miles in harsh conditions and in rugged, uncharted lands. He is credited with the conversion of over 80,000 Indians in Guatemala alone, founding missions in Costa Rica, Nicaragua, Guatemala, and México, and with countless miracles. The best known of his wondrous deeds, what some call a *miracle,* was performed in 1718 at the *Mission Nuestra Senora de Guadalupe* in Nacogdoches. Legend tells of a long period of severe drought that caused much loss of life and crops. One day, after a long night of prayer, Father Margil went to the dry bed of the LaNana Creek and struck a rock with his staff. Water poured forth giving the people much needed relief from the long drought. For this reason, the sight along the LaNana Trail in Nacogdoches was commemorated by the Texas Historical Commission in 1978 as *Los Ojos de Padre Margil* to symbolize the faith and endurance of the Spanish missionaries.

In 1936, Father Margil was raised to the status of venerable, one level below sainthood, by Pope Gregory XVI. He now awaits additional documentation, which should be obtained through his intercession, before he can be conferred sainthood, the highest of holy honors bestowed by the Vatican. Although his ecclesiastical leadership in Texas was brief, on the day he is raised to sainthood, Texas will receive its first patron saint.

Espinas, written as a historical novel, follows the life and accomplishments of this honorable man in the form of fictitious stories. The historical events told in this book really happened, but not exactly in the way told in the book. First published in Spanish in spring of 2012, it was later translated to English with the assistance of Peggy Arriola Jasso and Linda Arriola Austin. The book has ecclesiastical support from the Franciscan Province of Saints Peter and Paul of Michoacán, and the former bishop of the Diocese of Tyler in Texas, Bishop Alvaro Corrado del Rio, S. J. Several historical books have been written on Father Margil, but the author believes the style of Espinas will help its readers better understand the epoch adventures of Father Antonio Margil de Jesús, the great Apostle of the Americas.

PART ONE: SPAIN

I

Very Noble, Illustrious and Twice Loyal City of Valencia
August 1657

The city of Valencia overlooking the Mediterranean Sea sparkled like a jewel atop a flat plateau. Heat radiated from the clay rooftops as the breeze from the nearby sea offered relief from the sticky moist air of the Levantine summer. The birds sang somewhere high in the arched sky, but the lucid songsters were lost in the trees encircling the ancient market square. Floating through the air was an aromatic blend of roasted pumpkin, oranges, celery, artichokes, sliced chicken, and lard so pungent it adhered to everything it caressed.

The central plaza in front of the *Llotja de la Seda,* the silk trading building, covered one hundred sixty acres and was renowned for its vastness. It bustled with activity and incessant noise as the populace loitered through the gardens, visited with friends and purchased their daily supplies. At the center of the huge open square, a minstrel sang the praises of the heroic battles of Don Rodrigo Diaz de Vivar, *El Cid Campeador,* recalling the way he regained the Kingdom of Valencia from the dominance of the Moors in ancient times. The attentive children listened and imagined the brave knight swinging his *Colada* and *Tizona* swords in fierce battles against the dreaded infidels. Tucked away in a corner, a fortune teller invoked deities with her tarot cards as jesters, acrobats and buskers entertained the crowds.

Still fresh on the minds of most of the Valencianos was the tragedy that occurred in the square forty years earlier. It was when a make-shift scaffold collapsed during a bullfight and killed sixty onlookers and injured and maimed many more. Although these numbers were staggering, they were nothing compared to the Algerian plague that decimated the entire city ten years earlier.

From their home located near the center, Don Antonio Fradella and his wife Doña Paula solemnly walked along the narrow, cobbled streets toward their parish church. Doña Castillo was elegantly dressed, from head to toe, in a black lace dress and a matching lace mantilla. She carried her godson swaddled tightly in her veil. They passed the magnificent trade building, with its imposing battlement tower and splendid halls. Following closely behind, the baby's father Juan Margil was stately dressed in a fine black coat and trousers and was trailed by a scurrying female servant.

With a firm commitment, they walked across the market square amid the various carts of fish, vegetables and fruits. They passed the white outdoor stands, which lined the market place, where the vendors sold fabrics, blankets, linens and lace, fans, flowers, oils, and a wide variety of other products. Neatly arranged in wooden boxes, were fruits and vegetables, and delicious hams and sausages hung from poles. Elsewhere Spanish traders, with their mules laden with goods, shouted vulgarities and struck their beasts while trying to break through the crowds.

The party continued across the plaza, where they passed sailors from all over the Mediterranean: Portuguese, Italians, Greek, and many more. Mixed among the seafarers was a roving band of gypsies, with itchy fingers, polluting the air with the blue, sweet smoke from their *cigarillos*. Aristocratic ladies, with their noses in the air and maids at their beck and call, haughtily walked past the distinguished gentlemen, humble monks, and valiant soldiers. Young maidens, peeking from behind their delicate lace fans, were vigilantly guarded by their matronly chaperones.

The marketplace authorities daily monitored the goods for molded, bitten, rotten, and damaged merchandise and made sure the retailers did not enter the square before eleven o'clock in order to prevent rising prices. They also kept an eye out for the occasional wily thief.

As the party passed near the market square, they saw the Church of Saint Johns, also known as the *Esglesia de Sant Joan del Mercat* with its belfry and lofty slender tower. It was named for both John the Baptist and John the Evangelist. The church faced into the square where the facade of the Plaza del Mercado was highlighted by a central sculpture of The Lady of the Rosary. Over the sculpture, the gothic images of Saint John the Baptist and Saint John the Evangelist flanked the clock tower.

Don Antonio shuddered as he remembered a story his father told him when he was a young child. He said if a boy was naughty, he was taken to the square to see what was hanging from the vane at the top of the clock tower. When the boy was distracted by trying to figure out what kind of bird was hanging there, he was abandoned by his father. It was said that traders would then pick him up and force him to work in exchange for food and shelter. The story was that after a few years, the father would return to reclaim the boy, who by then had learned both an important lesson and a skill.

Throughout Don Antonio's childhood, he harbored the fear of being left to the traders in the back of his mind. It was many years later when he learned the church's weathercock, with an inkwell hanging from its beak, actually represented the eagle of the Book of Revelation of the Apostle John, and in reality, fathers did not actually abandon their sons in the plaza.

The baptismal party continued down the old street of the *Paja*, which separates the church and the central market square. When they reached the corner and turned left, they stood directly in front of the imposing facade of the church.

Don Antonio saw the large circle above the entrance that dominated a great part of the huge temple wall. The people used to call it "The 'O' of Saint John." Don Antonio thought as he smiled at the popular ingenuity. In actuality, the huge circular cavity should have contained a large polychrome, stained glass, rose window that was never built, and because of its absence a great, blind opening was left at the top of the dome.

On the main gate they admired the allegorical figures of an eagle which represented Saint John the Evangelist, and a lamb which represented Saint John the Baptist.

Slowing her pace, Doña Paula, now beside her maid, adjusted the infant in her arms to allow his elegant flowing white gown to unfold. The cherub face of the innocent child glowed like a beacon of light in a dark night as he smiled at the unfamiliar face. Following closely behind, were Don Antonio, Juan Margil, friends and family; all were an important part of welcoming the child into the faith community. His mother Esperanza Ros remained at home under a strict quarantine as was the custom.

"You must purify yourself," she was told sternly by her midwife who shook her finger as she talked. "You shall not go out for forty days and you shall not make any efforts to do so, and you must not touch water, and no weaving during this time of purification!"

They reached the temple and mingled with family and friends waiting there. Soon the priest met them at the door of the church and gave a brief welcome speech, and asked the godfather if the child had been baptized, and he responded negatively.

Then he asked, "Have you chosen the name for this child?"

"Agapito Luis Paulino Antonio, your Reverence," respectfully replied the godfather.

"And what do you ask of the Church for this child?"

"Baptism," the godfather replied.

The priest proceeded to breathe three times on the child's face to exorcise the evil spirit, the one who comes with original sin.

Ceremoniously he made the sign of the cross on the baby's forehead and chest, as a symbol of redemption, and then laid his hands on the child and put a bit of salt in the newborn's mouth.

Placing the end of his stole over the child, the priest and the sponsors entered the church followed by the crowd of family and friends. On the way to the baptistery, they recited in unison the *Apostles' Creed* and the *Our Father.*

Don Antonio was always amazed at the lavish decorations in the chamber of the Church of Saints Johns. Stretching across the ceiling and the sides of the vast nave were large medallions adorned with scenes from the lives of Saint John the Baptist and the Apostle John. Although the temple of the church was still being rebuilt after the terrible fire at the end of the last century, the beautiful frescos with biblical themes had been saved and were still visible to be admired by all.

At the baptistery, the priest recited a prayer of exorcism from a large black book. He touched his thumb to his mouth and then rubbed the child's ears with a small bit of saliva, and said, "Be opened."

Then the priest rubbed the baby's tiny pink nose and continued, "For a savor of sweetness, and to you, Oh devil, be gone! For the judgment of God is at hand."

The priest then asked the boy, "Antonio, do you renounce Satan?"

"I do renounce him," replied the godfather for the child.

The priest then changed his violet stole for a white one and poured water from the baptismal font over the head of the child three times. He proclaimed profoundly, "I baptize you in the name of the Father, and of the Son, and of the Holy Spirit."

With these words in the very noble, illustrious and twice loyal city of Valencia, on the twentieth day of August, in the year of one thousand six hundred and fifty-seven, the two days old legitimate son of Juan Margil and Esperanza Ros was baptized. The ancient and solemn ceremony set into motion the wheels of a most glorious and epic journey for the Venerable Father Antonio Margil de Jesús, the Apostle of the Americas.

II

"Who are the men playing the drums, *Mamá*?" asked little Antonio.

"They are our King's Royal Guard, my son," answered his mother who could hardly be heard over the cadence of the drums.

"They are leading the procession," she added.

Antonio's family was in the *Plaça de la Mare de Deu*, the Mother of God Square, opposite the beautiful gate of the Apostles at the Cathedral of Valencia. The figures of the Disciples of Christ were carved in stone and were all depicted in long robes and with beards except for the Apostle John. Some of the images appeared to be looking toward the crowd, some toward the square and others faced the temple. Above the vestibule, stood the image of the Blessed Virgin Mary with Jesus cradled in her arms, and surrounded by eight musical angels. Overhead, the Star of David was formed in a huge rosette of precious stone filigree.

The cathedral bells rang melodiously in the giant octagonal bell-tower of *El Micalet*, which was attached to the Cathedral of Valencia, and visible all over the city. On the hundreds of steps leading up to the cathedral, the worshipers pushed and shoved trying to gain a favorable position for the fantastic view.

The number of people who came to participate in the great procession of the Corpus Christi was staggering. As the crowds swelled, the fences bulged and the guards struggled to keep the pathways free for the passing caravan.

A few days earlier, the *trompeta public*, the heraldic trumpet player, had gained the attention of the crowds so the event could be announced by the town criers and bailiffs. In the proclamation, the people were reminded of the Solemnity of the Feast of the Body and Blood of Christ and the route the procession would take. In anticipation of the event, pathways were adorned with fragrant herbs and colorful flowers while balconies and windows were beautifully decorated with flags, tapestries and banners.

Fortunately Antonio and his family, consisting of his mother and two sisters, found a small hollow near the door of the church where they stood to witness the seemingly endless procession leaving the gates of the cathedral.

The parade began with the Royal Guard, in gala attire, marching stately in front of the procession. Behind the guards were the Kings of Arms elegantly dressed in coats of silk, white gloves and high collars and carrying banners, They carried the Catalonian flag with its four red stripes on a yellow background topped with a blue stripe on its standard, as did every parade entry

Next in the procession came the Archbishop's cross and candlesticks, followed by the city parishes, led by their chaplains elegantly attired with white taffeta capes and holding ornately carved crosses high overhead. For as long as anyone could remember, the parishes competed against each other for the best decorated cross during these parades. Members of each parish carried their patron saint on a litter and were followed by the parish guilds proudly carrying their banners. Antonio and his family could see the contingent from the Church of Saint Michael carrying Saint Michael the Archangel. Another was the Parish of Saints Johns carrying images of both Saint John the Baptist and Saint John the Evangelist; and another was the Parish of the Santa Cruz carrying on their shoulders the figure of Saint Helen, and so on.

The procession ended with workers from trade unions carrying their union flags and cheerfully waving them in the air to form colorful antics. Each guild also carried their respective patron saint on a litter. The guild of pack-saddle makers carried the image of Saint Anthony Abad; the carpenters displayed Saint Joseph; the boilermakers carried Saint John the Evangelist; the glove makers displayed Saint Bartholomew, and the many other guilds proudly marched with their respective saints.

"Look, *Mamá*, here comes father," said young Antonio with joy, while stretching as far as he could to see his father marching among the workers.

Antonio's family was poor, modest and had no pretentiousness. The legacy Esperanza and John Margil wanted to leave their children was, above all, a solid spiritual foundation. It was this lifestyle that provided the pathway to consecrated religious life for Antonio and one of his sisters.

"Isn't it wonderful to see your father, children?" Esperanza said happily.

Next in the procession came the characters from both the Old and New Testament. Moses carried the Tablets of the Law; the Ark of the Covenant was carried on the shoulders of the representation of eight ancient priests; King David, dressed elegantly, wore his crown. Tobias, Saint John the Baptist, the Apostles, and many more were also a part of the event.

Of special interest to Antonio, were the monks dressed in the brown sackcloth of penitents, with a white rope tied humbly around their waists. Some wore humble sandals, and others were barefoot.

"Who are they?" he asked.

"Franciscan friars, my son, followers of Saint Francis," replied his mother.

The charisma of all the religious men impressed young Antonio, and he was particularly drawn to the Franciscans who carried a statue of their patron saint proudly on their shoulders.

"Who is that saint?" Antonio asked, pointing to the figure of the Saint Francis of Assisi.

"He was an Italian friar and preacher who was a friend to the poor. Oh, his history is fascinating, I will tell you his story in the quiet of our home," she said.

The procession continued with the Order of Dominican, in black and white habits with Saint Dominic on their shoulders, and the Mercedarians with Saint Raymond Nonatus.

Next marched the twenty-four venerable old men called *Els Cirialots* who represented the Elders of the Apocalypse. They were impeccably dressed, had long white beards, and carried enormous, white candlesticks more than nine feet tall.

Then from the cathedral came the senior figures, both civil and religious, including the Canons, with red robes and brocaded capes, the Honorable President of the Court, and the Honorable Valentian Counselors, elegantly dressed in their black damask robes with their medals and awards.

With great reverence, the crowd humbly watched as loud bursts of artillery announced the entrance of the most Blessed Sacrament, the holy body of our Lord Jesus Christ. Clouds of incense gave way to a great gold and silver monstrance, fourteen feet tall, ornately carved, adorned with precious stones, and covered by a beautiful canopy embroidered in gold. It was accompanied by six young men wearing elegant costumes of red and white velvet and silk.

As the Body of Christ passed, everyone, old and young alike, knelt and reverently blessed themselves, "In the name of the Father, Son and Holy Spirit."

Lastly, twenty-four chaplains carried the sedan chair of the illustrious and Most Reverend Archbishop of Valencia, Don Martin Lopez Ontiveros. He was accompanied by a tender group of children dressed in white, like angels.

Closing the procession was a marching band, followed by the townspeople including Esperanza holding the hands of her children. By this time, the entire street was lined with a variety of flowers, and the air was filled with the lingering smell of incense.

The parade route, no more than a mile, was the same route taken by Kings in their centuries of visits to Valencia. Although short, everyone including Esperanza and her family were delayed several hours on their return to the gate of Almoina, on the opposite side of the cathedral, due to the great number of people in the city for the most solemn and holy holiday of the year.

Young Antonio was mesmerized by the reverence of the celebration, and every nuance of the courtship was indelibly recorded in his mind. As soon as he returned to his home, he took tiny pieces of wood, with fabric, stones and other materials, and reproduced small altars and the holy men. He then reenacted the reverent processions and ceremonies. He imagined that the little figures came to life, and he joined them in celebrating the glory to God, as he so yearned to do.

Antonio's virtues were not merely outward signs, but his love for others burned within his soul. Often at school he lovingly shared the lunch his mother prepared for him with the poorest of his classmates.

Most of all, he preferred spending time in the church rather than playing like the other children. His preference was with Benediction when the priest at the temple blessed the people with the Blessed Sacrament displayed in an elaborate monstrance. Despite his young age, Antonio became enthralled in constant prayer and reflection, and often stayed in the church in Eucharistic adoration late into the night.

"Antonio," his mother scolded him, "where have you been? You have not eaten all day!"

"Do not be mad at me," the little boy answered innocently, "I have been in the presence of Our Blessed Sacrament today, but it seemed as though I was there for just a moment."

With a sad face, he added, "I did not realize how long I stayed, until the sacristan reminded me it was time to go home."

"Oh, my boy, come here!" said his mother with tears in her eyes, "someday you will be a saint!"

Many years later the memories and experiences with his mother, "the old holy woman" as he so lovingly called her, would be cherished and embraced as he faced difficult moments in the faraway lands of New Spain.

III

𝔉riar Antonio looked up to see the imposing castle perched atop a rocky ledge overlooking city of Denia and the sea below. Since he lived at the Convent of Saint Anthony of Padua, located only a musket shot from the stately castle, he had witnessed the mass of solid stone many times, and each time great emotion exploded within his soul.

He was now nineteen years old and found his life in the convent calm and peaceful. He very much enjoyed the mild weather of his home in Valencia, but he found the weather in Denia a close rival as it was an envy of the entire kingdom.

When he meditated on his short life, he felt as if it was just yesterday when he was fifteen and entered the *Order of Friars Minor,* also known as the Franciscan Order. It was there at the Convent of the Crown of Our Lord, on the river Turia in Valencia, that he took his first vows. He remembered the convent church where his neighbors worshiped a relic of a piece Christ's crown of thorns. Unbelievably three years had passed since that time.

In the solemn and emotional ceremony, he received his first Franciscan habit from the hands of the Reverend Father Guardian Joseph Salelles and the Provincial Minister and Very Reverend Friar Diego Bernabéu. As a novice, he was guided by Friar Francisco Ordano, an exemplary teacher in the works and a wise judge of the words. For the next year of probationary period, he prayed and fasted continuously to show his willingness to serve God for the rest of his holy life. After successfully passing all requirements of a novitiate, he made his profession to become a Franciscan friar and took his vows of poverty, chastity, and obedience on the 25th day of April 1674.

In complete obedience to the holy orders from his superiors, he went to the Convent of Saint Anthony of Padua in the Marquesat of Denia to continue his studies in the course of arts. While there, he was an excellent student who astonished his teachers with his exceptional ability in the field of philosophy. His dedication to the study was so great, that even when he went into the city to beg for food, he mentally reviewed the philosophical teachings of the Church.

The traditional families of Denia opened their arms to Friar Antonio and he found them both hospitable and kind and his work among them uncomplicated. Often he and his parishioners gathered around an outdoor stone fireplace preparing scrumptious dishes of native food. His favorite was *paella*, rice flavored with saffron and olive oil prepared in a huge iron skillet. This local delicacy was composed of all sorts of ingredients including: shrimp, tomato, crab, green beans, oysters, sausage, squid, pork, sausage, artichokes, and more. However, he found the best ingredient of all was the delightful conversation that took place around the fire as they cooked.

"Truthfully, wives and mothers are role models for families," an old Valenciano said with pride.

"Mothers love their families, living solely for love and reverence for the elderly. They are dedicated homemakers and devoted to religious services. They view their lives with serenity, without fanaticism and judicious detail. Their hard work is extraordinary, but they also like to be cheerful and optimistic all the time, even when life is hard for them," they continued.

This made Father Margil remember the pleasant evenings as a child, when he and his sisters sat at the feet of his reverent mother as she quickly and artfully hand stitched their clothes.

"Your father hasn't money for a new coat," she told them affectionately, "but with this mending, it will look as good as a new one."
While she worked, his mother told them stories about the saints. Little Antonio loved to listen to the stories, especially the ones about the life of Saint Francis of Assisi.

"Tell it to us once again, Mamá."

"But you have already heard it many times, children."

"We want to hear it again!"

His mother didn't hesitate to leave her handiwork and turn her attention to her children as she began the story with renewed enthusiasm:

"Once upon a time, there was a young Italian man, rich and cheerful, who wanted to be a great gentleman. One day, while preparing to go to war, he heard a voice saying…" Antonio's mother paused to allow the children to move closer to hear what she was about to say, as if it was the first time they heard the story.

"Francis, Francis," said his mother with a hoarse voice, like the voice of God coming from the sky, "go and repair my Church which, as you see, is falling into ruins."

"Did he repair it?" asked Antonio. They all knew the rest of the story, but they wanted to hear their loving mother tell the story again.

"That's right, children. Saint Francis rebuilt the little *Church of San Damiano*, but actually the voice of the crucifix was not referring to that little chapel but to the whole Church as an institution."

"I want to be a Franciscan!" Antonio cried excitedly.

"And I want to be a religious, too!" enthusiastically said his sister.

"And ... I ... I ... no ... no," the other sister said with a sob, "I want to get married and have children."

"Do not cry, my child," her mother said while taking her child in hers arms. "Consecrated life is important, but marriage is also very important because it is the cradle of the new religious. Imagine if everyone wanted to be religious, how would anyone be born later to be devoted to our Lord?"

The children smiled and hugged their mother.

"Tell us another story!" they said in unison.

"Well, but only one more time because your father will return home from work soon and it will be time for dinner," she said.

Little Antonio fulfilled his dream a few years later when he became Friar Antonio Margil de Jesús at a tender age. In doing so, he entered a new life as a Franciscan friar, and in return he found a new family. Now his brothers were the friars, and his new home was the convent. He knew by wearing the habit, made of simple brown sackcloth, he was not only changing his clothes but was also profoundly changing his life. The cord around his waist with three knots would be a constant reminder of the three vows that now ruled his life: poverty, chastity and obedience. Humble sandals, made from crude leather and tied to his feet, replaced his luxurious footwear and reinforced his detachment from material things.

"From now on," the Reverend Father Guardian told the novices the day they took their habit. "You will have to avoid not only what is evil, but what seems evil, or gives occasion to evil. You will have to serve as an example to all people, and you will have to avoid anything that might serve as a scandal to the faithful."

"Of special care, in this new way of life," warned the Father Guardian. "Is the way you treat women."

Father Guardian warned them that special care must be taken with the opposite sex.

"You will have to avoid frequent dealings with women, even those that are models of modesty and piety," noted the Father. "Chastity must be preserved in the midst of women, or it will be hard to keep your reputation intact."

"So," continued the Reverend Father. "To avoid even the slightest occasion of scandal or suspicion, follow the rule of Saint Bonaventure: 'With women, not excepting those of high rank and virtue, be brief in your conversation, and never receive them in your home without a witnesses even if you are going to give them health advice."

All of these maxims and precepts Father Margil kept in his mind and remembered throughout his life. Surprisingly, this new way of life was not foreign to Friar Antonio. He was happy with the change. His new family was now what he loved most, and he devoted all of his time with great enthusiasm to his pastoral duties. However, his heart sank every time he thought of his homeland and his friends and family, but he never forgot the words of his mother in their fireside sessions. They were the words of Saint Francis of Assisi to his disciples:

> *Go, my dear brothers, two by two through different parts of the world, announcing peace to the people and penance for the remission of sins. Be patient in trials, confident that the Lord will fulfill his plan and promise. Respond humbly to those who question you. Bless those who persecute you. Give thanks to those who harm you and bring false charges against you, for because of these things an eternal kingdom isis prepared for us.*

It was here in this most austere countryside and among the most mundane people, he was called by the Lord to serve in a different realm by the way of simplicity and humility. His calling was to imitate the life of Saint Francis and go forth into a life of hardship and mortification carrying the word of God to heathens and infidels in foreign lands. An idea so exceptional and unheard of that Friar Antonio dared not to speak of it aloud.

IV

"Welcome home, Reverend Father," said the officer of the Trading House of the Indies, *Casa y Audiencia de Indias*, as he respectfully handed Father Linaz de Jesús Maria his papers.

"Thank you, Your Honor," the religious replied politely without much thought.

He was back, it was true, but returning to Spain now, Father Linaz knew he was not the same as he was when he left for the New World a few years earlier. He had undergone a radical change, a total transformation, a profound conversion.

Father Linaz watched as the galleon, loaded with goods from the New World, failed to maneuver the depths of the Guadalquivir River making disembarkment at Seville impossible. The cargo, the passengers, and Father Linaz instead unloaded at the Port of Cadiz.

The solemn priest took his papers from the officer and started walking in the direction of the Convent of San Francisco el Real. As he walked, the experiences of his recent years flashed through his mind like the pages of an open book.

Father Linaz was born into a noble family in Mallorca, Spain. It was on this Mediterranean island, in the Convent of Jesús Extramuros of Palma, that he joined the Order of the Friars Minor. While there he had performed his duties outstandingly and had specialized in philosophy and theology. So great were his achievements that he was awarded the post of preacher, *predicador,* in the Holy Church of Mallorca at the young age of twenty-five years. His skill and art in the delivery of homilies drew people from all over the country. With his great success, he next set his goal on the prestigious post of Franciscan teacher, a lector, but he was disappointed when he learned he was not chosen for the position.

Soon afterwards, he met the custodian and pro-minister of the Franciscan Province of San Pedro y San Pablo de Michoacán in New Spain, Very Reverend Father Juan Gutierrez de la Fuente. He had come from the West Indies to attend a meeting of the General Chapter of the Order of Friars Minor held in Rome and was now in Spain to recruit religious to return with him to the new lands.

Father Linaz became one of his new recruits. Soon thereafter, the new missionaries obtained proper permission from the Provincial Minister to embark to the New World where new adventures of religious life waited.

When he arrived in New Spain at the province of San Pedro y San Pablo de Michoacán, Father Linaz rose quickly. In just a few months, he was appointed as lector in arts at the Convent of Querétaro. Shortly thereafter, he was transferred to Zelaya as lector, and shortly after that he became the chair of theology at the Convent of Valladolid.

At Zelaya, he performed his work so impeccably, that in a few months, he was awarded the appointment of guardian of the convent. In those times, a monk was not allowed to hold the chairs of lector and guardian at the same time, but in the case of Father Linaz, the Franciscan provincial definitory made a special petition to the general commissary, Friar Hernando de la Rua, in México City, to allow an exception for him.

Father Linaz' work as guardian was a great responsibility, but the added heavy burden of lector, made his job almost impossible. As if through divine intervention, he was able to accomplish both tasks with ease and efficiency. Often times due to his great eloquence, the parishioners asked that he give the homily during special celebrations. They all loved his preaching.

Besides his virtues as lector and preacher, Father Linaz was an outstanding musician, playing the organ and the ancient *vihuela*, similar to a violin, for the delight of the religious and laity.

Having all these extraordinary gifts and talents, along with youth, Father Linaz was an easy target for the evils of vanity and self-indulgence. At about the age of thirty, he strayed from the righteous path and became vain and consumed by worldly things that he had vowed to avoid.

Father Linaz paused for a moment on his walk to the convent and smiled wryly, recalling the care he had once taken in his dress and shoes during that dark period in his life at the Convent of Zelaya. There he had ventured far from his professed vow of poverty.

With embarrassment, he recalled when he wore fine thin shirts under his habit, instead of the usual raw wool shirt called a *sayalete.* His meals were not simple, but were lavish and tasty delicacies. His cell was excessively decorated with mirrors, curtains and many luxuries to which he had become enamored. It was very different from the simple cells of the rest of his brothers in his order; in other words, Father Linaz had been enslaved by vanity.

With a shudder, Father Linaz recalled the terrible vision of death that came to him one night while at the Convent of Zelaya. The vision transformed him forever. Afterwards, he radically changed his lifestyle eagerly asking the Father Guardian to give him a robe of coarse sackcloth, raw wool underwear, and the most humble sandals. He used fasting and a *cilice,* a spiked belt used by penitents, to punish his body and bend his moral spirit. As penance for his sins, he was consumed with the great desire to spread the name of Christ to the entire world to compensate for his previous lightness and lapse of moral turpitude.

Inflamed by this new desire, his sermons began exuding emotion and spirit. His every word became a fiery dart. The worshippers, unable to defend against the flaming arrows, began to sob and beg God for forgiveness for their past regressions.

He declined an offer for the appointment as Guardian of the Convent of Zelaya when he retired from the job of lector, and with the consent of the Illustrious Bishop and Provincial Superiors, he dedicated his time to visiting the missions around the Bishopric of Michoacán.

For more than six months, he focused on his missionary work in the small towns and villages, and while traveling around the countryside, a seed began to grow in his mind. This seed would eventually grow into the greatest missionary project ever brought to the New World, one that would last for all ages.

The next great step in his life came when, at a Provincial Chapter meeting, he was asked by the guardian to represent the Province of San Pedro y San Pablo de Michoacán at the General Chapter meeting to be held in the City of Toledo in his homeland of Spain.

Complying humbly and with obedience, he embarked on a ship to Spain by way of the Indies fleet. During the long journey, when the monotony of the endless days at sea allowed him time for meditation, Father Linaz continued shaping his new idea. Upon arrival in Spain, he learned that the General Chapter of Toledo meeting would not begin for two more years. He felt this was enough time to present his new idea to the Minister General of the Order of Friars Minor. He was determined to bring to fruition his goal of disbursing the Gospel of our Lord to all corners of the Earth.

Arriving at the end of the cobblestone street, Father Linaz peered at the facade of the Convent of San Francisco el Real. It was here the friars waited to embark on a galleon to New Spain and where those returning would find temporary shelter.

With his heart pounding in his chest, he let out a deep sigh and started the familiar march up the incline to the convent, but this time he had a new vision.

V

𝕱ather Margil and his brother of habit stood along the winding path leading to the convent no more than a half mile from the village of Onda. He looked up at the Convent of Santa Catarina de Onda, nestled in the nearby hillside which was now no more than two hundred-fifty feet away.

However, the heat from the sun was burning the soil and the pace of Father Margil was exhausting. His brother, sweating profusely, complained to his companion. "I can't keep up with you, Father Margil," he said gasping. "You walk too fast!"

Father Margil stopped and waited for his partner and smiled sympathetically. Despite his young twenty-five years and his short stature, he seemed fragile at first glance. The truth was that when Father Margil undertook a march, he was like an arrow, able to soar long distances in the blink of an eye.

"Let me rest, brother," groaned the friar.

The road was rather dry, but they found a little shade under a tree where they could rest and catch their breath.

Father Margil took the opportunity to admire the breathtakingly beautiful view of the valley. At the center of the village, he saw the stately *Castell d' Onda,* with several lines of walls and numerous towers. It was situated on the top of a mountain, the twin to the one on which they stood. It was said that the castle and the village of Onda had as many towers as there were days in a year.

"We are not far from arriving," Father Margil said, encouraging his friend to begin the walk toward the convent.

While he waited for his brother, Father Margil remembered the history of the convent as it was told to him by one of the friars.

"The people of Onda asked for the Franciscans friars to be established in their village," his brother told him. "And the ladies of the Third Order of Saint Francis graciously gave them their *beaterio,* a religious house located on top of the hill. When the Franciscans first arrived, the villagers greeted them with open arms and showed them great affection and sympathy."

Father Margil turned his head to look at his colleague to make sure he could start the march again. His companion stared at the ground with his elbows against his knees. Sweat ran down his reddened cheeks. He pulled out the collar of his habit and fanned his face trying to get a bit of fresh air.

"It seems that you have wings on your feet," his companion said. Father Margil smiled with charity, not knowing that these words would resonate in his ears many more times throughout his life.

A few months before, Father Margil had completed his studies and received his ordination at Denia. He was now ready to go forth and deliver the Epistle and Gospel.

Soon after, the Provincial Minister received special approval and permission to appoint him *predicador* and confessor, and soon he was ordained for these saintly ministries. He was then sent to the village of Onda, about forty-four miles north of Valencia.

When in the village of Onda, he began his work for the priesthood. While there, his superiors and fellow novices observed his charity, his humility, and his willingness to help others. When he was in the laundry room, he didn't wash only his clothes, but often washed everyone else's clothes as well. His director, Friar Joseph Feliu, the theology lector, was surprised but pleased by his patience, delivery and kindness.

He was devoted to his work, and with great joy and enthusiasm, he performed each task assigned to him by the Provincial with great care. In his sermons, Father Margil was profound and clearly preferred subtleties and truth to vain gallantry.

"Compliments serve to flatter the eyes and ears," he would say, "but they leave the listeners with dry and arid hearts."

Shortly after starting his duties in Onda, he was given a new assignment back in Denia; he humbly obeyed his superiors without question. The village of Denia would now receive the fruits of his teachings and wisdom.

Soon the unimaginable call came to Father Antonio to fulfill his dream of disbursing the Gospel to unknown lands.

VI

On this day, the feast of the Ascension of Our Lord Jesus Christ, the majestic church of *San Juan de los Reyes* was overflowing with worshipers. The ancient temple, commissioned by King Fernando and Queen Isabel of Spain, was completed in 1504. It was a magnificent architectural structure of monumental dimensions situated in the western edge of the imperial city of Toledo. Its Gothic-Mudejar artistic splendor left everyone speechless; in fact, most believed the gigantic temple was the largest sanctuary for monks in all of Spain.

Adding to the revelry of the day was the fact that so many had come to be a witness to the first day of the meeting of the General Chapter held by the Order of Friars Minor. The crowds attracted by the transcendental event arrived early from Toledo and the surrounding areas, but the biggest attraction was the enormous fame of the Very Reverend Father Fray Pedro de Mena, preacher of His Majesty and the Franciscan Provincial government of the same province. The Reverend Father Fray Damian Cornejo, Custody of the Franciscan Province of Castilla, General Chronicler of the Order of Friars Minor, and Bishop-elect of Castelamar from the Kingdom of Naples, presided over the mass.

With great vehemence, Father Mena gave the homily and proclaimed his passionate rhetoric from the pulpit of the magnificent church. His words overwhelmed the congregation and tears flowed from the eyes of countless souls, some were mere tears of emotion and others of true repentance.

"I consider this cenacle of *San Juan de los Reyes* as holy as the *Sancta*

35

Santorum of the Temple of Solomon," proclaimed Father Mena. "Inside the oracle of the temple are doors of hope made of olive wood. I look to them once again: *Fecit ostiola.* The doors are very small, without a place for ambition, or the pride we find within us. Only Christ and one successor of San Francisco fit through these doors. They are as closed as the small bed of Solomon's shepherdess. *Lectulus noster floridus. Ostiola.* I look toward these doors with admiration. Outside these doors will remain six days of work, outside will remain all the creatures, and outside will remain all worldly goods. There is only space for prayer. And in prayer, said Saint Bernardo, "even the sunlight offends and clogs the interior light: *Lux impedit interiorem.* Get out vanity and showcase! Get out ostentatiousness and disrespect! Oh! Solomon's Franciscan doors! Oh! Seraphic oracle, Oh! Most Holy *Sancta Santorum* of Friars Minor!"

Father Linaz listened attentively to the words of the illustrious Father Mena overwhelmed by his fervor. Although he was sitting on a bench far from the pulpit, he squirmed as he felt the remarks were directed straight at him. As if they were painful daggers that pierced his soul, a bitter pill to swallow, the words reminded him of his sad past from which he now daily repented. It was a past he wanted to leave far behind.

Two years earlier, when he arrived at the port of Cadiz, he was sick and needed a few days of rest. Once recovered, he went to the Court of Madrid where he presented himself to his superiors, who immediately recognized him for his reputation of modest words and religious bearing. Encouraged by his many positive references, the Court offered him the position of missionary preacher This post allowed him to do mission work in all the kingdoms of Spain and in all religious convents, both male and female. In order to perform these duties, they allowed him the help of two friars, to be personally selected from any Franciscan Province of Spain. This license was granted with the approval of Friar Juan Luengo, the General Commissary of the Indies, and Reverend Father Fray Miguel de Avengózar, the Apostolic Nuncio and the General Commissary of the Order of Friars Minor.

The licenses were upheld by the archbishops and bishops of the places where he would journey giving homilies, confessions, and doing mission work. As part of his duties, he was to spend one year on the island of Mallorca, his country home, where his parents and family lived. While there, he found favor with his old friends and family as he developed his homily skills with extraordinary precision.

Such was the affection and esteem of Father Linaz to the local people, that when he left the village to embark on his trip, he was followed by a large crowd. With great devotion, many ripped pieces of his habit to keep as a memento. By the time Father Linaz arrived at the port, his habit was ripped to shreds and had to be replaced. The Viceroy, in anticipation of his greatness, preserved what was left of his frayed habit as a holy relic.

Arriving in the Iberian Peninsula, he preached in Barcelona and Lleida. By summer, he was back at the Court of Madrid where he preached in the squares and convents until the end of that year. In Madrid, he met with the Minister General of the Order of Friars Minor, Father Joseph Ximenes Samaniego, who was successor seventy-two of San Francisco de Asis. The Minister had just returned to Madrid after attending several Provincial Chapter meetings. Father Linaz politely informed him of the details of his future evangelical mission project in the New World.

"In the fields of America are countless heathen Indians, indigenous infidels," Father Linaz told the General Minister. "They are condemned without a remedy because of a shortage of preachers and ministers. Recalling the words of Our Lord Jesus Christ, I respectfully say to your Paternity: *The harvest is abundant but the workers are few.*"

With the grace of the Holy Spirit, Father Linaz asked if a petition for a missionary monastery in the Indies could be made at the General Chapter. It would be designed to allow him to perform as a missionary apostolate in those faraway lands. He felt the religious from Spain could especially help the inhabitants from the Sierra Gorda and the region comprised of the Franciscan Custody of Rio Verde. According to his proposal, the new convent of the missionaries would be placed in the town of San Juan del Rio.

"We already have convents of our brethren in those lands, Father Linaz, isn't it true?"

"Yes, Your Paternity, but the work of the Franciscan friars remains in the towns they serve, often doctrinas or parish chairs. But there are many other towns and small villages, which actually are not reached by the convent's work. Remote lands at the borders, on top of the mountains or in the jungle, places where the infidels have yet to hear the word of our Lord. We want to reach those places with missionaries from the new convent. The idea is not to wait for such infidel souls to come to us; but rather, we go out of the convents and reach them in their most remote lands."

After thinking for a moment, the Minister General agreed with the points raised by Father Linaz, but he suggested that it should not just include a project for the Sierra Gorda and the Custody of Rio Verde, but a more ambitious, far-reaching project.

"My proposal, Father Linaz, is the creation of a College of the Propagation of Faith, *Colegio de Propaganda Fide,* for the West Indies."

The friar was astonished! This was more than he had dreamed. He was shocked when the Minister General continued saying:

"I think it's best to appoint a friar as head of a group of twenty-four Apostolic preachers for New Spain."

The minister paused, thinking about the project, and then added, "I also suggest to your paternity, that the competent authority of these missionaries should be the General Commissary of the Order in the New Spain."

To carry out the project, the minister asked Father Linaz to prepare a detailed report to be submitted to the definitory of the Order of Friars Minor, during the General Chapter meeting to be held in Toledo the following year, to the Royal Council of Indies, *Consejo Real de Indias,* and to the King of Spain as well.

Several months later, with great enthusiasm, Father Linaz came to the Imperial city of Toledo. As the friar walked towards the town, he paused as he crossed the Tajo River. Few sensations made such an impact as to leave an indelible image in his mind, as the one of crossing the river. He always loved this walk and above all, seeing the imposing castle of *Alcazar of Toledo.* Continuing his march, Father Linaz was filled with emotion and with great anticipation.

When the General Chapter in Toledo ended after eighteen days, Father Linaz was convinced his new mission project was very near a beautiful reality.

VII

Royal Palace and Village of Aranjuez
Spring of 1682

𝕱ather Linaz looked around the spacious hall of the Royal Palace located in the village of Aranjuez. It was just one of the many rooms of the royal estate located south of Madrid where the Tagus River and the Jarama River merge. The living room was small compared to the size of the palace, but enormous in the eyes of the Father Linaz. It was richly decorated with large, crystal-cut chandeliers hanging from the ceiling like a sparkling waterfall. The walls were covered with oversized paintings depicting scenes of biblical subjects and large mirrors elegantly framed in gold. The doors were covered with majestic curtains of golden velvet cloth. Father Linaz, seated on an extravagant high-backed chair, silently wondered where the countless doors led. Against each wall, tables were lined with stately sculptures of alabaster and porcelain. Splendid murals covered the ceilings and depicted sacred scenes from the Bible. Father Linaz was overwhelmed. To anyone who was not accustomed to such majesty, a visit to the Royal Palace was breathtaking.

The Royal Palace of Aranjuez was used each year during the spring to relieve the royalty residents from the dust and drought because they were able to use the water from the adjacent rivers. For this reason, the entire court moved to the picturesque town with its extensive gardens annually where they found pleasure promenading among the many fountains and beautiful marble statues.

Along with the members of his Majesty's Royal Court were the Royal

Council of Indies which had no headquarters because it needed to always be as close to the King as possible. The Council advised the King on administrative, military, justice, and government issues pertaining to the West Indies.

For this reason, Father Linaz had traveled to Aranjuez to present his proposal to create the Franciscan missionaries' College for the Propagation of the Faith in the West Indies to the Council. He knew a favorable decision from the Council was of vital importance to the success of his great mission project. It had already been approved by the definitory of the Order of Friars Minor during the Chapter General of Toledo, and now he just needed the support of the Crown, the King of Spain.

After a long wait that seemed eternal to Father Linaz, a door opened and a court bailiff appeared dressed soberly in a velvet jacket and black cape, a ruffled neck of white silk, white gloves, a stylish hat touched with a fine broad red feather and sturdy black boots. His military attire greatly contrasted with the simple brown hooded habit tied with a white rope and humble leather sandals of the penitent friar.

With elegant manners, the bailiff led the friar into the grand hall where the Council of the Indies had been deliberating for several hours.

As they walked into the imposing room, Father Linaz was overwhelmed. A score of advisors, persons of high and noble rank, elegantly dressed in their finest wardrobe, were on high podiums on either side of the large hall. On another platform was His Excellency Don Vicente Gonzaga Doria, Interim Governor of the Council of the Indies. On each side were two secretaries, one for New Spain and one for the Vice-Royalty of Peru, each with his own corresponding senior officer and treasurer. At a small desk placed at one end of the room was the notary who was in charge of writing down all the agreements, and the chancellor, the custodian of the Royal Seal who authenticated the council's decisions. Among the members of the council were an astronomer, a cosmographer, a chronicler of the Indies, and lawyer for the poor.

Father Linaz sat on a chair at the center of the room. His hands were sweaty and his stomach was queasy as all eyes were riveted on him. The friar picked up the ends of the white cord tied around his waist and placed them on his lap. His fingers nervously fidgeted with each of the three knots. The spokesman for the Fiscal Council spoke:

"The next item on our agenda, Illustrious Lords," said the prosecutor of the council, "is the proposal of the Reverend Father Friar Antonio Linaz of Jesús Maria: the barefoot religious of the Order of St. Francis, son of the Franciscan Province of Mallorca, retired *Lector* in Arts and Theology, *predicador* and confessor, former Guardian of the Convent of Valladolid in New Spain, Custodian of the Province of San Pedro y San Pablo de Michoacán to the General Chapter and apostolic preacher. We appreciate your presence in this supreme council. I should add that Father Linaz has arrived at this Honorable Council with the illustrious recommendations of the Minister General of the Order of Friars Minor, His Excellency and Most Reverend Brother Joseph Ximenes Samaniego."

The prosecutor and the Father Linaz exchanged friendly nods.

"It is my understanding, honorable Father Linaz, that it is your intention to create a College for the Propagation of the Faith in the West Indies," said the prosecutor. "For which you make a formal request of approval to this Supreme Council to be allowed to recruit twenty-four religious from the Franciscan Provinces of Spain."

"Yes, Your Excellency," Father Linaz answered. "The college would be a training center for preparing Franciscan friars for the arduous missionary work in those lands."

"I ask you, your reverence, aren't these works already being carried out in the convents of the New Spain?"

"Not really, your Lordship," said the friar. "The problem is that the work of the convents and provinces that already exists in the New World has been focused on the pastoral work and has left out missionary work. Indigenous people at the borders are lagging behind and are forgotten. We want to reach them through the missionary work of the College for the Propagation of the Faith. We think that the college should be under the authority of the General Commissary of the Indies and not under the supervision of the Provincial Ministers."

"Are you criticizing the work of the Provincials of the convents overseas, Your Reverence?" questioned the prosecutor.

"No, no, your honor," replied the friar with visible embarrassment, "What we want with the College is to complement the work already performed. It never crossed my mind to criticize the work of the Provincials. The problem is precisely that because of the good work they had done, they are so overworked in their doctrines that it is very difficult to carry out further missionary work in remote areas. That's where this project fits in."

Satisfied with the proceedings, the prosecutor looked at the Governor Gonzaga and slightly nodded his head.

"Gentlemen," said the Governor addressing all those present, "I would like to hear your comments."

"I think, Your Excellency," said one of the Advisors, "the idea of the Provincial Ministers consolidating the Christianization of the actual villages is correct."

"I agree with Your Lordship and I feel extremely bold to judge so lightly the work of the Provincials in the New World," said another of the counselors glancing inquisitorially at Father Linaz.

"I agree too", said another of the counselors. "If we want to win some small 'barbarous nations,' we may neglect and lose a large number of Indians who have already been taught."

"Let me disagree with Your Lordships," said another of the advisors, "but my thinking is similar that of Father Linaz, that the missionary work is also required in those regions where we have not yet arrived and where they have not had the opportunity to accept the Gospel."

"It´s true," said another of the advisors. "If convents actually do not attend them, someone has to go to these Indians. They cannot stay without being catechized."

"It is my understanding," said the first one of the advisors. "that in some cases they have spent huge fortunes, with the help of many soldiers and still have not mastered those small 'barbarian nations,' as we should rightly call them, my illustrious colleagues."

"I intend to approach these people not with the sword but with the cross," Father Linaz responded quickly.

The advisor turned to look at the monk with a scathing look.

"Let me continue, Your Reverence. A few years ago, in the confines of the kingdom, the Governor Arias Maldonado tried to subdue the 'barbarians' of those lands with one hundred and ten heavily armed men and sixty thousand *pesos*. The reports we have are that the Governor was ruined and that this area is, as it was before, an ill-fated expedition. How do you intend to carry out your mission with just two dozen friars?"

"Our mission in the New World will be to convert Indians to Christianity, not kill them," replied the friar emphatically.

"Those Indians are not only 'barbarians' but are wild creatures with animalistic habits, like eating each other," said the advisor with a grimace of disgust.

"Those savages," replied Father Linaz with irritation, "are also sons of God, as are you and I, Your Honor."

The advisor jumped up with his face suffused with anger.

"What insolence! Be known that my family is most honorable and has the purest lineage in the Kingdom. I shall not tolerate the offense of being compared to a wild Indian!"

Putting his hand on the hilt of his sword, he snapped, "I won't challenge you to death for your priestly investiture, but I demand an immediate apology from you!"

A murmur of surprise and alarm spread throughout the hall, but the monk replied with moderation:

"I apologize profusely, Your Honor," said Father Linaz, "I did not intend to offend you. I would never challenge your noble birth. I just wanted to make clear that before the eyes of God, all creatures, even the humblest and the most sinful, deserve to be saved by Him."

"I accept your apology," said the advisor as he returned to his seat. "But I insist it's a waste of time wanting to catechize those natives."

"Do not get lost in vain discussions, Your Honors," the Governor cut in. "I think the question is not whether these people deserve to be saved or not, but who is going to do it. Certainly, the Crown has a strong interest in the conversion and Christianity of indigenous peoples, and our Monarchs have stated it clearly on several occasions through various laws and decrees. Remember in 1493 the Pope Alexander VI, through the Papal bull *Inter Caetera*, entrusted to our Majesties the salvation of those souls."

"I agree that we should strongly support this mission project in the West Indies. If Father Linaz has instituted this enterprise, I think we should give him our support," said another of the advisors.

"Yes, he should be supported," said another, and the rest of the advisors nodded in agreement.

"If the consensus is in favor, the question to our treasurer is if the Crown can financially support this project," asked the Governor to the Treasurer.

"The Royal Treasury can well cover the cost of the transfer of the twenty-four monks selected by Father Linaz, and because his request is not dependent on the Provincials, a pension of three hundred *pesos* a year can be granted for maintenance of each missionary."

"Very well," concluded the Governor. "Then, if Your Distinguished Honors agree to this request, I do not see any impediment to ask His Sacred Majesty, our Catholic King and Lord, who in his infinite mercy, to approve the establishment of the College for the Propagation of the Faith in New Spain."

"Your Honor," said the Governor looking at the advisor who had initially opposed the project, "Have you any objection?"

"If Father Linaz thinks a handful of missionaries can accomplish the conversion of those *barbarians*, then I do not contest," said the advisor curtly. He turned to view the religious and declared, "But I think you will need exceptional men to carry out this feat, because a normal person would be exhausted just by traveling to these remote locations, and that is before he even begins his work as a missionary."

"I believe, Your Honor," said Father Linaz looking into the eyes of the advisor, "That the Lord will give us the strength to carry out our work!"

The advisor raised his shoulders and arms, as if to say it was a doomed enterprise, but the case was closed, and it was no longer his responsibility.

The Governor turned his head to both sides, looking at the advisors for more comments, but there were none.

"Very well," said the Governor as he rapped the gavel, "If there are no other objections, the creation of the College for the Propagation of the Faith in New Spain is approved by this Council."

"I thank Your Excellencies for your extraordinary magnanimity," said Father Linaz with a slight bow.

The prosecutor went to the center of the hall and said to the friar: "I think we still need to clarify a point, Your Reverence."

Father Linaz turned bewildered to see the prosecutor.

"Do you have an idea of the most appropriate location for the creation of this college?" asked the Prosecutor.

"Because the Sierra Gorda and the Custody of the Rio Verde are the regions where the missionary work needs to be conducted, I think the best location would be in the small town of San Juan del Rio, about one hundred miles to north of México City."

"Are you thinking, Your Reverence, of building a new convent?" asked the Prosecutor, who had led Father Linaz subtly to a particularly point.

"Yes, your honor," said the priest with a slight hesitation.

The Advisors immediately flinched in their seats. The Prosecutor withdrew quietly, after making his pointed remarks.

"As I mentioned, Father Linaz," clarified the Governor, "It is the highest interest of this Council of the Indies to support your missionary work; however, I must make it clear that the Crown cannot afford, in any way, the building of a new convent."

"But, then, where will the college be installed?" asked Father Linaz alarmed.

The Governor looked at the Advisors, "Any suggestions, honorable Gentlemen?"

"It is my suggestion," said an Advisor, "That they use any of the existing convents."

Addressing the head member in charge of the affairs of New Spain, the Governor asked, "Could you make a comment on that, Gentleman Secretary?"

The Secretary reviewed a voluminous book given to him by his senior officer. He spent a few moments leafing through the pages, quickly reading some notes and then said:

"According to reports sent to us each year from New Spain, there are two convents of Franciscan friars in the city of Querétaro which is within thirty-three miles of the location that Father Linaz suggests."

He turned more pages and said, with a smile of satisfaction for having the data at hand:

"Here it is," he said pointing to one of the texts. "In this town, there is a large convent dedicated to San Francisco and a smaller one about one thousand yards away dedicated to the Santa Cruz. Perhaps the latter could be granted to the college."

"That is a good idea," said the Governor.

Weighing the suggestion for a moment, he addressed everyone:

"If the Honorable Advisors agree, it is the decision of the Royal Council of the Indies to grant permission to use the Convent of Santa Cruz in Querétaro for Father Linaz' missionary work."

"We agree," chorused the Advisors.

With a tap of the gavel the Governor approved the proposal and the Chancellor proceeded to seal the document that he received from the Chief Clerk that underwrote the decision.

"After a few days we will deliver to you the Royal Charter with the seal and signature of His Majesty, the King Carlos II of Spain," said the Secretary.

The Prosecutor approached Father Linaz signaling that his presence was no longer required. As he left the room, Father Linaz felt a sudden apprehension. He did not like the idea of evicting his brothers of the province of San Pedro y San Pablo de Michoacán, but the decision made by the Council of the Indies was irrevocable.

Within ten days, as if that decision needed greater moral weight, the act was confirmed by means of Apostolic Brief the *Sacrosancti Apostolatus Officium* and signed in Rome by His Holiness Innocent XI. Father Linaz was given the signed and sealed documents, and the College for the Propagation of the Faith was approved.

With patent in hand, he could now start searching for twenty-four religious who would join his missionary work in the West Indies. His great mission project was finally underway.

VIII

"Vou are going to the West Indies where you will suffer greatly from harsh weather and much manual labor," said Father Linaz to the crowd. "What I offer is thorns, no conveniences, no comfort and safety. Be known that where ever you go, only the thorns of the crown of Christ will follow you, day and night as you journey through the strange lands."

From the crowd, Father Linaz heard a small but profound voice, "If Your Paternity accepts me, I am willing to suffer these thorns in silence and without hesitation." It was the voice of the newly ordained Father Antonio Margil de Jesús.

Father Linaz stared at the young priest, slight of build and barely visible, as he peered from under the hood of his robe. He was not tall but carried himself as a tall man. At first glance, the iron strength of the twenty-five year old was overshadowed by his fragile and wispy appearance. As Father Linaz stared into his eyes, he saw fortitude rarely seen in religious his age, and he saw a determination and assurance which he admired and needed for the mission.

Prior to receiving the permission and the proper licenses from the Order of Friars Minor, the Council of the Indies, and the Apostolic Brief of the Holy See, Father Linaz had mentally begun the recruitment process for the religious. In order to get the right men to accompany him to the New World, he would have to search several provinces of Spain for the twenty-four Franciscan missionaries needed.

Friar Linaz wanted the missionaries to be a unique breed of Godly men. They should possess a combination of youth, physical strength, careful training and experience. Retired *lectors*, experts in sacred theology, and outstanding *predicadores* would be perfect for his brigade of exceptional Franciscan friars.

In the province of Castilla, Father Linaz enlisted the first man for his group. He was the Reverend Father Friar Melchor Lopez de Jesús, *predicador* and confessor of the Convent of Santa Maria del Castañar. Despite his age of forty-four years, he possessed great ability and exceptional strength, which was later proven in his short time in the Indies.

From the Convent of San Juan de los Reyes in the City of Toledo, Father Friar Joseph Diez, a twenty one year old *predicador* and confessor joined the army of men. He excelled in his studies at the Novitiate of San Diego de Alcala.

Others joined from the Province of Castilla. They were Father Friar Pedro Sitjar, confessor and *lector* of Sacred Theology; Father Friar Sebastian Bisquerra, predicador, confessor and *lector*; Father Friar Antonio Torres, *predicador*, confessor and theology *lector;* Father Friar Francisco Frutos, confessor, and the lay brother Friar Joseph Martinez.

From the southern Iberian Peninsula, of the province of Andalucía, a new member selected for the group of young missionaries was the young Friar Tomás de León, who despite still being a student, was known for his exceptional religious qualities, as noted by Father Linaz in his acceptance as part of the team.

From the province of Los Angeles, near the city of Cordoba, Father Friar Francisco Hidalgo, a twenty-four year old *predicador,* joined. He was extremely humble but very zealous in his faithful duties. His reputation as a tireless worker would later be confirmed during his work as a missionary in the West Indies.

From the Island of Tenerife in the Province of the Canaries, a request came from Father Friar Francisco Estevez, a young *predicador* and confessor. Despite being thirty-one years old, Father Estevez' references were impeccable. Father Linaz believed him perfect for the missionary work and gave him a patent to join the group. It should be noted here that upon the death of Father Linaz, Father Estevez was appointed his successor as the Commissary of the Indies and Apostolic Prefect of the West Indies.

After gathering the group of twenty-four missionaries, Father Linaz was given a departure date of June 24, the feast day of Saint John the Baptist.

On this faithful day, the men boarded their ships and journeyed from the inner harbor of Sevilla some distance down the winding Guadalquivir River to the coast of Andalusia. They rounded the bar of Sanlúcar de Barrameda, and were happy to reach the port of Cadiz, their last stop before entering the sea. They could hardly wait for their sea journey to begin.

Unfortunately, upon their arrival at Cadiz, Father Linaz learned, much to his and the group of missionaries' despair and dismay, the departure of the fleet to the Indies was postponed for a year. The delay was a catastrophe, as most had to return to their respective convents, and the rest were dispersed to various regions while they waited the next departure.

Now a second recruitment the following year would be necessary. Father Linaz did not know at the time that the postponement was actually a blessing from God. It allowed time for a decree from the Holy Congregation for the Propagation of the Faith to appoint Father Linaz as the Prefect of Missions for the West Indies and a Decree from the Holy Inquisition to ratify his powers. The new appointment gave him far more control and authority to perform his duties in the New World.

With renewed vigor and far more influence, Father Linaz began a new search for his twenty-four missionaries praying he could find some of his earlier disciples. With his old determination, he went back to the island of Mallorca where he felt certain he could find some of the old and maybe some new prospects.

This was true indeed, as several of the missionaries that finally accompanied Father Linaz to the West Indies, came precisely from this area.

Among the ones joining the group was the former Provincial Definitor, Reverend Father Friar Pedro Antonio Frontera, who despite being fifty-three years old and totally bald, showed an exceptional strength and was in good health. His body was more mobile than most men half his age.

In the same province, Reverend Father Friar Juan Bautista Lázaro, scarcely thirty-two years old, joined the group. He was retired from the office of Lector where he was preacher and confessor. His burly frame and premature baldness gave him a bold appearance.

Other brothers joining Father Linaz in the Province of Mallorca were: Father Fray Antonio Llanzor, preacher of theology; Father Fray Miguel Fontcuberta, preacher and confessor; Father Fray Miguel Roche, preacher, Father Fray Antonio Pereda, preacher and confessor; Father Fray Damian

Massanet, preacher and confessor; the theological student Fray Antonio Bordoy, and Friar Jaime Linaz, lay brother.

After recruiting missionaries in Mallorca, he returned to the Iberian Peninsula by way of Barcelona. While in the province of Catalonia, Father Friar Francisco de Jesús Maria Casañes, a twenty-six year old confessor, decided to come along.

One of his last selections came when Divine Providence intervened in Valencia. While he was at the Convent of Corona de Cristo, he crossed paths with the young, but very determined and enthusiastic young priest named Father Antonio Margil de Jesús. The humble young man had only recently been ordained as a priest, but Father Linaz immediately knew Father Antonio was perfectly suited for the mission.

"I welcome you into to our group of missionaries," Father Linaz happily told him.

IX

Port of the Most Noble and Loyal City of Sevilla
March 1683

The notary of the Trading House in Sevilla took a fine goose pen, soaked the tip in an ink well sitting on the desk, and started to write the words dictated to him by the customs officer. There in the Book of Acts, in a script still visible today, he wrote:

A group of barefoot religious of the Order of San Francisco are presented to this Royal Audience of Indies intending to go to the New Spain at the expense of the Royal Exchequer, whose names, professions and sources are described below...

While the officer recorded the data, Father Linaz sadly recalled mourning the death of two friars in Cadiz and a layman from Cataluña. They died while they waited their second departure with Father Linaz to the New World.

The customs officer finished writing the names of the missionaries. Then he announced the total fare, including shipping costs, was seven hundred and fourteen and a half *reales* per man, to be charged to the Royal Exchequer. The amount was paid in cash to the newly appointed Most Reverend Father Friar Juan de Luzuriaga, General Commissary of the Order of Friars Minor for the New Spain and the Philippines, a position he first held in the New World.

"Excuse me, Your Honor, may I ask a pertinent question," said the Commissary to the Officer, "shouldn't it be one thousand *reales* for each one of our brothers?"

"No, Your Reverence," politely intervened the President of the House of Trade. "The amount you say, to be precise, one thousand and forty-nine *reales*, is the amount budgeted to the religious Order of San Agustín by the Fourteenth Law, Fifth Title of the Laws of the Indies. Look here it reads: "*If a priest who travels belongs to the Order of the Dominicans the amount to be allocated is nine hundred seven reales and ten maravedís. One thousand and forty-nine for the friars of the Order of San Agustín, and seven hundred and fourteen and a half reales for barefoot religious of the Order of San Francisco.*"

"I thank Your Excellency for your kind clarification," said the Commissary with a slight nod.

"My pleasure, Your Reverence," said the President with a friendly smile. "Also, let me inform you that the officials of New Spain will release an additional eighteen thousand, three hundred twenty-six Iberian coins of gold and silver called *maravedis* from the Royal Bank account for each one of the friars who reaches his destination."

The Officer intervened:

"By the way," said the Officer, "it is my obligation to remind Your Paternity that as a commissary it is your duty to make sure all friars do not abandon ship on any of the many islands where the vessels stop."

While the Officer was speaking, the Notary set aside the goose quill and took some powder from a small box. Very carefully, he dusted the documents to help the ink dry. After a few moments, he bent the paper and blew lightly to remove the dust.

"Also," said the officer, "you will make sure all friars reach the convent to which they are assigned and make sure they are not diverted elsewhere. They must not go to any other town!"

"I'll take special care with the duties assigned to me by His Royal and Sacred Majesty, our Most Beloved King. I promise, I will," said the Commissary.

Friar Juan de Luzuriaga was a retired *lector* and priest of the provinces of Cantabria and Valencia. He was appointed to the Chair of General Commissary but also held the title of Apostolic Preacher.

The Officer stamped the Commissary's patents with the Royal Seal which were then signed by the President of the House of Trade.

"Your papers, royal charters, patents and decrees, are good, Your Reverence. You may embark on the Royal Fleet. Have a safe trip and now please be so kind as to take your papers."

"Thank you, Your Excellencies," responded the commissary

enthusiastically, as he handed back the papers. Father Linaz accepted them graciously and tucked them safely away in his leather briefcase and put them in his saddlebag.

The large and magnificent building of the House of Trading of Sevilla was bustling with activity. Along the vast and endless corridors, the constant comings and goings of ship captains, officials, pilots, masters, merchants, sailors, stewards, officers, guards, priests, and many other travelers was visible to all.

The people of the beautiful city of Sevilla were celebrating the departure of the Royal Fleet. Since trade with the Western Indies had been established, the big bustling city had become one of the most important trade centers in the kingdom.

"If it's a marvelous city you want to see, in Sevilla you must be," the people often said.

As tradition would have it, Sevilla remained a deeply religious and Christian city. There were at least forty-five convents of friars and twenty-eight convents of nuns scattered around the countryside. The imposing Cathedral of Saint Mary of the See was said to be the largest Christian Gothic cathedral in the world. With its five naves, seventy pointed vaults, and fifteen doors on four facades, it was truly an impressive and grandiose site.

The beautiful bell tower of La Giralda was reminiscent of the control the *Almohad Caliphate* had over Spain during ancient times and was visible from everywhere in the city.

Nearby, along the Guadalquivir River, the huge galleons from the Indies fleet lined the coast. The ships looked like a row of tall buildings with their imposing castles on their sterns.

The galleons had three giant masts, rigged with square and Latin sails, and were heavily armed with cannons and mortars. Each galleon was more than one hundred-fifty feet in length. A person standing on the first ship, lost sight of the last one in the line. The normal size of a flotilla consisted of twelve ships, often called "the twelve Apostles." In command of each ship was a merchant captain, usually the owner of the ship, or a commander appointed by the ship's owner. The convoy included the Royal Navy, with its flagship, *Our Lady of the Rosary*, in the lead. The admiral's ship was at the rear, with many small war ships in between.

The decks of the ships teemed with activity as several hundred crew men worked diligently to get the ships ready to sail. Officers, sailors, cabin boys, pages, artillery men, soldiers, and passengers each had their specific duties and expectations for the journey. They worked nervously hand in hand not knowing what the next days, weeks, and months would bring.

Many of the pilots, masters, officers and, sailors of the ships had their nautical certification from the University of Mareantes in Seville. Others, like the pages and cabin boys, were from the Royal College of San Telmo, the charity institution that specialized in maritime studies for orphans. The reputation of the San Telmo was outstanding, as many of the orphans later became exceptional pilots or masters of the sea.

The varied cargoes were loaded onto the decks and secured for the long journey. The merchants, dressed in colorful attire, were from all over the Mediterranean and spoke a multitude of languages: Spanish, Italian, Portuguese, and Flemish. The water around the ship was chaotic with a melee of small boats and frigates fighting for a chance to get to the shoreline to unload their wares.

A multitude of products were in heaps along the banks of the river: ammunition stacked in heavy chests, steamer trunks, bulky bales of wool, large bags of seeds, iron, heavy anvils, flashlights, barrels of water, oil, wine, food, horses, pigs and poultry cages were among the array. The air was heavy with a general nervousness emanating from the departing crew, but it did not impede their action on the pier. The charged atmosphere was contagious and caused high anticipation and frayed nerves among the witnesses of the infrequent event.

As with any large event, ill-fated beggars sat on street corners in hopes of scavenging leftovers or damaged goods. Loitering on the streets and in dark alleys, gypsy gangs spread out like scavengers as they looked for the slightest opportunity to take advantage of an inattentive sailor.

When time came for the departure of the Indies fleet, the bell in the tower of Giralda rang loudly and continuously to announce the impending exodus of the fleet of ships

Father Luzuriaga hurriedly gathered his missionaries on the beach of the Betis River for last minute words of encouragement. With eloquent words, he said, "We are about to embark on the greatest mission of our lives, a mission to carry God's word." Using the topic of the Gospel of the day, he filled the new apostles with a flame and missionary zeal.

"When John the Baptist was arrested," Father Luzuriaga said to the friars, "Jesus went into Galilee proclaiming the Gospel of God."

With great determination the friar declared, "So, now my Brethren, you are being sent by the Holy Spirit to proclaim the Word of God in unknown lands. Trust the Lord will be with you until the end of the world."

After the Commissioner's final ceremonial speech, the monks scurried aboard their assigned ships, ready to embark on their dream trip to the West Indies. Father Margil and Father Linaz received the honor of travelling on the flagship of the Royal Navy, the first ship in the convoy; it was commanded by General Don Diego Fernandez de Zaldívar. On the same ship was the Royal Notary, whose duty was to record all movement of goods; and the overseer of His Majesty, who monitored the interests of the King. According to the Laws of the Indies, each vessel carried a minimum of two religious and the rest of the religious were to be scattered among the other ships.

Father Margil was happy to be assigned to the flagship, where the image of the Blessed Virgin Mary, in her role as the Patron Saint of the Seas, would be placed on her bow. Along with Father Linaz and Father Margil on the flagship were harquebusiers, drummers, a trumpeter and a flag bearer.

All the confraternities and militia of the city along with the masses of townspeople dressed in their finest and best attire joined in the ceremony. Four priests of the Order of Dominicans carried the image of the Virgin Mary of the Rosary on a stretcher carefully protected by an elegant canopy.

At the front of the group, marched the *harquebusiers* carrying their ancient rifles and heralding twelve martial flags. As the venerable image proceeded down the streets from the convent, it was heralded at each intersection by soldiers firing musket volleys into the air toward the seawall. The delegation paraded in front of each ship, as artillery saluted the Queen of the Seas. First they stopped at the galleon Saint Christ of Agustin, where Captain Don Luis de Zerantes saluted smartly. The next stop was the galleon Our Lady of Conception, commanded by Captain Don Leonardo de Lara. Then the procession stopped at *Our Lady of the Solitude*, under the command of Don Juan de Villalobos. With great excitement, they came upon the ship *Our Lady of Rosary*, where Captain Agustin Pardo gave a martial salute to the *Galeona* with the sound of artillery firing. Continuing, they stopped in front of *The Angel and the Souls*, property of Captain Don Antonio de Aspeliqueta. Then, they went onto the *Our Lady of Carmel*, property of Don Juan Mathias Valdobino and captained by Don Sebastian Sarco, Master Administrator. The procession next stopped in front of the *Our Lady of the Victory* galleon, owned by Don Francisco de Pineda with Don Juan de Yriarte as Master Captain. They then stopped at the *Our Lady of the Remedies,* commanded by Captain Don Diego Rosales Vallejo and the *Our Lady of the People and the Souls* galleon, commanded by Captain Don Geronimo. Lastly, they arrived at the admiral ship, *Most Blessed Sacrament;* with its impressive two rows of forty cannons each weighing about twenty-four pounds. After this they walked to the small war ships; the first, the second and then the *Margarita.*

Excitement rose to a maximum when the image of Our Blessed Virgin Mary, reverently called the *Galeona,* arrived. The roar from the crowd was overwhelming and mixed with cannon fire and musket blasts while the holy image was carefully loaded onto the ship's deck. Then there was silence, as the audience stood at attention and saluted the sacred image, elegantly dressed with her Imperial Crown and holding the Infant Jesus in her arms, as she was attached to the bow of the flagship. This tradition was so that the image of the Mother of Jesus could watch over the rest of ships in the fleet, as a mother would watch over her children.

Sword in hand, Captain Don Diego de Zaldívar gave a military salute to the Blessed Virgin and solemnly swore to look after her and return her home safely from the long trip to the New World. The captain had a reputation of being an expert seaman so they all believed the blessed Lady would be safely returned. For this act and many others acts of loyal services to the Royal Navy, Captain Zaldívar was later awarded the noble title of *Conde de Saucedilla* by King Charles II of Spain. The lives of many hundreds of men and many millions of pesos were now in his hands. Thinking to himself, Father Margil could not decide if it was the captain protecting Our Lady or if Our Lady was protecting the captain and his crew.

At last, the Spanish fleet was on its way to proclaim the word of God to the lost souls in the New World. Father Margil and the other young missionaries knew they were on a life changing journey and there was no turning back now.

At the completion of the ceremony, the galleons slowly sailed down the Guadalquivir River to the port of Cadiz, about fifty miles away. The flagship and the smaller war ships were easily maneuverable, but the heavily laden merchant ships had to move slowly and carefully down the waterway. The speed of the slowest ship marked the speed for the entire fleet; for this reason, officers from the House of Trading closely monitored the weight of the cargo ships. On more than one occasion, the greed of the merchants caused a ship to be stranded in the river or wrecked on the Sanlucar de Barrameda sandbar near the coastline.

By the time the convoy assembled at Cadiz, it was imperative that everything be perfect and in strict compliance with the rules. The time had come for the fleet and its crew to enter the vast sea. The flagship hoisted its flag up the main mast and fired a cannon shot to signal the lifting of the anchors. Gradually and slowly, in a long line, the ships sailed from the coast of Huelva and entered the vast blue ocean that lay ahead.

They headed southwest, towards the African coast, and then turned toward the Canary Islands where they stopped. They had been at sea for ten days. There the captains took advantage of the time on the island to do inspections for contraband goods. Any stowaways found were removed and sent back to the port of Andalusia.

The fleet replenished their supplies on the islands and after a short delay, returned to the sea. To take advantage of trade winds blowing from the stern, they turned sixteen degrees west. The first few days of the journey were very quiet and even boring to the veteran sailors. However, the days seemed endless to the young missionaries who had never sailed aboard a ship. Half way through the trip, the boredom of the veterans ended when a ferocious storm approached. With driving rains and heaving waters that seemed endless, the captain and crew soon feared the storm would sink the ships and jeopardize the entire mission. On deck, the situation was intolerable and very chaotic as the mates tried to batten down the hatches and save the cargo. The gigantic waves exploded against the ship and washed everything and anyone not tied down overboard. The panicked crew felt their end was near, especially the older sailors who remembered the story of *Our Lady of the Conception,* an old galleon sailing off the coast of the island of La Española, which fell victim to a hurricane forty-two years ago and was lost at sea.

Fearing the ships would collide in the unending storm, the Captain decided to split the fleet into two groups and allow them to navigate separately. After a few days, the storm abated, but not before it took a remarkable toll on the nerves of the men. Near the island of San Juan Bautista, the two groups met and were delighted to see their friends alive but saddened to learn of the loss of one ship and its courageous crew.

The misadventures caused by the storm delayed a voyage that should have taken seventy days, twenty extra days, which were agonizingly long even to the most experienced sailors.

Their next stop was the Santiago de Cuba Island, the last point before reaching the mainland of the New World. When they left the island, their route took them past the Cape of San Antonio, the westernmost tip of the island to avoid the dangerous reef of Los Alacranes. By now, Father Linaz and the other missionaries felt safety would not come to them until they set foot on the land of the New World.

When land was spotted a few days later, they fell to their knees to thank God for allowing them to finally reach their new home. It had been a long, arduous ordeal at sea, but they were glad to be in the place where their great missionary work could finally begin. These strange but welcomed lands would be where the Gospel of Our Lord could be spread. It was their new home.

Unfortunately at the time, they were unaware of the bitter welcome their New World would bring.

PART TWO: NEW SPAIN

X

"This is intolerable," a prisoner shouted in despair.

"We will die of hunger and thirst!" exclaimed another of the captives.

"Oh! God, have mercy on us!"

The several hundred prisoners, crammed inside the Cathedral of Veracruz, had been locked in the temple for four days in the sweltering May heat. The poor souls were trapped there with the doors and windows of the cathedral hammered shut to prevent their escape.

"Rumor is that the demon Lorencillo has threatened to blow up the cathedral like a keg of powder," bitterly claimed another prisoner. "You know he has wreaked havoc on the entire coastline of New World."

"Blow up the cathedral? What blasphemy against the house of God!"

"That pirate doesn't believe in God, just money, and he has no religion, only ambition!"

"Why would he want to blow up the cathedral?"

"We hear he has sent an ultimatum to His Majesty, the Viceroy Don Antonio de la Cerda, demanding the ransom of a million *pesos* or he will blow it up."

"A million pesos! Hasn't he looted enough so far?"

"We also hear the demand has been reduced to one hundred fifty thousand *pesos;* and that the viceroy has ten days to pay up."

"The bastard has no end. We hear he has emptied the Royal Treasury at the fort of San Juan de Ulúa."

"He has also looted our homes, businesses, stores, farms, inns, temples, the City Hall, and the market; everything has been destroyed by that ruthless pirate."

"His men have violated our women. They have all been dishonored: natives or whites, maids or married!"

"Blood of the Christ! These bandits are heathens!"

In the midst of the inhumane overcrowding, the sweating prisoners were starving. Children cried inconsolably while many wandered the confinement with dazed looks on their faces. The holy grounds of the church had become a cesspool as the smell of human waste permeated the air. The captives tried their best to relieve themselves in a single location far away from the crowd to avoid offending the temple of God, but the putrid stench of human waste was intolerable. It was so nauseating and unbearable that the poor souls begged God to have mercy of them, but their fate was uncertain.

"We were taken from our homes half naked on Tuesday morning and forced to sit in the main square. We were then herded through the doors of the cathedral and imprisoned. Today is Saturday, so we have been here five days now!"

"This treatment is inhumane! My poor starving wife has fainted two times; we shall all die soon!"

"We heard that Don Arturo, the silk merchant, was tortured to death when they tried to find his hidden treasures. Many rich men have suffered the same fate."

"They put a rope around the neck of Captain Gaspar de Herrera and hung him until he told where his treasure was hidden."

"The devils also hung Father Friar Fernando Ricardo, Guardian of the Convent of the Franciscan Friars. Only by the mercy of the God's hand did he survive, but he was left in a poor state."

"The pirates destroyed the Holy Sepulcher just to steal its silver. What blasphemy!"

"Those of us, who live, will still lose the battle."

"I've seen the square where they store the goods they looted. Their bounty also includes slaves and mulattos. Poor souls!"

"And what happened to our Royal Navy, the Winward Navy? It was supposed to defend us in situations like this. We pay high taxes for their protection!"

Unknown to the captives, the Royal Navy could not come to their defense, as they were in Campeche to block the Dutch from taking captured slaves to Jamaica.

"And what about our garrison? Don't we have more than a thousand men in the vast fortress of San Juan de Ulúa?"

"Don't you know? Those pirates surprised our soldiers early one morning and killed many of them. They were slaughtered like animals trying to defend us!"

The face of the city was now the face of death and desolation. The pirates led by the Dutchman Lorencillo; Nicholas Grammont; Bronon Nicholas; and John Jacques, were accompanied by about eight hundred men on this horrid night. After being forced into submission, the guards at the fort of San Juan de Ulúa were divided into groups. Then the band of pirates looted the houses and shops of the city, and stole everything of value. Amidst cries of pain and sorrow, they forced themselves on the women, young and old alike. After their forage through the town, they locked the townspeople behind the walls of the cathedral.

"This is sacrilege!" cried the priest when the pirates forced open the door of the cathedral. One of the pirates hit the priest on the head with a tremendous blow which hurled him to the ground. Showing little mercy for the holy man, he was taken the temple and locked away with the rest of the inhabitants, including all the City Council, the Royal Ensign, the Sheriff, the Notary, and the Officers. The Franciscan friars suffered the same fate.

In normal times, the population of Veracruz did not exceed one thousand inhabitants. Six hundred of those were African slaves and mulattos who worked on the ships and labored on farms growing crops to feed the village.

But with the arrival of the Royal Fleet that summer, the population had tripled. People came from other towns and villages, far and near, to buy and sell their products in a trading fair that lasted about three months. Merchants, royal officials, customs officials, military and government officials, and residents of Jalapa, a village fifty-five miles from Veracruz, all moved to the port. The food, accommodations, health and other services, reached exorbitant prices during these months.

Valuable merchandise, that was to be shipped to Spain in the Royal Fleet, was stored in San Juan de Ulúa, an imposing fortress with massive defenses. But the pirates must have known of these riches and came to steal all of the estimated one thousand pounds of silver and four to seven million pesos of treasure. Also stored there were the many treasures from the Philippines and other products including: cabinets, silk, porcelain, spices, gunpowder, jewelry, gold, silver, vases, weapons, cocoa, and flour.

For a few short days, the village of Veracruz was the richest city in the world. And now, all had been plundered by Lorencillo and his pirates in an orgy of destruction and death.

Once the pillage was complete, they took some of the prisoners from the cathedral to the Isle of Sacrifices, which was a couple of miles away by sea. Among the prisoners were twenty of the most prominent male citizens of the area, including the Governor, the Officers of the Regiment of Militia, members of City Council and the Prelates of Religious Orders.

"Poor men, only God knows their fate! And what about our Governor Don Luis Fernandez de Cordoba?"

"If he comes out of this alive, he'll need a good story to tell His Majesty the Viceroy, who'll be very unhappy with this situation. Rumors have it that Lorencillo may have had the support of insiders within the Governor's staff, or otherwise he could not have taken the fortress so easily."

"Do no say that! Do not accuse without evidence."

"Well, I do agree that it sounds impossible for a formidable and impregnable fortress like San Juan de Ulúa to fall so easily."

"Lorencillo used to live in the city and knew its defenses well; he even served in the Winward Fleet!"

"Well, I think strengthing the city is long overdue. Protection has to be built around this city, with ramparts and bastions, to make it a stronghold. Strengthening the city is way overdue."

"I agree with you; it should only have two doors, one toward the shore and one toward to the inland. A city like Veracruz can't be an open city, now that we see the drawbacks."

"Don't speak foolish words! First, we must live through this situation and then think of the future."

The hope that the Royal Navy would save the towns' people from the ruthless pirates was in vain. The citizens remained captives until Sunday, when the bandits noticed the presence of the Royal Navy's first ship on the horizon. They quickly loaded their vast bounty, the Viceroy's ransom money and more than a thousand black slaves and mulattos, and set sail into the vast open waters.

When the Royal Fleet arrived in Veracruz, the pirates were long gone. The bitter picture of death and desolation was evident in all directions and was all that they left behind. The pirates killed more than four hundred men, women and children, including countless numbers of soldiers. They had sacrificed a huge numbers of animals, including mules, horses and dogs. Houses and shops were ransacked, looted, and often burned to the ground. In temples, the tabernacles were violated and destroyed, and the sacred images tossed on the ground. The women were raped. The men tortured and assaulted. Only hunger, despair, desolation, and ruin remained. The smell of death permeated the city!

It was May thirtieth in the year of 1683, the feast day of *San Fernando*, knight of Christ, servant of the Blessed Virgin, and ensign of Apostle St. James. It was also the day Father Linaz, Father Margil, and the rest of his missionaries arrived with the Royal Fleet, after their long and arduous journey of more than ninety days. As the shipped sailed into the harbor, the passengers stepped off the ship into the horror and aftermath of the rampage of Lorencillo. This was the scene that began Father Antonio Margil de Jesús' epic journey into the New World.

XI

Sangremal Hill, Santiago de Querétaro
July 1531

𝕿he mighty warriors agreed on a symbolic battle. One without weapons. The meeting of the two great armies was a display of courage, and only the strength of the combatants would determine the victor. The hand-to-hand combat was a pure and basic display of human strength.

Two indomitable forces fought. On one hand was the fearless *Chichimecas* Indians and on the other the *Otomi* warriors. The *Chichimecas* were led by warlord Cimatario, and the *Otomis* by Don Fernando de Tapia, a Christian convert formerly known as *Conin*.

On the morning of July 25th, on Sangremal Hill near Querétaro, the battle began. The fierce *Chichimeca* warriors, from the highlands, were dressed handsomely in white, brown and black animal skins and wore pachxochitl-green quetzal hats over their long black hair. They bore red earmuffs and carried shields called *tlahuitolli* made of eagle feathers. In keeping with the predetermined agreement between their leaders, their obsidian weapons, swords, and arrows were banned from the skirmish.

The brave *Otomis*, from the southern valley, were also dressed in pelts of wolves, coyotes and cougars. On their heads, they wore wooden masks carved into animal faces and covered with leather. Although unarmed, they were fierce looking in their intimidating regalia and body tattoos.

At first, the battle was simply a demonstration of power as the fighters pranced around, shook their fists, and shouted boorish insults at one another. This lasted for hours before it finally escalated into a bareknuckle encounter. The physical superiority of the *Chichimecas* gave them an edge over the *Otomi*. The *Otomi*, smaller in stature but stronger in will, did not give up easily. Equally matched, the struggle continued for hours with much pain, anguish and bloodshed on both sides.

All of a sudden in the middle of the thunderous fracas, a strong wind began to blow and quickly formed a large dust cloud. The skies darkened. The combatants instantly stopped and looked upwards to the heavens.

There in the cloud of dust, they saw the image of Saint James riding a white horse and carrying a large red and white cross.

"Look, the Holy Cross and Lord James!" shouted one of the Christian warriors. "Our wicked ways have angered our Lord!"

When the few fighters, who were still trading blows, heard these words, they stopped fighting immediately. Startled by what was happening, they all fell to their knees and gazed at the holy sign of Jesus Christ. All the anger they felt for one another was gone. Now, all they felt in their hearts was serenity and benevolence. Somehow, they knew this was a sign from God telling them to make peace not war.

The next day, as a sign of peace, warriors from both sides worked together and erected a huge pine cross, twelve feet tall and six feet wide. They placed it on the battlefield in the exact location of the apparition. There they held the first Holy Mass to commemorate the occasion, and thus the ville of Santiago de Querétaro was born.

In months to come, the Indians asked the religious to replace the wooden cross with a solid one of stone. This more enduring cross was a seven foot, octagonal piece of stone, smaller but more permanent than the original wooden cross. At the urgings of Don Fernando de Tapia, a chapel next to the cross was built from branches and was adorned with beautiful wild flowers.

Over the years, wondrous deeds began to happen on the little hill. Often the soft sweet smell of lilies and roses permeated the air. This was a smell the Iberians knew only from their homeland in the Kingdom of Castile. The sight became legendary as the people, now mostly Christians, stopped and prayed at the holy cross when they passed on their way to and from Querétaro.

In a few years and with the permission of His Majesty Philip IV, priests from the Franciscan order were assigned to the little convent. For the next hundred years, they worked with the Indians and even helped build a nursery, a novitiate and several guest rooms at the nearby Convent of San Francisco. The whole time they were happy to be assigned to the much small and quieter Convent of Santa Cruz.

The peace and solitude of the isolated friars was short lived. In years to come, the pious Father Antonio Margil and his fellow brothers would grace the halls of the convent. With the appearance of these first messengers of God, trained to carry the Gospel to far reaching places, life at the Convent of San Cruz would never be the same. In history the small convent would grow to be known as the radiating center of all missionary work in the fledgling Kingdom of New Spain.

XII

𝕬s Father Margil approached México City, he was awed by the panoramic view before him. The magnificent old town was perfectly laid out in sprawling expanses in a large valley. It was accented by beautiful tall buildings not seen in most regions, and was completely surrounded by Lake Texcoco. Its main accesses were over several long bridges and wide roads leading into the city.

"This magnificent and beautiful city loses nothing in comparison to the cities in the Old World!" said Father Margil.

He and his Franciscan brother, Father Joseph Diez, crossed the bridge entering the city by way of the Avenue of the Conquerors. It had been a month since they left Vera Cruz, and they were now in the city to rendezvous with their fellow Franciscan brothers on their way to Querétaro.

Stopping for a minute to rest, Father Margil thought back to the difficulty they encountered upon their arrival at the port of Vera Cruz. The suffering inflicted on the poor people by the loathsome pirates and the ravages of the city was still fresh on his mind. He thought of how the dangerous sea voyage had not dampened his excitement for coming to the New World, and the misery of the good Christians made him realize the importance of God's plan for the mission.

Prophetically, his first duty in the New World was to give Christian burials to the dead. It was a horrific sight to see so many corpses: four hundred soldiers and civilians and thirty-five pirates. The burials brought back memories of childhood stories about the devastating epidemic of plague that decimated the Kingdom of Valencia and left thousands dead.

After the burials, the friars cleaned and repaired the holy cathedral and the Convent of San Francisco. With tears in their eyes, the men picked up fallen and battered Holy images that once stood gloriously inside the convent. With much reverence, they also found and ceremoniously collected the Holy Eucharist that lay on the floor amid the garbage left behind. The travesty and sacrilege of the devil pirates was unbelievable.

One of the first casualties was the Reverend Father Guardian of the Convent of San Francisco who was hung by the pirates. Holding the aging man as he struggled to breathe, they saw the raw skin on his neck from the thick noose. It was a miracle he had not succumbed to the treachery of the pirates. After performing all the corporal works of mercy bestowed by the church, the friars helped minister to the sick and wounded. Later in the month, they even helped repair and rebuild homes and businesses.

It took weeks for the people to slowly recover from the utter devastation. When their feelings of violation and sadness began to subside, they realized that the merciful Lord had saved them from the hands of Lorencillo. Their anger turned into gratitude. To preserve the dreadful date in history, they held a festival to celebrate their freedom from the pirates. The streets filled with joy and euphoria, as the people danced and partied through the alleys in a carnival-like atmosphere.

With a faint smile, Father Margil quickly put away thoughts of his first mission work in Vera Cruz. Now it was time to begin a new undertaking.

It had been about a month since Father Linaz gathered his followers for a final blessing at Vera Cruz, and he did so in the same manner as St. Francis of Assisi, the Seraphic Father, had gathered his followers a hundred years earlier. Father Linaz told them:

It's time for you to go, my brothers. Preach as you pass through the towns and villages. Enter carrying the cross high, and singing litanies to the Virgin Mary. Always, carry your sheep hook, a breviary, and a crucifix. Your journey will take you in the direction of the setting sun. Forty leagues ahead, you will find a town called Puebla de Los Angeles, where we will meet again.

With this simple valediction, the Franciscan brothers were sent through the new lands to begin their work. Father Margil and Father Joseph were partnered. Father Margil, at the youthful age of twenty-five and with an innate ability to travel long distances, knew he could travel faster alone. But because of his charity and consideration for others, he walked a slower pace with his companion brother, who was equally young, but not nearly as agile. On their way, they came to an endless succession of high peaks that were beautiful but also the most difficult part of their journey.

Complying with the instructions given to them by Father Linaz, they performed God's work in the small towns of Huatusco, Costastla, San Lorenzo de los Negros, San Martin, San Salvador el Verde and a few other villages along the way.

Not being accustomed to the seasonal rains, they struggled with the mucky roads and often were covered with mud upon arrival in the towns. Having no spare habit, they continued to walk in their damp, dirty clothes that eventually dried in the sun. On occasion, a passing convoy offered them a ride to the next town, and they took it as a temporary relief from their long, hot journey.

After several days, the brothers converged at the Convent of San Francisco in Puebla where they also met Father Linaz. They were filled with elation and sat for hours talking about their many adventures and conquests in the towns that they visited. The next day, Father Linaz once again gathered them for a blessing and instructions and disbursed them, two by two, to México City. Father Margil was again paired with his old friend Father Joseph.

It was another long journey to the capital city, but along the way good fortune led them to a young friar, from the Convent of San Francisco, who had the same destination.

A few days later, they reached the long road that crossed over the lake surrounding México City. The road took them to the customs hut of La Candelaria, where after logging in they entered the vast city. They looked around and admired the beautiful buildings and palaces.

"This is the square of the flying man," said their new friend, "The site of the Royal and Pontifical University. His Majesty King Philip II ordered the establishment of this superior institution so it would be like the one at Salamanca."

With admiration, Father Margil recalled that in his years of study, he had learned that the prestigious and venerable institution in Salamanca, which was more than four hundred years old, once proudly bore the title of University in Spain.

When they turned the next corner and passed near the House of the City Council, they saw the bridge over the royal channel. It was here that merchandise arrived on small boats, called *trajineras*. The goods, consisting of flowers, fruit and a wide variety of products, were sold directly from the docks by the hawkers. On the other side of the bridge was the stately main square.

"This is the Royal Palace," said their guide pointing to a massive building across the street. "His Majesty, the Viceroy Tomas Antonio de la Cerda is happy today because his charming wife is about to give birth. A great feast to mark the event is being prepared."

They crossed the street.

"Here you can see the city market, called the *Parián*," said the young friar pointing to a giant trade site bustling with activity.

"In the front is our beautiful cathedral," he added. "It's not quite finished, but you can still admire its beauty."

Looking towards the center of the square, the foreigners observed a large, magnificent church partially constructed. Inside of it were huge scaffoldings, large ceiling beams, and countless laborers toiling in the heat. They had not yet begun the bell towers and main vault, but the building was already of colossal dimensions.

"Today, like every Thursday," he told them, "we celebrate the solemn Holy Mass of the Blessed Sacrament in the cathedral."

When the clock reached the top of the hour, the bells began to ring. Everyone in the square stopped in their tracks, took off their hats and bowed their heads in silence. They knelt as a carriage with the Holy Body of Christ passed them. As soon as the coach went by, activity returned to normal, and the friars continued their journey.

They passed the merchant area and continued down the street named San Francisco. They passed one side of the Professed House of the Society of Jesus for priests and brothers, whose temple was known as the *profesa* church. Six hundred yards further, they arrived at the large Convent of San Francisco.

"We have made it, brothers," said the young guide. He opened the heavy gate, framed by a beautiful stone-carved arch, unfolded his arms and proudly said, "This is your home!"

"Rest here and await the arrival of the rest of your brothers."

They entered the courtyard through the side door and marveled at the size of the property occupied by the convent. They were in awe at the huge temple and its many chapels.

"Legend is that this magnificent place was once the private zoo of Montezuma. It was his palace of birds and his house of wild beasts," said their guide.

As they entered the convent, they could see the side of the temple of San Francisco. On the left was the chapel called Our Lady of Aránzazu, and on the right was the chapel of the Third Order of San Francisco. Surrounding the temple, they saw the front of the cloister arches and the imposing baroque quarry façade of the temple. Touring the court, they found other chapels, of which the largest was the San Jose of the Natives. They were pleasantly surprised when they learned the convent had enough rooms to house nearly three hundred religious.

"It is a great convent, isn't it?" asked Father Joseph.

"Yes, brothers," said the friar. "I understand it is the largest religious convent in this city, and maybe in the entire New World. When you walk through it, you will find several chapels, two cloisters, a cemetery, and a vast garden. We have plenty of water from two channels surrounding the monastery. It has a beautiful garden, an infirmary and a vast library, which may be the most complete of all New Spain."

To the monks, the most impressive and reverent sight was a giant wooden cross placed at the center of the main square.

"It is very large," said Father Margil. "It seems to reach up to heaven."

"That's right," said his confrere. "It is the highest in the city. In fact, if you remember, you can see it before crossing the bridge outside the city. It's made from a large cypress tree that grew on the hill of Chapultepec."

"It is a relief to feel the protection of this blessed cross," said Father Margil. "Soon we will be on our way to Querétaro."

XIII

Convent of San Francisco in Querétaro
August 1683

$\mathbf{F}$eeling somewhat overwhelmed by the large stack of papers in front of him, Very Reverend Father Antonio Alonso, the Provincial Minister of the Convent of San Francisco, quickly read through the documents. They included a Papal Bull of His Holiness Innocent XI, three Royal Decrees of His Royal Majesty, Patents of the Very Reverend Minister General of the Order, and the Very Reverend Commissioner General of the Indies, and two decrees, one of the Sacred Congregation of Propaganda Faith and another of the Holy Inquisition.

The papers were delivered to him by a congregation of priests led by Father Juan Bautista Lázaro who had come from San Juan del Rio about thirty-three miles away. The members of the religious troupe were Friar Pedro Antonio Frontera, Friar Francisco Estevez and Father Antonio Margil de Jesús.

Upon arrival at the convent, which belonged to the Franciscan province of Saints Peter and Paul of Michoacán, the young men entered the peaceful silence of the spacious chapter room. They walked through the chambers, to the pounding of their hearts, into the cold and impersonal surroundings.

Toward the back of the room, the Provincial Minister sat with the friars from the convent who were members of the Provincial Definitory and the Provincial Vicar, the secretary, the receiver, the guardian of the convent and few others.

With a sigh, the Father Provincial spoke in a loud voice, "This patent clearly orders us to allow Father Linaz to occupy the Convent of Santa Cruz. Further, it states the College will be created under the supervision of Commissioner General and it won't be dependent on this province." He hesitated for a moment, "It is very clear and we must obey!"

The members of the definitory couldn't believe their ears and many expressed their surprise and dissatisfaction. The room was filled with murmurs and complaints from the friars of the Franciscan Province.

"But ... but that's inconceivable!"

"It's impossible! Why would the college be here, and not dependent on our Province?"

"That goes against the structure of the Order!"

"It's an outrage! This convent belongs to us and nobody can take it away!"

"This is thievery!"

"For sure we will not allow it!"

"Never!"

"Father Linaz has betrayed us!"

"Yes! He left as custodian of our Franciscan Province and returned as our enemy! "He did not have the courage to come before us himself; instead, he sent his errand boys."

In a loud voice, the Provincial Minister cut them short, and said, "That's enough, brethren! I will not tolerate any action against the venerable Father Linaz!"

With his head tilted downward and peering above his glasses, he said in a slow but serious voice, "Should I remind your paternity that we are here to obey orders and not question them? Have you forgotten your vows of obedience? We are a part of a religious order, not a court of judges. It is not for us to question the provisions that are given to us."

The Father Provincial glared at each one of them, and they quickly settled into their chairs and began to listen attentively.

He proceeded in a pleasant but deliberant tone, "Listen to me very carefully, and this is meant for all of you!" he said as he stared at each man. He wanted to make sure his words were very clear, "Nobody, I repeat, nobody in this room shall ever discuss the foolish argument we had today!"

Taking his seat he said, "Never, I mean, never shall you question the motives or the actions of Father Linaz. If the Minister General has determined that we should give up the Convent of Santa Cruz, as is confirmed by His Holiness and His Majesty the King, then we must not rebel against the Royal commands!"

"Besides," he concluded with all the power his position held, "I must warn your Illustrious Paternities that this decision has a decree approved by the Holy Office of the Inquisition!"

Then turning to Father Linaz' quartet, he said, "You can take possession. Our friars will be asked to vacate the Convent of Santa Cruz and immediately move to San Miguel el Grande. They will not take anything from the convent; no ornaments, no clothes, no furniture, no books, nothing at all."

The Minister returned the papers to the friars and said, "We will prepare the corresponding bills which will be delivered to you in the coming days. May God be with you all!"

The four brothers bowed and gave thanks to the Father Provincial. They left the chapter room in silence and briskly walked across the cloister and headed toward the cemetery. They walked beside the Chapel of Our Lady of Loreto and soon arrived at the street called Cinco Señores. They turned left and travelled down Serafin Street, to Malfajadas Street, and continued their ascent up the streets of Flor Alta and Cornelius. After crossing a small plain, the convent, which was no more than fifteen hundred feet from the Convent of San Francisco, was in sight.

They fell to their knees and thanked God for keeping them safe during their long arduous journey to their new home. They entered the gates of the convent to await the arrival Father Linaz so they could begin their mission. With this simple act, the College of the Propagation of the Faith founded by Father Margil and his brothers in faith at the Convent of Santa Cruz, became the first and most famous Spanish college for missionaries in New Spain.

XIV

𝔉ather Margil filled the last wooden bucket with water and handed it to his brother in habit who was waiting on the shoreline. On this first trip they each carried two buckets, precariously dangling from a pole balanced across their shoulders. After this trip, they only had two more trips to the river to have the convent's water quota for a whole day.

Slowly they began the arduous journey up the hill to the convent. Frequently, Father Margil's companion stopped to catch his breath, while the tireless Father Margil waited patiently. When they finally arrived at the convent, a distance of about a half mile, they poured the water into a round brick urn built into the ground. They prepared themselves to return to the river for the next load.

As they walked through the tiny corridor of the cloister, Father Margil surveyed his new home with much joy and enthusiasm. He knew the Convent of Santa Cruz was small, very small. The cloister was barely thirty feet square, with twelve rooms on a single level. It was no comparison to the huge building at the Convent of San Francisco, which was fifteen to twenty times larger and had rooms for the novitiate, nursing and hospice care. Thinking back to his days in Spain, both paled in comparison to the great convents he had left behind in his homeland.

Yes, the Convent of the Santa Cruz was small, but to Father Margil it was absolutely stunning. He knew it was now his new home, his most wonderful home.

He was quite satisfied living in the beautiful city of Querétaro with its many large squares, well laid out blocks and wide streets. A traveler might describe it as one of the most beautiful, large, and wealthy cities of New Spain. Some even said the soil around the city was so fertile that it could compete with Italy's very best. In every home, luscious gardens abounded, where almost anything could grow. The trees were full of delicious apples, avocados, bananas, guava, pitayas, plums, peaches, pomegranates, quinces, apricots, pears, oranges and lemons. They were all so scrumptious to the palate that one could hardly choose a favorite. In addition to the fruit trees, reeds, sweet melons of all kinds, and vegetables grew abundantly. Also remarkable were the variety of vines and aromatic and colorful flowers, including roses and lilies, found in the gardens.

The houses were very beautiful, well made of adobe, and almost always one story. What was striking about them was that they had a thick thatched roof instead of tile which was common in other cities. The very few homes that were two stories were richly decorated with expensive iron railings and usually marked the abode of the very wealthy.

The friars were thankful they were in a city of divine worship. One with a large number of convents, churches, homes and schools where the devoted actively participated in the frequent liturgical celebrations and belonged to religious guilds of their choice. They felt here everyone, both Spanish and Indians, could worship and be served.

Now, it was true that Querétaro, like all large cities, had its own share of social problems. Many men spent their time in the squalid *pulquerías* where they drank in excess a native wine called *pulque* which was made from the fermented juice of the maguey cactus. Some loved gambling on the streets and watching obscene comedies. With a pause, Father Margil knew in his heart that he would find a way to fight these evils.

Quickly, his thoughts returned to the new home that he admired so much. Yes, the Convent of Santa Cruz was small, but it was destined for extraordinary greatness as their missionary work grew and overlapped into the borders of the kingdom.

XV

Palace of the Archbishop in México City
October 1683

"You are extremely kind to be here on this day of prayer and penance," said the Archbishop. "Especially since you were installed in the College of the Propagation of the Faith in Querétaro only two months ago."

"It's our pleasure, Your Eminence," replied Father Linaz. "It's a real honor to be invited to participate in this grand event. We came as soon as the Franciscan general commissioner informed us of your summons."

Earlier in the day, Father Linaz and his eleven brothers had arrived at the magnificent Palace of the Archbishop in México City. The palace was located a few steps from the Metropolitan Cathedral and next to the viceroyalty palace. The directive came from the Don Francisco Aguiar y Seixas, Archbishop of New Spain, and was delivered by Fray Juan de Luzuriaga, the commissioner general of the Order of Friars Minor to the West Indies.

His Holy Archbishop Aguiar y Seixas, a native of Galicia, Spain, had been promoted to his prestigious position only two years earlier. Prior to his appointment by Pope Innocent IX, he held the position of bishopric of Valladolid. The Archbishop belonged to the Third Order of Penance, one of three orders founded by St. Francis of Assisi. Its members were called Franciscan tertiaries.

The new Archbishop was known for his detachment from worldly possessions and his charity toward the poor. Often it was said the Archbishop contributed his entire salary, and a good portion of the tithes of the church to the poor and to the sick in hospitals.

As with any good deed, the Archbishop had supporters who praised his actions. They approved of his contributions to the poor girls and repentant prostitutes at the College of San Miguel de Belén, and his plans to build a mental hospital, a house of Mercy, and the Theological Seminary of México. On the other hand, his opponents were angry because it appeared as if he was too strict with moral rules and extremely conservative.

The Archbishop was fifty-six years old, but his neatly trimmed, gray hair, mustache and beard made him look much older than his years. As a symbol of his austerity, he wore a simple wooden cross around his neck, in contrast to the ostentatious gold cross embolden by precious stones worn by his predecessors. Under his heavy black coat, which matched his grim expression, he wore a discreet and simple vestment. Unlike other Archbishops in the high office, he rarely used white gloves. Those who knew him, from his days at the Colegio Mayor de Cuenca of the Royal and Pontifical University of Salamanca and from his days at the Royal University of Santiago de Compostela, knew his simplicity was genuine. It was not a mere pretense because his affinity to austerity and morality had been with him most of his life. In fact, he became more rigid and strict over the years from his many years of sacrifices, strict discipline and penance. Sometimes his suffering appeared to be almost intolerable.

After each Franciscan brother approached and kissed the ring of the Archbishop, they were invited to sit in his spacious but empty office. The commissioner was there as well. As the fathers looked around the great hall, they remembered being told that the Archbishop had sold the expensive and ostentatious furniture in almost all the rooms of the palace. Keeping with his strict practices, he donated the proceeds to help the poor in the diocese. Also missing from the Archbishop's palace were women. Not a single woman was present, not a maid or a cook. The Franciscan fathers had heard that the bishop had ordered that no women be in the palace under threat of immediate excommunication, *ipso facto incurrenda*.

After taking his seat, the Archbishop took a deep breath and turned toward the window and said, "You must know that decency and morality have relaxed too much in these lands. Modesty in dress for our women has given way to scandalous fashions and cosmetics. Too many look exaggerated and frankly highly improper."

Turning and looking at the group of fathers, he continued, "In the near future, we will prohibit certain corruptive activities, such as those infernal cockfights and bullfights. They are insulting and promote vice. We will also prohibit the comical theatrics which make a mockery of our faith, dignity, and good manners."

One by one, he glared at each man, and said, "That's why I called you here today, dear fathers. I want you to support me in this cause during your daily prayer, penance, and in your preaching. I am sure, with your eloquent passion and mission, you will find a way to touch the deepest fiber of the faithful. It will be necessary for you to preach morality and lash out at the promotion of this corruption."

He stood up and continued his stern oration, "It is intolerable that, even in our nuns' convents, morals are relaxed and enforcement of monastic rules in nonexistent. Increasingly the religious women are not committed to their vows and only look forward to parlor visits with family and friends. Especially annoying are the men in their lives who disguise themselves as devotees and only come to disturb their meditation and prayers. In many convents, these overindulgences have become more frequent, as is the number of servants each of them has at their beck and call. I have personally witnessed scandalous behavior in some sisters. They seem to care more for worldly possessions and frivolity than for devotion, fasting and contemplation. Some even offer more time to writing letters than to their perpetual profession and permanent solemn vows!"

With a sober expression, he said, "Sometimes, I wonder if it was really a genuine religious vocation which led them to the seclusion of the monasteries!"

"On another subject, it seems intolerable that even prominent persons of nobility, whose names I shall not mention, nightly attend those vulgar street comedies, dances, and parties. And they think they are hidden in the darkness of the gardens. It disgusts me to see such displays of cheapness."

With a deep sigh, he continued, "It's time, dear fathers, to stop this serious tawdriness! It is time for us to put a halt to the demons! I`m sure you know what needs to done to help in this apostolic mission."

Overwhelmed by what he was hearing, Father Linaz said, "Do not worry, Your Eminence, we will do our best to curb these moral blunders."

And they did! During the first week of missions, many solemn Eucharistic celebrations were performed in the cathedral. On the first day, Archbishop Seixas, himself, preached the first homily. On the second day the Commissioner General Friar Juan de Luzuriaga preached. And on the third day, Father Linaz honorably preached in the revered cathedral. Simultaneously, all the other brothers from the college, including Father Margil, fanned out and preached in surrounding parishes and in the many convents of friars and nuns.

During the second week of the mission, four groups of missionaries, accompanied by religious from the Convent of San Francisco, went on a walking procession through the city streets. The pageant was led by a religious carrying a large and high cross, as the others prayed the Rosary and sang short verses. These short verses were called *saetas* because they were like arrows shot directly into the heart. They were accompanied by five soldiers in a formation of three in the front and two behind, wearing traditional regalia and playing the drums. They sang to the crowd:

> "Confess sinner,
> that the more neglected
> you can die in sin.
> Men who are in sin, if you die tonight,
> look where you will go.
> God calls you, and you do not listen,
> Time will come, sinner
> when God won´t hear you.
>
> If pursuing this life,
> do the eternal sin,
> be your eternal Hell"

They preached in the squares. They preached in the streets. And every corner throughout the city was graced with the holy word. Each day the crowds grew larger, and the Franciscan friars became more admired. Demand for confessions from both the Spanish and Indians alike was greater than it had ever been.

On the last Friday in October, there was a solemn procession of penance and the Way of the Cross. At each of the fourteen stations, beautiful scenes of the crucifixion of Jesus Christ were displayed. This procession of faith was a means for the people to make contact with God, to adore him, to thank him and to increase their love for him. It started at the Convent of San Francisco where they prayed the first station. The second station was in the Chapel of Sorrows, at the main entrance of the convent; and the next nine stations continued through the chapels of the Sacred Way, next to the Alameda Park. The last three stations were prayed in the Chapel of Calvary.

This procession was so emotional and so memorable, that long after it was over people remembered its passion and often spoke about it with great piety.

Subsequently, a thanksgiving procession, which ended in the cathedral, was held where for four days and three nights they sustained the *Forty Hours Devotion* in solemn prayer before the exposition of the Holy Eucharist. Sermons were preached to the devotees, both day and night, while they reflected on the sacrifice of Our Lord.

On November 2nd there was a celebration for *All Souls*, with a funeral sermon by the commissioner general. At the end of the journey, at the request of the Archbishop, Father Linaz gave private sermons at the numerous monasteries of the nuns. His eloquence revived the devotion and religious virtues of the many holy sisters.

The success of the Franciscan fathers of the Apostolic College of Propagation of Faith of Querétaro was extraordinary. They put so much effort into the conversion of souls that Friar Antonio de Escaray, the father guardian of the Convent of San Francisco, gave up his guardianship and requested to join their mission.

Father Linaz and his friars were satisfied that the first mission of the College of Propagation of the Faith had been a great success. The seeds for the greater missions had been planted in the fertile soil around Querétaro. Now it was time to for them to spread the word to the remotest corners of this New World.

XVI

"**I**s it possible that your unfortunate adventures with the pirates and your frightening nights at sea could have actually been a sign from heaven? One that is telling you to stop and examine your conscience for past transgressions!" said the commissioner general.

"Are you referring to the decision I made not to accept the chair guardian of the newly formed Recollect Institute in the Provincial Chapter of Merida?" asked Father Melchor.

"Exactly, Father! That's what I mean!" answered the Commissioner.

"Reverend father, with great respect, as I expressed previously, I feel a strong calling from Our Lord to work with the College of Propagation of the Faith. I prefer their mission to convert the infidels over the contemplation that I observe in my convent at Santa Maria del Castañar in Castile," said Father Melchor.

"Be careful! When the desires of Our Lord are much like our own desires, it's hard to distinguish between the voice of Christ and our own voice and will," said the commissioner.

With a solemn face, which indicated some discomfort, he firmly said, "Retire to prayer for now. Maybe it will help you clearly discern the will of God."

The four friars were from the Apostolic College of Santa Cruz, which had been founded only months earlier. The group consisted of four young missionaries: Friar Melchor Lopez, Friar Antonio Margil, Friar José Díez and Friar Francisco Casañas.

Shortly after the establishment of the College of the Santa Cruz, they decided they needed to branch out with their missionary work. They left Querétaro and traveled to the Yucatán Province in the southern regions of New Spain. Their journey had not been free of disaster and problem, and often their trials overshadowed their joys.

Father Margil and his companions first went to the port of Vera Cruz, a place they knew well. There they met with the commissioner general, who arrived at the port after completing a successful mission in Puebla de Los Angeles. After performing mission work in and around Vera Cruz, the friars went by sea to San Francisco de Campeche and arrived several days later. They evangelized in the picturesque town with much success before going to Merida, where the Provincial Chapter meeting had just adjourned. The General Commissioner Luzuriaga had proposed to the chapter the restoration of the Recollect Institute in the city, and the proposal was approved by the attendees of the chapter meeting. They also appointed Father Melchor Lopez as the guardian of the newly created institution. When Father Melchor was told of his new appointment, he was caught off guard by the move. He quickly but reverently refused the position saying he had come with the hope of converting infidels and could not take the position.

He then asked the commissioner for permission to travel with his three brothers to the southern regions of Guatemala, Tabasco and Chiapas. After the commissioner reluctantly gave them permission, they set sail for Tabasco hoping to arrive in the city of Santa Maria de la Victoria in a few days. Eight days later when they were about to enter the bar of the Tabasco River, near the town of Santa Maria de la Victoria, they spotted pirates ship in their pursuit.

For the next eight days, they were followed day and night. Frightened that they would soon be over taken by the brigands, they quickly sailed for the refuge of the Port of Campeche from where they had originally come. It was on their return that the commissioner counseled them to pray and search their hearts to discern the will of God.

After an appropriate time, the commissioner again called the four missionaries to meet with him. "You have had enough time for prayer, reflection and discernment. May I ask what you have in mind for your future?" he asked.

Fray Melchor was the first who dared to answer, "Very Reverend

Commissioner, after meditating on this issue and applying good judgment, we are still confused about what to do. Perhaps *confusion* is not the right word but *undecided* as to God's will. Let me explain. If one of the two decisions would separate us from the kingdom of God, we would know clearly that it was not His will but ours. But, we are confident that both decisions will lead us to the Kingdom of God. First of all, the Recollect Institute in Merida is certainly a way to bring us to the Supreme Being, but also the missionary work in the land of infidels is something which no doubt pleases the Kingdom of God as well."

"I understand your concern and personally do not want to oppose the designs of the Lord. Perhaps he has prepared you for a greater task in mission work," replied the commissioner.

The four friars smiled at each other rejoicing in the commissioner's understanding and goodwill.

"This situation reminds me of when the Apostles had to decide who would replace Judas Iscariot and they cast lots to make the decision," he told them. "As you well know, the decision fell on Matthias. So, to be more certain of God's divine will, we will shuffle the cards three times and let a child choose a card for each man randomly."

They did so. The first lot was that everyone would stay, but the second lot determined only two of them would stay, and the third lot was for Father José Díez and Father Francisco Casañas to stay. All of the friars readily agreed on the lots.

Thus with the permission of the commissioner general, Father Margil and Father Melchor embarked for Guatemala on the 13th of April. To prevent another pirate attack, they were escorted by a frigate to their destination and accompanied by Commissioner Luzuriaga. They arrived in the town of Santa Maria de la Victoria on the Tabasco River and from there they began their pilgrimage. Before they left, a kindly gentleman carved them a wooden crucifix to carry on their mission.

PART THREE: SOUTHERN TERRITORIES

XVII

Royal City of Chiapa
September 1684

The caravan traveling to the Royal City of Chiapa made its way through the rugged carriageway of endless curves and bends. In a litter pulled by two mules, Commissioner Luzuriaga rode comfortably protected from the falling drizzle. It was a daunting task for the muleteers who nervously guided the animals and the precious cargo.

Behind was a legion of soldiers called *dragóns*, consisting of a sergeant and eight armed and mounted soldiers, smartly uniformed in their blue jackets, military boots, and matching great coats. Traversing the challenging terrain was difficult for the soldier but was even tougher for the horses and mules. They snorted and reared under their heavy load as they inched their way forward. There were two extra mules that served as replacements should the need arise.

The royal city, surrounded by mountains, was also known as Chiapa of the Spanish, *Chiapa de Españoles*. It was nestled in a plateau in the southern most regions of New Spain. It was a renowned city, but its equatorial weather of constant fog and the fresh scent of pine and oak trees made it seem disconcerting at times.

The commissioner carried his holy ornaments and sacred vessels in the front seat and held silver beads in his left hand, while he prayed the mysteries of the Rosary. On the second Glorious Mystery, he felt a slight shiver as his mind wondered to the rich history of the city. He remembered the days of the early Spanish conquerors when the indigenous of the region fought Captain Don Diego de Mazariegos, of the Hernán Cortes expedition, in the famous battle of Tepechtia. The Indians were hold-up in the security of the mountains above the Tabasco River Canyon and were surrounded by the Spanish soldiers. With no hope of escape, they martyred themselves by jumping to their death on the rocks and river one mile below. The legend was that for days the river water ran red with blood of the proud warriors. Feeling compassion, Captain Mazariegos called a truce and with the surviving Indians, he founded the first settlement in the region which now included the Royal City of Chiapa.

The commissioner had just finished the Rosary when they reached the cobbled streets on their way to the large main square. They passed along one side of the cathedral and in a few minutes they reached the Church of St. Nicholas, located behind the cathedral. The simple church, framed by two large pillars, had a belfry with three bells and was where the Holy Mass was celebrated for the Indians.

When the mules stopped, the commissioner peered from behind the cotton curtains at the front door. He waited for his servants to open the door before he stepped down from the litter. While the muleteers and laborers took care of luggage and the mules, the commissioner walked briskly to the church. Entering through the side columns, he walked in, knelt, and made the sign of the cross before the altar and entered the vestry.

There he found Father Margil and Father Melchor, who arrived earlier, and gave them a warm fraternal embrace.

"My dear brothers," he said with tears in his eyes, "I am thankful to see you alive!"

The friars were sincerely moved by his trepidation.

"From the news received about you, I thought I would never see you again," said the commissioner.

"To tell the truth, we had a very difficult journey! Many times we feared we would succumb to the elements, Your Paternity," said Father Margil.

"We became very ill on the way to the town of San Marcos Evangelista Tuchtla," said Father Melchor. "By the time we arrived, we were almost dead. Father Margil received the last rites, and the townspeople made our coffins!"

"It was truly a miracle that you recovered and survived the treacherous journey," said the commissioner.

"We are thankful," answered Father Margil. "But my recovery has been slow."

"The Indians kindly carried us in hammocks to Chiapa of the Indians, *Chiapa de Indios,* where we convalesced until they brought us here," said Father Melchor.

"Ah, what kindness! You know your objective is to recover completely so your missionary work can continue," concluded the commissioner.

"Yes, Your Excellency, that is what we want most of all," said Father Margil.

"I will not be able to spend much time with you," said the commissioner. "I just came to see for myself that you were alive and able to continue your journey. Now that I have seen for myself, I must continue on my trip. As for you, my holy fathers, I want your health to be completely restored before you continue. Remember your goal is to reach the confines of the kingdom of New Spain where the natives have not heard the word of God for many years. But I urge you to go at a slower pace! There is plenty of time to convert souls on your way."

"For now and until we meet again, I bid you farewell."

XVIII

Very Noble and Very Loyal City of Santiago
of the Knights in Guatemala
July 1685

Nervousness and anticipation was clearly exhibited on the faces of people as they awaited the arrival of the Major Mail from Spain. This solemn ceremony, at the Stone Cross on the outskirts of the city, was a tradition held once or twice a year. The Governor and the chief authorities were present, all wearing distinctive garments adorned with a chest full of medals, as was, the illustrious bishop of Guatemala, Friar Andres de las Navas y Quevedo, and the superiors of the convents of the various religious orders. Knights and ladies, richly dressed, were also part of that huge crowd.

The letters, royal dispatches, and other documents sent from Seville were received in the House of Major Mail of the Indies. The correspondence was then shipped in huge crates aboard the Indies Fleet. On arrival in New Spain, the crates were transported to the Palace of the Viceroy in México City where the viceroy personally oversaw the opening of the vessels. Then with the viceroy's approval, the drivers called mail lieutenants and disbursed the correspondence to the various cities. It took months, and sometimes almost a year, for the mail to finally reach its destination.

"It's coming!" shouted one of the guards, who had been watching the road with a telescope. A general murmur fell upon the crowd as their excitement grew.

The correspondence convoy approached slowly. In the lead, the gallant mail marshal rode galloping on a black stallion. He was elegantly dressed in his royal blue coat and pants and high black boots. Next in the caravan came the correspondence wagon and its driver, who was assigned by the mayor of mail to assure the cargo was delivered timely and without problems. Behind him, two foremen rode horses carrying the mail saddlebags. The military escorts, consisting of a lieutenant and four soldiers, were last in the line.

When the contingent arrived at the stone cross, they slowed for a rendezvoused with the people. They dismounted from their horses to the solemn sound of the marching band as background. They turned to the crowd and saluted the authorities, who responded the same.

Then they walked to the huge stone cross where they knelt on one knee and bowed their heads. The proceedings then continued with the Bishop giving a thanksgiving prayer and blessing the mail bags in honor of a safe arrival.

At the conclusion of the religious ceremony, the postilion gave the Governor the news report, and the driver made a formal delivery of the bags to the authorities of the city. People burst into loud applause and cheered loudly. The officials congratulated the members of the convoy on their success in weathering the dangerous seas, the pirate attacks, many accidents and assaults, and even thieves on the roads. Then with great joy, they began the distribution of the precious cargo. The recipients of the letters showed their feelings with tears, anger, laughter, sighs and the occasional fainting after reading the letters from their loved ones back home.

The Bishop received the largest bulk of the mail, and after a final blessing he excused himself from the authorities and began his journey back to the palace. The people were so busy reading the news that they paid little attention to the prelate. He left quietly with only the superiors of the religious orders joining him on the return trip.

As the Bishop and his companions were on their way back to the city, they stopped at the stone cross on the hill and admired the beauty of the city in the luscious valley surrounded by mountains.

The prosperous and charming city of Santiago was known for its fertile soil and abundant evergreen. Its grassy fields were an excellent food source for the plentiful wildlife and domestic animals. Two rivers served as the water supply for the generous gardens that produced an abundance of fruits, vegetables, and flowers. The mild year-round climate was like an eternal spring. A visitor once said, "The gift and comfort of this place leaves nothing to be desired."

The modest homes and buildings were extremely neat and well kept. The people were well dressed and happy and often gathered to enjoy good food and fun at church feasts and festivities.

When the Archbishop's party arrived at the main building of the Bishopric, he invited the superiors of the various religious orders a cup of tea. The fathers accepted the kind invitation which was held in a private room.

The Bishop of Guatemala belonged to the Order of Mercy and had been appointed such due to his outstanding performance as Bishop of Leon in Nicaragua. He received the appointment only one year earlier. Now he was loved by the Guatemalan people and regarded as one of their most illustrious prelates. He had a very stern look with prominent eyebrows, a large nose, and small mouth, but his large dark eyes expressed kindness. He strived for direct contact with his parishioners and promised to personally visit each of the parishes in his area. He did not want to be limited to exercising apostolic from the pulpit.

Once they all were served tea, Bishop Navas started the conversation, "I thank you fathers for taking the time to speak with me."

"Our thanks go to you, Your Excellency," responded the fathers.

Included in the round table were representatives from the orders of the Dominicans, Franciscans, and Our Lady of Mercy.

"I shall ask you, Honorable Fathers, to make every effort to ensure that each member of your religious order not only becomes proficient in the Indian languages but also good teachers in the languages."

He took a sip of his tea and then said, "You all need to learn how to speak the different dialects of the Indians. This is the only way you can communicate with them effectively; the more capable and intelligent you are in their language, the more sincere you will come across to the natives and the more you will touch their conscience," remarked the Bishop.

"I think we all agree with Your Eminence, and I am sure that each of us will work hard to respect your orders," said one of the fathers.

"I'm sure you will try your best," said the Bishop with a friendly smile. "But the truth is that it will not be easy. It seems the devil is up to his crafty tricks in these lands. He plants the seeds of discord that adds to the confusion of so many different languages. Nevertheless, we must remember that His Majesty Philip III, may God give him glory, dictated that no fathers could serve and preach religious doctrine in any area where they did not know the language of the natives."

"Don't worry, illustrious Bishop, we will take great care that all our priests and friars, especially those designed to address the natives, master the language of the Indians," said one of the superiors as the others nodded in agreement.

"You still have much work to do to ready yourselves for the missionary work in these lands," concluded the Bishop, and standing, he said "So I will count on you, fathers, and in all your exceptional brothers to carry out this work."

XIX

The magnificent temple of the Holy Cathedral of Guatemala was brimming with people from all over the kingdom. The president, the Royal Court, His Excellency the Bishop, all civil and religious authorities, and many socialites were present. There was not an inch of space for another person. From the elevated pulpit, the young and confident Father Margil addressed the faithful. As he spoke, his audience listened attentively, as they did not want to miss a word from the mouth of the holy priest. After all, he was the one the Indians called a saint.

The words of Father Margil fell upon the audience like a thick blanket and weighed heavy on the hearts of the parishioners. His words, like daggers, pointed out the dangers that lust, envy, greed, and pride would bring upon the lives of those who dared to commit these deadly sins. He preached that the family unit was endangered by the carefree lifestyle many had chosen to follow.

At the climax of his oration, Father Margil lifted a chain and with a firm hand whirled the metal through the air and struck his back. The sound of the lash filled the room as his flesh split open. Horrified, the crowd watched as not a grimace or a sound came from the pious man.

The audience was shocked! Color faded from the faces of the women and many fell to the floor. The men let out a weak cry of dismay.

Every sentence spoken from the mouth of Father Margil was accompanied by a hard lashing of the chain. Tears streamed down the faces of women. The men wanting to show their manliness said nothing but clutched their fists so hard that their nails brought blood to their hands.

To add to the dismay blood seeped onto Father Margil's habit. His act of penance and sacrifice astonished the people. Feeling the need to examine their consciences, they bowed their heads and looked deep into their souls. After this, the confessionals were crowded with the faithful who wanted atonement from their sins. As they lined up to wait their turn, the most desperate souls began to scream loudly their regret for their past deeds. Without doubt, it was a most remarkable celebration, one that would be remembered for many years to come.

The preaching continued the next day when Father Melchor vehemently provoked sighs and tears.

In the crowd, a quiet murmur resonated, "He preaches like a saint!"

The orations of both priests caused a huge stir among the people. Even the other friars and priests commented to each other, "God has sent Father Margil and Father Melchor to us. With their abject humility, charity and truth, they can show us the way to Our Lord. They will not force us, but will call us to action by their examples. They only ask us, who are the preachers, to preach with truth and humility and to see the face of the crucified Christ in the faces of the poor and the lame."

Father Margil and Father Melchor ministered to the people of Guatemala City for almost a year and a half before they continued their trek across the country.

Their travels took them to Ciudad Real and Soconusco, the southwest corner of the state of Chiapas, Mexico, along its border with Guatemala. Everywhere they went a congregation of Indians followed. By now their fame preceded them as they were regarded as saints by most people in the lands. In every town and village along the coast, the arrival of the holy fathers was anticipated. On the roads, caravans of people who wanted to hear them speak were endless. There were hundreds and maybe thousands of people no matter where they went. Two, three, and maybe four thousand Indians followed them bearing palms. In the words of a witness to these events, "It seemed as if the forests were moving."

The fathers did not like the attention they drew and felt it was a hindrance to their ability to spread the word of God effectively to the faithful. They did not want the pageantry of the Indians! They repeatedly asked them not to march with them, but the Indians ignored the requests. Instead they marched behind them. Soon, it was necessary for the fathers to warn the people that they would not go any further, until these demonstrations ceased. Although the parades stopped, the people continued to follow. This the fathers could not stop. Along the way, Father Margil taught the Indians how to sing, and as they walked, they sang songs of praise and thanksgiving.

When the fathers neared Guatemala City, they stopped and waited for the late hours of the night so the people would be asleep when they entered the city on their way to the temple of San Francisco. Nevertheless, throughout the early morning hours, the Indians came and settled into the atrium located near the cemetery. There they waited to catch a glimpse of the priests. When Father Margil and Father Melchor arrived to see the Bishop, the crowds of both Indians and Spaniards accompanied them. Once again the fathers expressed their dissatisfaction to the people, but there was no way for them to avoid their notoriety. The fathers, still wearing the same torn and tattered habits of their journey, introduced themselves to the Bishop and the captain general. They looked tired and forlorn in their garments that had been mended countless times and washed far less.

The fathers' mission at the cathedral was postponed due to an imminent attack from the mischievous pirates stationed off their coast. In fear, the people went to the temple and prayed as the pirates fired volleys as impending threats of invasion. The authorities knew the danger was real since only one year earlier the pirates had overrun the Fort San Felipe in the Gulf of Rio Dulce. There they burned buildings and stole the military's ammunition and artillery.

While waiting for their mission to begin, on the 18th of October, the priests were dispatched to the villa of Escuintla to help ease tensions between two factions inside the military. After Father Margil and Father Melchor made peace among the soldiers, they returned to Guatemala City.

On the 13th of January, their long awaited mission began in the capital city. Soon it extended into the neighborhoods and squares, into the convents of friars and nuns, and later extended into neighboring towns. The mission moved fast and lasted a little over six months. At the end of their mission, the fathers were content to see the large number of people who repented for their sinful pasts and the many converts brought into the Church.

Pleased with the outcome, they set their sights further south. Now it was time to enter the lands of Nicaragua, Honduras, and Costa Rica.

XX

Territory of Grand Nicoya, Providence of Costa Rica
January 1688

The Indian Nanbueme adjusted the colorful plume of feathers around his head. He was a majestic man with a muscular chest and chiseled arms emblazoned with tattoos of wild animals. Naked, except for a canvas loin cloth that covered his noble parts, he stood proud to represent his people. On his arms and legs, he wore bracelets of shells and feathers, and around his neck he wore a necklace of colorful seashells. His face was painted with black stripes.

He was accompanied by the Indian Urzaryrey, his best friend. They entered the town of Nicoya in northwestern Costa Rica late in the afternoon. The town was located on the peninsula carrying the same name. When they arrived at the main square, the townspeople were celebrating the arrival of the new moon, a traditional Indian feast day. The ceremonial event lasted for hours because the Indians believed it was a symbol of brotherhood and coexistence and strengthened the group's social identity.

Immediately, they began to mix with the crowds in front of the *teyopa* building, a wide hut in the center of the square. Inside the hut, stone steps led to a mound of dirt and rocks that served as a sacrificial altar. Scattered about the steps lay carved wood or stone idols depicting half man and half animals, along with primitive weapons. Nanbueme watched the arrival of the *cacique*, the chief of the town. He was surrounded by nobles, courtiers, warriors, and knights, along with the feared and arrogant Indian knights called *galpones*. The prestigious elders, called *huehues*, stood next to the chief.

The town was one of the largest in the territory of Grand Nicoya, whose dominions extended to the banks of Lake Cocibolca in Nicaragua. The body of water was one of the largest in the West Indies, and some said it was the only lake where sharks could be found in its depths.

When the ceremony started, the women held hands in a big circle around the sacred stone of sacrifice. They wore loincloths and sleeveless shirts, and like the men, were adorned with tattoos, necklaces, and new black *gutaras.*[1] Five or six steps behind them was another circle composed of only men. In between the two groups stood attendants who served the participants an extremely strong, acidic beverage from fig shaped clay jars. The brew, prepared well in advance of the ceremony, was made by placing chewed corn into a jar with sugar cane, which then had to ferment. Each participant received three or four sips at a time from the drab container. The chief then ordered the servants to bring the dancers crude cigars which were lighted and passed around from hand to hand. Each person inhaled deeply and held the smoke as long as possible, before exhaling through their nose and mouth.

To the beat of drums and accompanied by ritual music, men and women danced wildly around, rolling their bodies and heads, moving their feet, and drinking excessively. Drums and rattles, made from gourds with pebbles inside, accompanied the performance.

The Indians celebrated well into the night as the participants, full of alcohol and the devil weed, made frantic and jerking movements as they stumbled around. The dances became wild and exotic. Some laughed, some cried, and some jumped in an endless frenzy of movement.

In midst of the magical ritual, the climax was reached when a victim was led to the high priest by four warriors. He was made to lie on the sacrificial stone, and then with a single blow, he was stabbed in the heart.

At the moment of death, the women went crazy, crying loudly and running frantically into the surrounding forests and mountains.

The sober men tried to stop their partners any way they could. Some used bribery, others prayed, and some even used brute force to stop them. The frantic race of the women was a planned event and part of the ceremonial ritual. In fact, the woman who ran the farthest without being stopped would be recognized by the people. Nanbueme quickly stopped his wife, and she returned to the crowd without incident.

---

1   Indian made shoes.

Urzaryre`s wife did not suffer the same fate. She was stopped with blows from a stick and then tied up and taken into the town. There she was kept tied until the next day. When the effects of drunkenness wore off, she was freed.

XXI

After a long march to the Province of Costa Rica, Father Margil and Father Melchor stopped at the top of a hill overlooking the beautiful town of Cartago. In front of them lay a colorful valley surrounded by luscious green hills. The clear blue skies and the emerald green pastures framed the small, picturesque village. Dotted along the valley were no more than seventy houses of adobe with tile roofs. The town was one of the last Spanish villas in southern New Spain. The only other Spanish villa in all of Costa Rica was the village of Esparza.

Long before they reached the town, the barefoot Indians came to greet them. Accompanying the Indians were the friars of the Convent of San Francisco in Cartago.

Carrying their cross high in the air, the friars entered the town singing *Alabado*, a song of praise and glory written a long ago time ago by Father Margil. With great solemnity and joy, they sang:

> Lift up your hearts in joy and praise Him
> In the Blessed Sacrament Most Holy,
> Where the Lord, His glory veiled,
> Assists souls faithful and lowly.
> All praise to the glorious Conception
> Of the Queen of Heaven,
> For She, remaining Virgin and stainless
> Is the Mother of the Word Eternal.

Blessed be St. Joseph, spouse of Mary,
The one chosen by God on high.
To his paternal care so tender
The Word Incarnate was given.

And so for endless ages
Shall it be for evermore.
Amen! Jesus and Mary!
Jesus, Mary, and Joseph!

O dearest Jesus,
To Thee I give my heart.
Imprint on it, dear Lord,
Thy most holy Passion.

O Our Lady of Sorrows,
Grant that at the moment of death,
We may surrender our souls to God
Through thy most holy hands.

Whoever seeks to follow God
And strives to enter into His glory.
One thing he must do and say with all his heart:
"Die rather than sin.
Rather than sin, die!"

When they arrived, they headed straight to the temple of Saint James which had two adjacent chapels, one for the rosaries and other for the souls. Here they gave thanks to our Heavenly Father for allowing them the good fortune to reach their destination located close to the southern border of New Spain.

After their prayers, Father Guardian helped them settle into their rooms in the convent and offered an attendant to doctor their wounds. Their aching feet were covered with cuts and bruises caused by the harsh elements encountered during their journey.

"It's a great joy and honor for you to be at our convent," said Father Guardian. "We have received good news about the mission work you have been doing. It is truly amazing that the two of you alone have helped the inhabitants of the peninsula of Nicoya stop their horrible vice of drunkenness and their ritual acts of human sacrifice."

"It's not a vice," said Father Margil. "Believe it or not, these binges are part of ancient pagan rituals. We were blessed to have the wisdom of the *Guatuso* Indians. After bringing the word of Our Lord to them, they were baptized with the understanding that the rituals were bad and not pleasing to God. I believe they will follow our way."

As they spoke, the church's assistant continued to wash their feet, dry them, and sprinkle them with a healing powder made from the root of a plant the Indians called *güerequi.*

"Nevertheless it was not easy!" Father Melchor said. "The Indian chief told us that when he tried to convince his people to stop such practices, he feared he was being criticized for looking weak and not defending their traditions."

The fathers looked at their feet, deformed from the many calluses, sores, cuts, and bruises and thought it would take a miracle for the assistant to heal the pitiful looking limbs.

"It has not been easy to approach the Indians," said Father Margil," often in the Indian villages of Liberia, Nicoya, Bagaces, Canas and more, we were met with suspicion and distrust."

"Yes, it is true they are distrusting," Father Guardian said, "but it's because they have been abused so many times in the past. Often times their villages are raided and their people enslaved by wicked men."

"Once they realized that we were not the evil ones, they talked to us freely, and told us that the Nicoya population was greatly diminished by these foreign abductions," said Father Margil.

"Not only in Nicoya," said Father Guardian, "Also in Matina and several other local towns along the way. They have all suffered beatings, mutilation, and thefts. Fortunately, our voice was heard by the president of the Royal Audience of Guatemala, and he quickly banned such practices by his soldiers in the future."

"I'm glad to hear that," said Father Guardian. "We can't be complicit in such practices," chimed in Father Melchor.

"Sometimes, I wonder who is more difficult and dangerous, our own people or the Indians. '*Of our soldiers, free us, our Lord,*' is the prayer of one of our own friars," said the guardian.

"I can assure you, Sir, that our work as missionaries is not to be witnesses of injustices but to combat them. Our obligation is to stand at the side of the oppressed, as Jesus stood near the lepers and the homeless," said Father Margil.

"Unfortunately, there are still sectors of our population who think the Indians are inferior beings and that they have no intelligence or aspirations," said the father guardian.

"Right now, I think the Indians are crushed and subjugated but once we support them, they will rise and be able to walk forward, understanding the Gospel, and integrate into our lifestyles just fine. Then, they will be able to contribute to our society."

"Fortunately, our sermons were also heard by our own people. Captain Sebastian Guillen told us ..."

"Ah, indeed! You're talking about the friendly officer who accompanied us from the town of Esparza!" said Father Margil.

"The same," Father Guardian said. "He told us how he witnessed a number of Spanish men, who formerly lived unmarried with native paramours, listen to your sermons and then corrected these situations by marrying the women."

"It was the Holy Spirit who opened their ears and moved their conscience," said Father Margil.

The assistant finished working on their wounded feet and wrapped them with clean white cloths. The friars felt uncomfortable with all the attention they received, as they were unaccustomed to such care. The Father Guardian seemed to guess their thoughts, so he approached them and put his hand on their shoulders thanking them for their sacrifices.

"The work you have ahead of you will not be easy fathers," said Father Guardian with a sigh.

"We are blessed by the favor of God, the intercession of the Blessed Virgin Mary, and the support of our patron saint, Saint Francis of Assisi. We look forward to our next stop in the lands of the *Talamanca* Indians. We wish to get there as soon as possible," said Father Margil.

"God be with you, my friends! It is well known that those strange and dangerous lands remain untouched. It has been more than a century since our Dominican brother Father Peter Fray Alonso de Betanzos lived among the natives. No civilized man or holy man has ventured into the region since."

Father Guardian went to the window and looked southward where he could see the lofty peaks overlooking the lands about which he was speaking.

"The paths opened by the venerable Father Betanzos have long been closed. He made a sixteen year pilgrimage there, until he died in Chomes near the Gulf of Nicoya. Since then, not a soul has walked in those jungles!"

Father Margil walked to the window and stood beside Father Guardian so he too could see the lofty peaks of the Chirripó Mountains. His heart beat quickly as he yearned to reach the coveted territory of the *Talamanca* Indians.

"God will reopen the paths for us!" he said firmly.

PART FOUR:
INLAND PROVINCES

XXII

𝕿he *Bribri* Indian woman left her hut and looked about for a sign of life, but there was none. She grimaced in pain as she gazed beyond the huts into the lush vegetation of the dense forest bordering the village. In the deep damp valley surrounded by hills not a soul could be seen and not a sound could be heard. The people had left a few days earlier because they feared contamination and even death if they stayed while she gave birth. The animals had also gone, and now not a squirrel, parrot, macaw, or any living creature remained in the desolate village. She was utterly alone.

Her husband and her sisters, who were also wives of her husband, had departed as well. But she was not sad or resentful for she knew all the women of her village faced the birth of a child in this same manner. For as long as anyone could remember, this traditional birthing rite had been their custom.

She waddled slowly into the dank jungle wearing only a skimpy loin cloth made of banana leaves that partially cover her naked body. Her protruding stomach revealed her impending fate. The dark nipples of her breast were perched atop her large sagging breasts, as if they were lifeless blemishes on her dark brown skin. Her hair fell upon her neck and shoulders and was entangled with her coral necklaces.

On swollen bare fee,t she stumbled further into the woods looking for the clearing where her husband had built a birthing shack a few days earlier. When she found it, she knew she would remain here until the time of birth. In a few hours, the labor pains began. Unaided and scared, she drew all the strength she could muster to endure the agony and exhausting labor of delivery. As time passed, she quietly hoped to please her husband with the birth of a son. Lying on the hard floor, she choked back cries of pain and pushed as hard as she could to expel the child but nothing happened. With a blank stare and sweat running down her face, she took both hands and pressed hard on the top of her stomach. She pushed several more times with her legs drawn as near as possible to her breasts, trying to end her suffering. But, her pain grew more intense with each contraction. She felt her world would surely be coming to an end. Soon thereafter, the intolerable pain subsided as the child slipped from her womb and gave a loud cry.

Exhausted, she lay quietly for a few minutes, unable to attend to the immediate needs of the child. A charitable old woman came near the cabin and left outside the door a sharp piece of cane to cut the umbilical cord. Then fearing contamination, the old woman quickly ran back into the forest to avoid the *bucur* or maternity sickness.

With great effort, the mother crawled from the cabin with the baby in tow. She took the knife and quickly cut the cord. Carefully, she made a knot, and cut it near the baby. Then, she washed the newborn with a bit of warm water left in a banana leaf outside the door by the old woman. Sore and tired, with little strength, she walked slowly to the nearby river holding the baby. There she bathed and started the decontamination process.

When she returned to the shack, a shaman sorcerer called an *awá* was there to help her with the rest of the rite of purification. The elderly healer was extremely thin with a sunburned face that marked his many years. His wide dark eyes were glassy and darted around as if he was looking for something in the deserted landscape of the jungle. Then looking upwards and speaking in a language unknown to the young mother, he began communicating with supernatural spirits. To the woman, he appeared to be completely entranced and out of touch with reality. The dutiful woman was called to stand in front of him where he began to chant softly. He stuck his skinny trembling fingers into a container of water and began washing the woman all over. When finished, the shaman drank the water to swallow the impurities removed from the woman.

Next, he lit a carved pipe of tobacco and blew the smoke over the impure woman, from head to toe. The magical smoke and its pungent odor penetrated every inch of her body.

With the same fire in the pipe, the shaman burned magical plant leaves and passed them over the woman's bare chest while mumbling the ritualistic prayers. Next he washed his hands as a sign of purification. To symbolize the end of the ritual, he next took his magic stones of sacred power and healing and placed them in the palm of his hand. While speaking to the stones, he ceremoniously blew on them, and they began to spin. Once the stones stopped, the *awá's* musical chant of unfamiliar words quietly drifted into the wind.

What the woman did not know was that he had spoken to the spirits of animals so they could assist him in the cleansing. He had to find the right animal that could help him liberate the woman from the evil spirits that resided in her from childbirth.

Now his work was complete. They could return home where she and the child would gladly be received by the rest of the village without fear of death.

The shaman's last gesture of faith for the child was to put a tiger's tooth on its stomach to ensure he would be a good hunter. He also touched the baby's skin with horsehair to give it horse qualities, so he would be strong and able to carry large loads.

As customs dictated, this primitive but routine ritual was performed in the solitude of the jungle with only the mother, the healer, and the baby present. Everyone knew that no one could see the mother or the baby until she was purified from the illness caused by the birth of a child.

The ancient rituals practiced by the *Talamanca* Indians were taught to the shaman by Sibö, the supreme god who created the world. They believed these ceremonies would cure diseases, purify parturient, cast spells, predict the future, and even create magic. For this reason, the *awá* was highly respected and feared by the natives who knew their fate depended on him. His mere presence caused them nervousness and concern. No one dared to contradict or cast doubt on the wise man's claims. They all feared the fate of a non-believer.

Not even the dead were beyond the control of the shaman, for they served as the intermediary who drove spirits to their final resting places. According to custom, a body could not be buried immediately after death because it would contaminate the land. In a death ritual, the shaman would cover the deceased with large leaves and cotton cloth. The bodies were then hung in hammocks outside the village. There they remained for a year. During this time, the Indians believed the shaman led the souls of the dead by the delicate cotton thread to all the places they visited in his lifetime. They also believed the thread kept the soul from getting lost. It was an important issue, because a lost soul could not return to its bones. After time passed, the *awá* returned the skeleton to the arena. Around a ceremonial fire and amid chants, the shaman opened the cotton bundle and allowed the four souls of the departed to be reunited to the bones. The four souls were the soul of the outer body, the soul of the eyes, the soul of liver and heart, and soul of the bones.

Finally with a howl, the wise old man announced the souls had reached their destination and the remains of the deceased could be buried in the family graveyard in three to four months. If the deceased had been brave in his life, he was given the glory of being buried with a macaw so the feathers could serve him in the afterlife. Likewise, if the deceased had slaves at that time of his death, then the slaves were buried with him to serve him in his afterlife.

Throughout their existence, from birth to death, all activities of the Indians were hopelessly tied to the *awá*. All daily activities, like hunting or warfare, were governed by those magical stones of shamans. Nothing was done without the interdiction of the *awá*. Nothing was allowed if it was not authorized by the shaman. In all diseases, in all spells, in all the ceremonies, the precious magical stones were present. Only they could communicate with the divine spirits, and only they could transmit gifts from the deity. Only they could establish a link between man and the spiritual world.

The *awá* was satisfied with the work he had done. After all, it had been many years ago when he learned the art and magic of the shaman and the wisdom of the sacred stones. He knew he alone could interpret their movements and he alone was the prophet of the village.

For this reason, he was firmly against the new visitors called Franciscans, and he was not going to allow them to enter his village. He knew they came from the other side of the sea to preach against their tradition and his magical talents.

XXIII

The persistent rain seemed endless. Since the previous afternoon, all day and all night, the storm clouds gathered above the priests and dropped torrential rain. Everything was now soaked. Even their temporary shelter, which had served them well until the wee hours of the night, was now in shambles, and the rising water had cut them off from their surroundings. The total darkness, except for the frequent lightning strikes, was overwhelming and very frightening. They sat alone and helpless on the wet floor huddled against a rock. They trembled from head to toe as they tried to keep warm. Never had they been in a rainstorm like this one.

When the rain finally stopped and the sun peeked from the darkened clouds, Father Margil and Father Melchor first thanked God for their survival. Then they looked around at their new surroundings and saw the beautiful green landscape of the far off jungles of the Talamancan Mountains full of life and color.

As they walked into the jungle, its dark and dangerous nature made it appear treacherous. Although at times the sun shined overhead, only a small fraction of its light penetrated into the forest below. The trees were much too tall and their leaves formed too wide of a canopy to allow the rays of sun to penetrate the dark, damp, cold soil below. For this reason, there was almost no vegetation, only a greenish slippery mold and a dry bed of leaves in a permanent state of decomposition. Most of the time, it rained.

To make their journey more difficult, the underbrush hid an assortment of venomous snakes, poisonous dart frogs, centipedes, tarantulas, scorpions, and other dangerous creatures. The humble friars found walking through the wet muddy ground almost impossible in the dense vegetation. With every step the danger of accidentally stepping on a snake and suffering a venomous insect bite increased. They feared the agonizing death caused from the bite of a huge serpent called the velvet, or yellow beard, that was plentiful in the lands. They were extremely careful not to mistake a fallen branch for the slumbering serpent. The banks of rivers and wetlands were also covered with man-eating crocodiles, jaguars, ocelots, and pumas. And to add to their distress, humidity and heat caused their tattered wet habits to stick to their skin. It seemed their journey to the Indian villages turned out to be extremely dangerous and terribly uncomfortable.

For several days, they walked through the jungles along the seacoast of the West Indies looking for the region of the Indians of Talamanca, but they had little success. When the rains finally stopped on the third day, they were completely disoriented from the many sleepless nights and constant rain.

Resting their tired bodies, they were startled awake by yells from fierce *Cabecar* warriors exiting from the dense forest with their spears, knives, and clubs. Every arrow was ominously pointed at the religious. Startled, but relieved, the priests knew they finally arrived at the Talamanca region and found its coveted Indian tribe.

The nearly naked Indians were covered only by a tiny loincloth similar to those seen many times in other regions. On their faces, necks, arms and legs, they had symmetrically lumpy scars which appeared to have been healed-over cuts made from sharp stones. Their mutilations were covered with dark tattoos.

In their nose and lower lips, small bones pierced the skin. They learned later that, to the warriors, each bone was a trophy for the number they had killed in combat. Father Margil observed that many of the warriors had many piercings in their lips.

To the menacing shouts of the Indians, the friars were led into a jungle clearing. Neither Father Margil nor Father Melchor understood what was being said, but they knew the Indians agitated voices and aggressive expressions were not good signs.

The Indians grabbed, stripped, and bound them to trees. Through an interpreter, the chief commanded the priests, with threats of death, to bow down and worship their village idols. The holy men, bare and naked, refused and instead knelt and prayed aloud the Rosary. The chief, hearing the unrecognizable chant, ordered them to be beaten again. Even after he left, the priest continued to pray.

Eventually, the mighty Indian chief came back, and with the help of an interpreter, he said, "You have come here to spy on us for the white soldiers in our lands! Now, you are our prisoners! We will keep you here until your soldiers come! We will use you to barter for our brave warriors they are holding. If you do not help us, we will kill you!"

The friars tried to explain that they were not spies, but the chief did not believe their words. He only turned his back and walked away leaving the friars guarded by his fierce-looking warriors.

For three days, the priests remained tied to the trees never once crying from their excruciating pain. They suffered in silence, and the only sound that came from them was a faint chant of continuous prayer. When hunger and thirst took over their bodies, they passed out only to be awakened by the swift blows of their captors. Day and night, they were watched and made to remain on their knees. They knew their end was near and their martyrdom for the Church would soon come. The days passed agonizingly slow. By the second day, their pain seemed eternal, and by the third they, had no awareness. Their lips were dry and swollen, and their lifeless eyes had gone blank. This is when the chief and his warriors returned.

"Where are your soldiers? asked the Indian chief, "We want them to come so we can attack and kill them, but they have not come to save you!"

"We did not bring soldiers. We came alone. It's only me and Father Melchor," whispered Father Margil.

"You lie! You are spies for the soldiers. We were warned by our medicine man, the awá. We know that you have come to rob us, and your soldiers will come parading around in their gleaming shields of armor. Their guns will spit fire and silence our warriors. We will suffer great destruction!" said the chief

"We are not spies; we are men of God!" muttered Father Margil.

"You lie! Many white men before you have come to kidnap our children and rape our women. They come to take our warriors and force them to work in your corn fields. We fight but always have to submit to their superior weapons, and then we are enslaved!" uttered the chief.

"We do not come to steal. We come to speak the word of God!" Father Melchor whispered.

"In the name of your god, you make us abandon our towns. You force us to build your towns. Then we have to live there and work your fields. You enslave our men and beat them to death!" said one of the warriors.

"We have not come to take your homes. We have come to meet you, live with you, learn your language, work with you, and bring you a message from God," said Father Margil in a begging tone of voice.

"A message of war, injustice, domination, and slavery!" said the Indian chief.

"It's not true. Our God wants peace, love, justice, and freedom for your people!" declared both priest in unison.

"So why have your warriors come at other times to steal our men and make slaves of them?" a warrior asked.

"Take my word as truth; it won´t happen again. Our Governor will not allow such practices by his soldiers in the future; they shall never again enslave your people. He has promised us!" cried Father Melchor.

"How can I believe you? I believe you are their spies. You want to oppress us too. You work for them; you are their servants!" loudly proclaimed the chief.

"It's not true; we have denounced injustice! We want to stand beside you; we have come to free you!" Father Margil said in a pleading tone.

"The *Sambos* and *Mosquitoes* tribes come to steal our people, too!" responded the chief.

"They are pirates. They are not our people, and we can't control them. I can't promise that they will not come again, but I can offer help to defend against them," said Father Margil

"And who will defend us from you?" said the chief.

"Believe me when I say that we come in peace. We do not bring weapons. We do not bring soldiers. Our weapons are the words of God. Our soldiers are the angels of heaven," declared Father Melchor.

For a few more days they remained tied to the tree, but after much persuasion from the friars, the Indian chief was finally convinced the soldiers were not coming. He felt the strange men were sincere about their religion so he ordered them to be untied and fed. Starving for nourishment, they ate bananas and drank a fermented beer.

From that day, with infinite patience, the friars began learning the Talamanca dialect in keeping with their holy orders. They knew they had to be able to catechize the Indians in their own language. Progress was slow, but eventually the Indians realized the fathers were truthful. In fact they were impressed with their sacrifices and knew they were not sent as disguises to deceive.

It took months for Father Margil and Father Melchor to finally begin their missionary work in the most untamed and difficult lands of the region, the land of the *Talamancans*. Every day they were thankful that divine grace had saved them from death and early martyrdom, but they knew this mission had a very long, long way to go.

XXIV

San Miguel de Cabec, Province of Costa Rica
February 1691

"Put it higher, brother," said Father Margil to a young Indian as the boy raised the cross high onto the trunk of a huge tree.

All the Indians worked hard. Some dragged poles cut from the nearby trees and others dug holes in the ground where the logs were placed.

"We must carefully select only the straightest poles for cutting," said Father Melchor to another group of Indians. "They must be twelve to fifteen feet tall, straight as an arrow, and have a fork at one end. They will be used to hold the rails of our new temple."

The entrance way of the building had four wooden columns placed eight steps apart. Each of the four posts had large triangular pediments covered with straw. The branches they used were tied with ropes made of fibers called *lianas*, which were kept flexible by submerging them inside gourds filled with water. When they were taken from the gourds and dried, they would remain tightly wound. Above the front entrance, the natives were building a smaller square enclosure with a thatched roof. This is where the wooden cross would hang.

Standing near the workers were some of the Indian children who were steadying the cross as they waited to hand it to the workers at the pinnacle of the temple. Even the Indian women worked on cane and palm screens to be used to form the walls.

Father Margil watched with joy as the wooden temple was erected, but he was more joyful to see the conversion of the natives who until recently were engaged in ancient practices of idolatry and human sacrifice.

The temple would be shaped like the letter *Tau*, the 19th letter of the Greek alphabet, and would be very large. When finished, it would be about ninety feet long and seventy feet wide except where it broadened to about seventy five feet at the forefront.

"It will be a "T", like what Our Seraphic Father San Francisco used to sign his writings," said Father Margil to his brother.

A neat altar was erected from pieces of wood bound with vines and decorated with beautiful wild flowers. Then, the tabernacle was artfully made by the good people of the village from corn stalks gathered from the fields. When they finished the temple, Father Margil and Father Melchor looked at each other and smiled. They were happy and satisfied for now it was truly the house of God. But, they were even prouder of the people, especially the children, who helped build the temple as richly and tastefully as possible. During an elaborate ceremony, a milestone in their mission work, the priests christened the new building by celebrating the Holy Mass. It had taken months of preaching in the desolate rainforest to convert the *Talamanca Indians* to Christianity, but now it seemed all these strange people wanted to be received into the Church through holy baptism.

When their work was done, the friars travelled onward building churches in the name of Jesus in every town where they arrived. They used the same pattern in Santo Domingo, San Antonio, The Name of Jesus, The Santa Cruz, San Pedro and San Pablo, San Jose, San Agustin, and San Juan Bautista. They were all places where the Indians could now come to the house of God.

One day, after finishing work at the Church of San Juan Bautista, they returned to the Church of San Jose only to find it in flames. Outraged, the fathers sought answers to the heresy. Quickly they were told that a group of rebel Indians, who lived in a nearby village on the top of the mountain, had decided to wreak havoc on the missionaries in their territory.

Father Margil and Father Melchor were determined to find the criminals responsible for these sacrilegious acts. For several days they travelled up the steep slopes of the mountain until they came to a single hut. Cautiously they entered but found it empty. Thinking someone would soon return, they stayed the night. They continued climbing the next morning and soon noticed women peering through the undergrowth and waving at them. Not long afterwards, they arrived at the rebel village. As instructed, they entered holding their crucifix high, but they were met with scorn. The villagers rushed them and spat upon them and the most holy crucifix. They were beaten with sticks and spears.

All they did was turn their heads and continue walking in silence. With much dignity, the fathers arrived at what appeared to be the hut of the village chief. Here they were treated no differently. They tried to talk to the chief in what they thought was his native language, but it was useless. The abuse continued.

The last straw came when the Indians took their sticks and struck the face of Christ on the holy cross. This sacrilege convinced the fathers that this was not the time to convert these rebels.

In Saint Luke's word as written in the Holy Bible, Father Margil said, "*And as for those who do not receive you, as you go out from that city, shake the dust off your feet as testimony against them.*"

With this, they left this mission for another day.

They decided to continue their mission in other areas, knowing in their minds that another day would come to convert the rebels on the top of the mountain.

"Father Melchor," lamented Father Margil to his brother of habit. "I think we should send a message to the highlander rebels."

"And what is the message?" said Father Melchor

"The message is '*so that you know we are not angry with you, we are only looking for your souls, pitiful and hurt by your perdition. And after we have converted the Terrabas Indians, your enemies, we will return to kiss your feet,*'" said Father Margil.

XXV

The *Boruca* Indian village sat atop a lofty ledge of a rock cliff and had a deep ravine on all sides expect for the two well-guarded entrances. These access ways were booby trapped with a large pit encircled with pointed bamboo stakes. These defenses made the village a fortress, impenetrable and difficult to attack.

Looking toward the village, Father Margil counted about eighty huts, perfectly aligned and harmoniously distributed through the large settlement. The huts of the egg shaped village were about fifteen feet tall and conical in shape. Compared to a common Indian village in the region, they were large. Each one was made of rough wooden pitchforks, covered with straw, and had only one door facing west. The Indians believed the westward orientation of the door allowed the evil night spirits to escape at sunrise, and it prevented them from entering from the opposite side where they were protected by the mountain's precipice.

Here, Father Margil and Father Melchor had been well received by the Indians, and in a very short time about a third of them converted to Christianity. With the help of God and the new converts, they had built a beautiful temple in the village.

This was another great accomplishment for Father Margil and Father Melchor because this barbaric tribe had a very bad reputation for being fierce, unrelenting warriors. They were known to kill every living creature that crossed their paths, man or beast. Now it was unbelievable how they coexisted with the Franciscan fathers. They learned to depend on the fathers who often served as the liaisons between Indians in other rebel villages.

One early morning, a group of Indian men asked Father Margil to accompany them to the river to fish.

He found this opportunity fascinating and was excited to be included. He and two dozen Indians travelled to the river and then divided into three groups. Father Margil was with the first group, whose task was to crush the bark of the *pejibaye* tree, a native palm, into a fine dust and put it into empty gourds.

The second group took large stones and lined them up in the river forming a half moon. This crude trap had only one entrance where the fish could enter or exit.

The third group headed downstream to find a school of *mojarra*, a local fish weighing about a pound. When a school of delectable fish was located, they began hitting the water violently with sticks to scare the fishes toward the half-moon trap.

Father Margil and his party got into the water and stood in two rows on each side of the rock formation to serve as a human channel. As the fish swam into the trap, they closed the door with more rocks, and quickly sprinkled the *pejibaye* dust over the top of the water. In a few minutes, the fish began floating to the top, first one or two, then three or four. Before long, floating fish covered the water in the trap. They appeared to have just fallen asleep. Quickly, the men and women jumped into the river and collected their prey. Carrying the fish to the banks of the river, they quickly cut them open to extract the paralyzing venom and washed them in the river. When all their catch was processed, they were divided among the entire village.

Father Margil was so excited that he could not wait to tell Father Melchor of his new experience. "I had a lesson in teamwork today!" he said enthusiastically.

"These friendly Indians are truly God's people!" responded Father Melchor. "Just think they didn't trust us at first because our countrymen have so badly mistreated them in the past."

"You know how many times they have talked to us about their people being enslaved and forced to work. And to think, it was our people who made them do their dirty work, like dyeing yarns and working in the fields; and they were often beaten until they bled," spoke Father Margil.

"I firmly believe God brought us here and caused them to receive us well," lamented Father Margil.

"Now it is our turn, we must help God!" he said, "We must ask him for the intercession of the Most Blessed Virgin Mary."

"Maybe this is a sign that it's time for us to enter the territory of the most feared tribe in these lands, the ones our own soldiers have not subdued."

"You are referring to the *Terrabas* Indians, aren't you Father Margil?" moaned his brother friar.

"Indeed, Father Melchor, I am talking about the fierce *Terrabas* Indians! I feel it is time," he paused before continuing. "May God be with us on our next journey; surely we will need all the help we can get!"

XXVI

Terraba Territory of Southern Costa Rica
July 1691

The middle aged woman walked briskly through the open doors of the Church of San Francisco with a broad grin across her wide bronze face. She was the most respected woman in the town. Her name was Doña Andrea – a holy woman.

Father Margil and Father Melchor greeted her at the door, "At last we are finished with our beautiful sanctuary, Doña Andrea," Fray Melchor said as he pointed to the picturesque temple. "We must now give thanks to Our Lord for allowing us to work together in peace and harmony Glory to God!"

Thinking back a few months, Father Melchor remembered how the *Boruca* Indians had treated them with scorn and suspicion. When they arrived during those dark days, the tribal leaders drove them away and would not allow them to enter the village. The *Boruca* Indians set up camp a few hundred yards outside the village and used mediators to speak to the tribesmen on their behalf. Their message to the eight *Terraba* chieftains was one of peace and love.

While they waited, what seemed like hours for the outcome of the peace negotiations, they were ecstatic to hear that their *Boruca* ambassadors had won over the chieftains. With a vote of seven to one, they voted to allow the friars to enter the village. There was one lone dissenting vote by a chieftain who vowed to kill the newcomers on sight.

Their first assignment was to win the favor of the reluctant elder. Lacking fear and with unwavering determination, the friars neared the area of the chief's hut. To their dismay, the dissenter actually received them warmly. Instead of aggression, the chief had his wives prepare food and drink for his guests. He openly thanked them for their blessings but soon informed them that final approval would have to come from Doña Andrea, the village priestess.

From the friars' past experiences, they knew encounters with the holy women were not usually pleasant. But in this case, it was necessary for the success of their mission. That night they prayed for God to intercede and allow his grace to flow into the heart and soul of the local priestess. Early the next morning, they were escorted to her abode. To their surprise, the sullen woman sat on the ground outside her hut in a large circle with her hand-picked allies.

Anxious to break the ice, Father Melchor kindly acknowledged her presence and opened the summit with words of the true God. Not knowing what else to say, he jumped into the anticipated subject of the need to destroy the strange images of their gods. He said, "You should not have idols, nor graven images, nor shall you raise up or bow down to a standing image, nor shall you set up any image of stone in your land from this day forward!"

"Understand, my daughter," announced Father Melchor, "that your idols of stone are abominations to the true God, our Lord and Savior Jesus Christ! You say they are your gods, but they are only a work made by your hands."

The old woman stood and approached the Christ crucifix that Father Margil was holding and slapped the image and said, "And your God? Isn't it a creation of your hands?"

"That is true," Father Melchor replied, "but the crucifix is only an image of our true God whom we believe is in heaven, a place beyond our imagination. Believe me when I say, heaven with God and Jesus will be a place of love for all of us. God, in his tender love, will wipe away all our tears and there will no longer be any death; there will no longer be any mourning, crying, or pain."

Listening attentively and waiting for silence from the friar, Doña Andrea said, "Now let me tell you what we believe! We believe that our god has many seeds."

"It is from him we get the seeds for our corn, the same way we get our children," our god gives us the seeds of birth," said Doña Andrea. "We also believe man has two souls, one for doing good and the other for doing bad. I am happy to say that at this time the good overshadows the bad," she explained.

They sat and talked a long time about their respective beliefs, each expressing their feelings openly. In the end, Father Melchor won out and convinced Senora Andrea to advise her people to embrace the new faith, Jesus, and the idea of a heaven as a place where angels will rejoice as heaven fills with righteous Christians.

To mark the occasion of the new celebrants entering into the Church, Father Melchor said, "I will build a fire where each of you will place a log. When the fire begins to blaze, you will toss your idols into the flames as you hold a holy cross high above your heads!"

With this ceremony, the period of catechesis in the village began. In the new spirit of faith, the friars were given permission to build two new temples, the first dedicated to San Buenaventura of Urachal and the second dedicated to San Andres.

Finding the right time to give admiration, Father Melchor said to Doña Andrea, "You are a good woman, a devout and God-fearing follower of Christ. I want you to be the first sacristan of the church." Grinning from ear to ear at this special act of kindness, the toothless former priestess accepted the responsibility to take care of the sacristy, the church, and its contents.

Thinking back over their months of travel, Father Margil and Father Melchor thought about the many missions they had founded along the way: *Santo Domingo, San Antonio, The Name of Jesus, Santa Cruz, San Pedro* and *San Pablo, San Jose de los Cabecaras,* the *Holy Trinity of Talamanca,* the *Conception of Our Lady, Santa Ana, San Francisco of Terrabas* and *Buenaventura.*

Satisfied with their most recent accomplishment, Father Melchor looked at Father Margil and said, "Now you have a promise to fulfill with the fierce Indians on the mountains."

Smiling Father Margil remembered the promise he had made to the rebels who had burned their holy Church of San Jose.

"This is true Father Melchor!" replied Father Margil, "This is true! Now it is time for me to venture back into the Talamanca Mountains and kiss the feet of my enemies."

"Do you want me to go with you?" asked Father Melchor.

"No, I have to go alone!" he said.

XXVII

High in the Talamanca Mountains, Father Margil carefully placed each of his steps into a crevice of the steep incline. It was not an easy task, but he felt no fear as he ascended from earth into the clouds of heaven. The vertical slope, not more than half a mile, was his path to the Indian village. The illusive Indians had built their village at the top of the mountain as a fortress to protect against the attacks of their nearby enemies who lived only ten or twelve miles away.

Not even mules and horses could make the ascent. It took a tempered spirit, accustomed to adversity, like that of Father Margil, to make this torturous and extremely dangerous journey. More times than he could count, his bare feet slipped on the wet rocks. If it had not been for his strong calloused hands, clinging to the rocks and vines, he would have surely slipped and fallen to his death many times.

Still climbing the jagged peaks, he felt as if he would soon enter the gates of heaven. He had long since left behind the beautiful landscapes and moist heat of the valley below. His new landscape was increasingly desolate and cold, very cold. There was no vegetation at these heights; nothing grew. The icy wind blew intensely and seeped into the seams of his habit chilling him to the bone. His feet turned blue and his jaw trembled, but he moved on unwilling to give up his task.

He had brought only a few rations for his trip up the mountain, but now they were gone. Looking around for something to quiet his stomach, he saw nothing more than stones. After a couple of days of arduous climbing, he arrived at the land of those who, not too long ago, beat and spit upon him and his brother, Father Melchor.

When he arrived, he was exhausted and fell on the ground. The Indians were in disbelief as they looked at the pitiful man who lay before them. Where had he come from? Surely he had not climbed the treacherous side of the mountain. Father Margil raised himself to his knees and began to kiss the feet of the nearest young warriors. Quickly they pulled away, not believing what was happening. With tenderness, the friar continued on his knees, from one to the other, each time tenderly caressing the feet of his enemies. With this act of love he said, "I have no resentment for your rebel acts against me or my God!"

Baffled, shocked but intrigued by the actions of this strange man, the warriors put down their spears. Their hearts began to soften and they said, "Please forgive us for our past actions. We want to ask your God for forgiveness for our souls!"

"My brothers," said Father Margil, "If you really want conversion and salvation for your souls, I ask you to make peace with your enemy, the *Terraba*."

"That's impossible!" cried the rebel chief. "They have been our sworn enemies for as long as our oldest people can remember and even longer! They will always be our enemy! Our children and the children of our children will be warriors against them!"

"That´s why you need to reconcile now," declared the friar. "Our Lord Jesus Christ said 'Love your enemies and pray for those who persecute you." Hesitating he continued, "Do you want the same future for your children?"

"But how can we love our enemies? That's impossible!" said the chief.

"No, it is not impossible," said Father Margil with a smile.

Wide eyed, the Indians approached to hear what he had to say.

"Please believe me!" cried Father Margil.

"Honestly, we don't trust you or believe you!" said another of the chieftains cynically.

"Well, what I´m telling you is what our Lord said is the key to the solution of many conflicts" said Father Margil.

"They have killed too many of our brave men in their human sacrifices to their gods." The chief spat on the ground, "How can we love them? How can we forgive them! How can we be friends with our enemies?"

With a sincere smile, Father Margil said, "There can´t be coexistence if there is no forgiveness." He then said, "Do you want to continue the killings? All of you must stop these barbarous acts! From this day forward, no one will be killed in this manner again!"

One chief shook his head doubtfully, "Father, do you really believe we can live in peace? What will they think of our cowardice? We can´t speak of peace, we only know war."

"I'm sure they want peace as much as you, but someone has to be the first to step up to begin the process. I want you to take the first step," he said

"But..."

"No, say no more! As from this day forward, your war against the *Terraba* Indians is over!"

The astonished young Indian warriors looked at each other puzzled by this strange man with these incredibly foreign ideas.

"How are we going to tell them that we will no longer pick up our weapons against them? Surely they will laugh at us for we have been fighting each other forever. And now you say the war is over?" laughed the chief.

Seeing his earnest confusion, Father Margil proposed, "I will go to the village of the *Terraba* and will ask their chief to lay down their arms and end the war against you and that you will do the same!"

The half-hearted chief got up and threw his spear to the ground, half way challenging Father Margil. "Father, if you will do that for us, then we are willing to do the same. We will give up our weapons!"

Father Margil stood and tearfully embraced the convert and said, "You will see God's words are words of wisdom, Alleluia!"

His mission on the mountain had begun but was not complete! All night, he prepared himself with prayer for his perilous journey to the enemy. The next morning, with only meager rations, he began to scale the other side of the mountain where he would find the *Terraba* tribesmen. "God please be my guide," he thought.

As he began his climb, he could hear the chief saying, "Father, do not go that way; it is too dangerous. There are trails you can use in other parts of the mountain."

"God will open the path for me," answered Father Margil with a smile. With these words, the Indians watched him climb until he was swallowed by the clouds.

XXVIII

Gazing out of the window with great sadness in his heart, Father Margil remembered the day he entered the Order of the Friars Minor in Valencia, Spain. He had made a public profession of faith and promised to follow the vows of chastity, poverty, and obedience. Now his pledge to practice the sacred vow of obedience was being tested in this strange new world.

He never imagined that a directive from Most Reverend Father Friar Juan Capistrano, the Commissioner General of the Indies, would cause him so much sorrow and conflict. He laid the letter that Father Melchor had given him aside. Continuing to stare out the window at the beautiful countryside, he thought maybe the Commissioner General was just new to his job and did not understand the importance of what they were doing. His predecessor, Friar Juan de Luzuriaga, understood, but he had been replaced in 1689. Coming back to his senses, Father Margil realized the letter was an order to immediately return to Querétaro. Neither he nor Father Melchor could challenge the directive.

Father Margil was not concerned that they were far away in the wilderness of Costa Rica, on the border of the Kingdom of Tierra Firme, more than twenty days from the nearest Spanish villa. It was a large territory in Central and South America, including lands from Panama to Peru, and Colombia and Venezuela. He was not concerned about the distance or time it would take to travel the more than eighteen hundred miles to reach the College of Querétaro. He was not concerned by the dangers they faced and the near death experiences they had experienced while preaching the gospel in those strange lands. He had forgotten the abuses and insults. He only thought of the faces of his converts and the confidence they had bestowed upon the young friars.

Father Margil knew he could manage his few possessions in the long trip back. He had never had a problem carrying the vessels for the Holy Mass, a pair of old sandals used during the celebration of the Eucharist, and the holy crucifix. They were his constant companions.

Father Margil was sad to think he would have to leave the beloved land he called home for the last few years and his many new friends. Here he and Father Melchor had opened so many new paths while converting thousands of Indians. He nostalgically remembered the fifteen temples that had been erected in various towns and the support and deep faith of the converted Indians.

He was sad because he wanted to continue evangelizing in these lands but knew he could not. Their plans had been to head south towards the coast to the South Sea, where there were still other tribes to convert like the *Guaymi* Indians.

Nostalgically, he reflected on the past two years realizing that without weapons, without soldiers, and armed only with their crucifixes, they had captured the hearts of the people. He had traveled to places that had not been penetrated by hosts, swords, or muskets for more than a hundred years. They had used the word of the Lord as a merciful redeemer, not whips or guns, to convince the people of God's love. Love had won where powerful armies had been defeated.

For these reasons, he did not want his work to end so abruptly. Contemplating his vow of obedience, he knew he had to humbly and without reservation follow the edict. Nevertheless, he would leave behind a small part of his life and a great part of his heart

"I want to stay in these lands," he told Father Melchor. "I don't think we should have to go back."

"If the Commissioner calls us, we must obey, my brother! You know that," said Father Melchor. Yes, Father Margil knew that his brother was right, and he knew he could no longer question the order. "We must be obedient!" they concluded in unison.

With great sorrow, they said goodbye to Doña Andrea and the rest of their friends in the territory of Talamanca.

"We were like little children, as helpless infants," said the old lady with tears in her eyes, "Sucking the sweet milk of your doctrine has now saved our souls."

Obediently but sadly, they began their long journey to Querétaro. They travelled by way of Matina, Pacuare, Cartago, Heredia, Leon, and Comayagua to the Captaincy General of Guatemala.

While on their way back, the mysterious hand of divine providence intervened and led them on a new challenge and a new adventure among the *Lacandon* Indians. It was not time for them to return to Querétaro. Not yet.

XXIX

The Secretary dipped the tip of the pen in the inkwell and waited for His Excellency Friar Nicholas Delgado, twenty-third Bishop of the Diocese of León, to dictate a letter to the Superior Council of the Indies, authorizing Father Margil's mission into Nicaragua and Guatemala.

He began:

Very powerful Lord, in execution of the command of the Royal decree issued to my pastoral office, I announce the news of the state of the conversion of the Caribe Indians living within the limits of my diocese and what is needed to promote it.

Sighing slightly to gain the attention of his fellow missionaries, he continued:

Father Melchor Lopez and Father Antonio Margil, religious of the Order of San Francisco and residents in Querétaro Seminar of the Order, came to the Bishopric of Nicaragua in the year of 1688, to comply, with ardent zeal, to their mission of converting souls, (I have no authority to canonize anyone in life or in death, but clearly do say what I have experienced, seen and heard). These men have executed, with such divine assistance, their missionary work and its wonderful effects until today.

The Bishop took a break and coughed, so the Secretary could re-ink the tip of his quill, and then continued:

With their assistance, their preaching and examples, they have been able to banish many abuses of the Indians who have become entrenched in the Catholic faith, with demonstrations of great comfort. Examining them, to discover their strength, they say, 'This was taught to us by the holy fathers during their mission, and we prefer to die than give way to sin.'

The Bishop stopped and took a drink of water before restarting:

And if some of the Indians experience the slightest slip, only with a slightest hint of the doctrine the fathers preached, the faith is restored back to them with happiness. The Spanish, the mestizos, and mulattos were reformed much in the same manner, for the duties in the performance of my pastoral charge have been soft and easy to reach.

They went into the mountains, called the Talamanca, in the Costa Rica Province, to begin the mission from the North and reached into the South. Indians lived in those mountains without knowledge of the Gospel and committed barbarous acts of idolatry. They were the Talamancas, the Terrabas, the Cabecares, the Chichahuas, the Usamboros, the Capces, the Usuros, the Mayagüez, and many others of all different nations but similar in false rites and diabolical practices. From the beginning, the natives were docile and friendly but not instructed in the truth of the evangelical law. The men were lazy and let the women do all hard work.

Their dwellings, ranches called palisades, consisted of three hundred inhabitants, more or less. They keep the lineage of their families by not allowing mixing with any other tribes and not allowing trade between the ranches.

They make their ranches in the highest reaches of the mountains, which are almost inaccessible and a distant of ten to twelve miles from each other. All of these mountains were penetrated by these religious Franciscan fathers, walking barefoot and preaching the holy gospel to the inhabitants. They loved these people as dearly as they could, and explained to them the truth of our Catholic faith. With signs, demonstrations, examples, and without an interpreter, the fathers instructed the Indians and established twelve churches in different locals.

These little 'seeds of faith' of their principles had just started to grow when these missionary fathers were urged to leave, compelled by obedience to comply with their superiors, who needed them for another purpose. It was a great distress to the new Christians. Having a natural propensity to idleness and rudeness to strangers, they very quickly forgot the teachings from the fathers. As soon as possible, I sent two very virtuous and valuable men: Fathers Friar Sebastian de Las Alas and Friar Pablo de Otalora, from the Franciscan Province of San Jorge de Nicaragua. But working on that land, rugged and uninhabitable, was nearly fatal to them. The common food was a beverage made from ground roots and herbs and sometimes bananas and yuccas that often made them extremely sick. If they hadn't returned, they would have surely died.

We can't work there anymore as all the men we have are occupied in the administration and conversions of Indians at other locations. As of today, the towns in the Talamanca Mountains have no minister because of the danger and bad experiences we have encountered, as we have seen the mountains are impracticable for the administration of Indians. It is necessary that Indians be reduced,[2] and made to leave the eminence of the hills where they live and come live in the valleys of these mountains where we can teach them.

The reduction of the Indians would be fruitful if the conquest is made by the divine word, good example, poverty, and nearly infinite patience in suffering by the Ministers work. I trust in divine providence that if Father Margil and Father Melchor are provided, we will be able to achieve what looks impossible with all the perfection that we need.

Your Highness will determine what will be the best way Our Lord should be served. God save your grace for many years and may you thrive in higher realms.

Father Nicholas, Bishop of Nicaragua

---

2   The general purpose of the missions was to "reduce" or congregate the Indians into a settlement, convert them to Christianity, and teach them crafts and agricultural techniques.

PART FIVE: LAND OF LACANDON

XXX

"**F**athers, we are grateful to you for coming to our land," the mayor of Alta Verapaz happily remarked.

"We came as soon as possible, Your Honor," said Father Melchor.

Father Margil and Father Melchor were in Santo Domingo de Coban, in the mountain region of north central Guatemala. They had come at the request of the mayor who sent messengers to find them.

"You should know," hesitantly said the mayor. "We have a big problem with the *Lacandon* Indians in our region."

"Yes, we have heard," said Father Margil.

"We consider the actions of these barbarians to be intolerable," emphasized the mayor.

"They not only abscond with our crops but rob our people of their precious possessions. They seem to target only our peaceful Indians, living in the misty forests far away from our Spanish towns. They are more ruthless than any other tribe in these lands. They act as if they are the masters of our region and make our people afraid. They even travel to the province of Chiapa, a distant of about fifty miles, with constant theft and abuse along the way. Their actions are intolerable!"

The mayor raked his hand through his hair in despair.

"Worst of all is that our peaceful Indians become instruments of these devils and hide the infidels from our soldiers. I don't know it this is from fear or for profit. For this reason, they have become more elusive then you can imagine!"

"What do you want us to do?" asked Father Melchor.

"I would ask, dear fathers, that with your great humility and power of conversion, you speak with the *Lacandon* chieftains and try to convince them to stop their hostile attacks against our neighboring villages."

"But you have said they were very elusive," stated Friar Melchor. "How can we find them?"

"Our brothers here," he said as he pointed to a group of indigenous. "Have offered to guide you to the village of the *Lacandon.*"

Father Margil and Father Melchor looked at the volunteers and were immediately struck by the fact they did not appear to be happy about their newly appointed duties.

"With good reason," thought Father Margil.

The next day, Father Margil and Father Melchor, accompanied by their reluctant volunteers, abandoned the humid highlands. As they travelled, they saw for the first time all types of unusual creatures like the beautiful emerald green quetzal, which were normally hard to see in their wooded habitats. When they reached the dense jungles, they trailed in single file behind their guides who hacked their way through the tangled vegetation. They were now in the home of the elusive *Lacandon* Indians.

For the next six months, the dismayed friars were led in circles by their guides. They never found one *Lacandon* village or saw one living soul. Father Margil questioned whether this was by accident or a plot among the guides. In his heart, he believed they were trying to sabotage their quest so they could return to Alta Verapaz, but he never spoke a word of his doubts.

When their supplies ran low, the guides quickly volunteered to go back for more. The volunteers promised the priests they would return soon with a load of supplies and they quickly vanished into the jungle.

For days the priests waited near the river bank, but the guides never returned. With no food or shelter, the friars languished in the jungle but never gave up hope. One day a young Indian boy passed down the river in a canoe. He stopped and offered to take Father Margil, the stronger one, to the next village.

When they arrived at the small village, the chief was very friendly and promised to punish the shameful guides who left them to die. He appointed eight new companions to go with Father Margil to retrieve Father Melchor. When they arrived, Father Margil feared he was dead because he lay motionless on the damp forest floor. Cradling his head in his arms to give him his last holy rites, Father Margil was quite surprised to see his eyes open. He said, "Finally, you have come for me. I am ready to resume our journey."

After a day of rest and with renewed health and spirit, the priests were led by their new guides to the elusive village of the *Lacandon* Indians. Caught totally off guard at the arrival of unexpected outsiders, the *Lacandon* were agitated to see their fortress breached. Quickly the men grabbed their weapons and fled the village in all directions. Only a few women and children were left behind.

The Indians regrouped a short distance away and watched the small party from the confines of the forest. Seeing the small number of intruders, they returned to the village and with viciousness, for which they were known, began to beat both the friars and the guides. The frightened trespassers fell to the ground and took the beatings never crying out. They were helpless against so many.

After a while, seeing the men carried no weapons and did not defend themselves, one of the chiefs intervened and called a halt to the aggression.

"Why have you come here?" asked the chief through an interpreter.

With a bloody face and an aching body, Father Margil responded with difficulty:

"We came to... speak ... of the one true God, and ... to ask you to make peace ... with the *Coban* Indians."

The chief sneered and gave orders to lock them in a nearby shrine where they were guarded day and night. For five days, they remained there and surely would have perished except for a kindly soul who secretly supplied them with a little food and water.

The most affected was Father Melchor who, already in poor health, lay lifeless. When a chief returned, he touched Father Margil's chest and said, "This one ...good."

Then he turned to Father Melchor and touched his weak chest and said: "This one...rotten." Then he left.

A few days passed before the chief returned and told them:

"We will see if you tell the truth! Twelve of my warriors will go with one of you to meet the *Coban* Indians. If they receive us well, it is a good sign that they want peace."

Father Melchor agreed to stay as a hostage and allow Father Margil to leave with twelve warriors and go to the village of the *Coban*.

Father Margil, anxious for illusive peace between the two tribes, shortened the journey as much as possible by taking a straight but difficult path. When they arrived at the *Coban* village, the warriors were surprised at the reception and the kindly offerings of peace they received. It was a great demonstration of friendship. Unfortunately, the drastic change in climate caused ten of the twelve *Lacandon* to become sick and they soon died.

Father Margil worried about reentering the *Lacandon* village for he knew the death of the warriors would not be understood by their chief. To make things worse, upon his arrival he learned the village had suffered a fire while they were gone. Now with the loss of nearly all of the warriors and the fire accidentally started by Father Melchor, the ire of the Indians was taken out on him. Once again they nearly beat him to death.

"Go back where you came from or you'll find death just like your partner who lies buried in the jungle," shouted the *Lacandon* chief. "We killed your brother for starting the fire that burned our fences."

With tears in his eyes, Father Margil responded to the Indians: "I won't go back without my brother. Take me to him. He must be buried in Christian lands!"

The Indians stopped their physical attack on him when they saw the sorrow he felt at the loss of his brother in Christ. When they left, feeling devastated and alone, he raised his beaten body and started to search for the remains of Father Melchor. After a while and to his surprise, he found him alive sitting under a tree. With tears in their eyes they greeted each other and thanked their merciful God for keeping them alive.

For several days they recuperated and when strong enough to walk, they went back into the village to try once again to convert the *Lacandon* Indians. This time they were not beaten. For several days the friars talked, but all their efforts were in vain. The *Lacandon* only responded that they did not want to leave their ancient gods and did not want to support any other god.

"And give thanks to our chiefs that they did not allow us to kill you," said one *Lacandon* warrior. "If it were not for them, long ago you would have died."

Seeing that any further attempt of dialogue was fruitless, the fathers returned to Guatemala.

XXXI

"𝕴n order to quickly subdue our enemy, our strategy is a three-pronged surprise attack on the region near the Lacantún lagoon," explained the captain general."

He spread a map onto a large table and pointed to the locations and explained his tactics.

"Governor, our plan is that you and six hundred men will start out in the township of Huehuetenango, accompanied by Fray Tomas de Mendoza y Guzman from High Cape and Fray Antonio Margil."

"Captain Rodriguez de Mazariegos and his contingents will go through the mountains of San Mateo Ixtatán," explained the captain. "He will be accompanied by Fray Pedro de la Concepción."

And finally, Captain Juan Diaz de Velasco and his men will enter through Cajabón, in the region of Verapaz, accompanied by Fray Agustin Cano.

"The three forces will serve as pincers as we encircle the *Lacandon* area. This approach will prevent the Indians from fleeing as they have done in the past. They will have no way out and will have to surrender. This campaign will be the largest and most overwhelming that we have had in a long time," said the captain general.

The Palace of the Captains where they met was the residency of the governor, the captain general and the Royal Court in Guatemala. It was a medium size facility, with adobe walls, tile roof, and a vaulted ceiling and porch.

Governor Jacinto de Barrios Leal, Knight of the Order of Calatrava, stood elegantly dressed in a heavy black velvet robe, known as *grenache*, which fell to his ankles, and a white collared shirt with long sleeves. His short black satin cape was lined in silk and had gold buttons. He placed his white silk gloves aside as he carefully studied the map before him.

"Captain, your plan is very interesting," said the governor. "But do you really think we can succeed in capturing these Indians? Do I need to remind you that we are dealing with the most militant and ruthless savages ever known."

"So far we have only used *entradas*," said the captain. "These were conducted by priests and rarely supported by our military. They have always been peaceful."

"This time it is reversed. We will have a large military force of soldiers who will be supported by priests. We will have Reverend Father Margil with us because he was there just last year trying to evangelize these heathens. We also have the support of Fray Diego de Ribas, the Illustrious Minister Provincial, and other loyal fathers."

"Certainly the goal of Father Margil and the other fathers to evangelize the Indians is commendable," the governor said. "But in the best interests of the Crown, we must recognize the enormous resources being spent on this expedition. Our ultimate purpose is not to reduce the *Lacandon* Indians but to gain a path linking the territories of Guatemala and the Yucatán. For this reason alone, we have obtained the support of His Excellency Don Roque de Soberanis y Riva, governor of the provinces of Yucatán, although his province is plagued with internal problems. The campaign will be coordinated by Sergeant Major Don Martin de Ursua, as acting governor. This campaign should be successful and produce the new road."

"By the way, Governor, as it refers to the Father Margil," interjected the secretary, "I must mention that he, like most of the venerable fathers from the Order of Preachers, does not support the strategy of attacking on three fronts. He says we will be wasting time going through uninhabited territories where we will not find a single Indian. He also says this territory has fallen to the Dominicans and that Father Margil and Friar Pedro de la Concepción are Franciscans, so..."

"Not applicable to these complaints," interrupted the governor. "Father Margil comes with me as my confessor!"

The captain general said:

"Let me address the problem of the venerable Dominican friars taking over the route we have chosen to follow through Chiapa. First of all, this route is the one recommended by His Serene Majesty Charles II, in his decree dated 24th November 1692. It is broadly supported by the members of the city council. Additionally, we have recently received reports that the *Lacandon* Indians have been seen near the village of Ocosingo. So I reiterate that this is the most suitable route for the purposes of this expedition!"

The governor appreciated the clarification and asked the secretary:

"Do you have the latest report of donations and support requested for this endeavor?"

"We have had a favorable response from both the people and the authorities of the different towns and even from the religious," replied the secretary with satisfaction. "The recruitment of men and the donations have been received. The donations both cash and in kind include such things as horses, weapons and supplies needed. The contributions to the Crown are extremely encouraging."

"For example," said the secretary reading a report to the governor, "Don Juan Jeronimo Mejia has given fourteen horses and one hundred *pesos*; Corregidor Don Miguel de Acañon sent thirty-four horses collected from the residents at Acasaguastlán village; the Adjutant General Deputy Mayor of Chiquimula sent sixty horses and fifty *pesos*; Lieutenant Captain of Soconusco, some thirty horses and six mules; the Governor of Arms of Guazacapán and Esquintepec villages contributed thirteen horses, two mules and one hundred and three *pesos*; captain general of the provinces San Salvador and San Miguel, have cooperated with sixty horses, two mules and two hundred *pesos*. And so follows a long list of people who have made contributions."

The secretary was encouraged to continue when he saw a smile appear on the governor's face.

"We also have news that in Huehuetenango we will be joined by a column of fifty more men, fully armed and on horseback. And we believe there will be more volunteers from neighboring towns."

"All these are good signs," said the governor.

Directing his gaze back to the map, he said:

"I have high hope that this time we will conquer these Indians. They are so obscure, and are so reluctant to live in our society; it seems they prefer to remain in ignorance and solitude in the rugged mountains where they reside now. I don´t understand why they always want to return to their tribes after we give them so much freedom here. It's as if they are ashamed to be Christians. Don't they understand the amount of money we are spending on this folly? I don't understand why they won't leave their nomadic life to build a comfortable home and wear proper clothing. I am not talking about elaborate clothing, just something to cover their nakedness. Why can't they see that we just want them to be civilized, learn a simple trade, such as woodworking? Can't they see into the future? Civilization is not bad!"

"I'm sure the influence of the missionaries will be especially important, governor, to help change and mold their opinions," said the captain.

"Too much emphasis has been made by the fathers, especially Father Margil," said the governor, "that the *reduction* of the Indians should be made with great charity and that weapons should only be used as a deterrent. He says this is clearly indicated by our Majesties the Kings of Spain, may God our Lord and Savior grant them long life."

"We have given precise instructions to our men to not attack the Indians unless provoked. However, I can assure you that if they become belligerent, we will use every means at our disposal to defend ourselves," said the captain.

"Make sure your men don´t attack first! We do not want to be accused before the courts and before the *Inquisition* of a military maneuver rather than a peaceful evangelization and reduction," sharply replied the governor.

The secretary coughing slightly, said to the governor:

"I want to commend you for accepting this most difficult and enormously dangerous assignment, considering your delicate state of health, Your Lordship. Some members of the city council wonder whether it would be better to delegate the command of the troops to another of your subordinates, so your life is not put at risk."

The handsome young governor, only forty-five years old, was in poor health from the stress of abuse of authority accusations previously leveled against him. The charges were from his family's previous activities, but the Crown ordered a full investigation against him personally. He was temporarily removed from office but emerged unscathed and resumed the reins of government. His health was still poor from the incident, but he wished to keep it a secret. He silently anticipated a military victory to improve his tarnished image.

With an air of benevolence, the governor replied:

"Reassure the council that I appreciate their concern and affection; however, my health is slightly improved and I look forward to a long and loyal service to Our Lord and our King, who both demand my leadership."

With a nod to the captain general he added:

"Also tell them that after much reflection and for their peace of mind, I have decided to grant direct command of this expedition to Captain General Don Bartolome de Amezquita, prosecutor of the city council. He has accepted the appointment."

"I am honored by the distinction Your Excellency has given to me," replied the captain general modesty tilting his head downward. "I will do my best for the success of this enterprise."

"You are very trustworthy! Although any member of the council could have been appointed, many did not qualify due to poor health," said the governor.

The governor returned to his chair and ordered the secretary:

"Inform the venerable Father Margil and the Provincial Minister Diego de Rivas that the expedition will begin shortly. Along the way they will have to negotiate with the mayors of the villages for accommodations for the troops to hasten the success of the expedition. Also send a dispatch to the Governor of Yucatán that the campaign has begun!"

And turning again to the Captain, he commanded:

"Prepare the weapons, ammunition, food, and supplies needed for the expedition. Then have Captain Don Tomas de Guzman take one hundred men and supplies to the town of Comitan. With the mercy of Our Lord and the protection of the Most Blessed Virgin Mary, we will depart on the 17th of January."

XXXII

Foothills of Ocosingo, Chiapa
March 1695

The young officer stood at attention as torrents of water spilled over the brim of his hat and down onto Royal uniform. His body trembled from head to foot as the raging storm continued throughout the night. The wind howled through the trees as the skies brightened with each flash of lightning.

"In these forsaken lands, it rains four times more than in Santiago," thought the captain.

He pondered whether to awaken the governor, who was sleeping soundly in the comfort of his makeshift tent and apparently oblivious to the threat from above. With uncertainty, he waited a few minutes to see if the commotion in the camp would do the job for him. It did not. He entered the shelter and quietly approached the bed of the governor.

"Your Excellency," he whispered.

"What's happening?" The Governor, immediately aroused, answered, "What's wrong?"

"Our people are really frightened tonight because of the relentless rain and the thunderous dark skies."

"It hasn't stopped raining?" asked the governor.

"No, Your Excellency. It rained all night and our people are terrified. They have no protection from the rain. Everyone is soaked. Our men can't sleep, and as you know, have not eaten for days. Their fatigue, along with the rain and the dark night, are making them very nervous. Some are hearing strange noises and voices in the night. They are fearful that the *Lacandon* will attack at day break. They also say they feel evil spirits all around us and that they are terrified and troubled," explained the young man.

Indignantly, the governor said, "I doubt the *Lacandon* Indians will attack in this weather. And given the size of our military, they would be crazy to do so!"

"I agree with Your Excellency, but if we don't do something soon, we may have a mutiny or a mass defection on our hands."

"Still no dawn?" asked the governor.

"No, it should come soon, but we can't wait that long."

"Go wake Father Margil and ask him to..."

"Sorry to interrupt you, Your Excellency, but Father Margil hasn't slept either. At midnight he began the Prayer of the Litany of the Hours, the Divine Office, and since has been hearing the confessions of our soldiers. The confessions have not stopped for one moment all through the night."

"Well, then please ask him to hold a Mass to drive away the evil spirits," he said sarcastically. "I guess they think the *Lacandon* Indians have cursed us and are trying to make us pray to their demon gods. Even their witches and warlocks are working overtime to put spells on us tonight." He hesitated, "Go light the torches and help Father Margil prepare for the Holy Eucharist."

The coalition of soldiers and religious had travelled into the thick jungle, which had no trails, or roads, for several days. The dense, almost impenetrable barrier of vines, branches, and fallen trees were only opened by machetes and heavy swords, and every step gained was a hard battle won. The countless slopes, up and down, were always wet, slippery, and very dangerous.

The governor cried desperately, "I do not see how anyone can live in this place. These conditions are dreadful."

The journey from the Guatemalan village of Santiago to Ocosingo was a colossal undertaking for the three Spanish companies and two companies of Indian warriors. To the nearly 500 men, nothing was easy; every river crossing, especially the marshes and swamps, held a surprise. The horses, laden with supplies, sank to their necks in the quick sand unable to move, and many perished. Others died from hunger as their normal food source of green grass was nowhere to be found. Even the great explorer Hernán Cortés who had passed this way many years before had called the same swamps, "*the scariest thing people ever saw.*"

It took a month and a half for soldiers and religious to finally reach Huehuetenango. When they reached Comitán, they took a short rest before they headed southeast to Ocosingo, the land of the *Lacandon*. Little did they know that a nightmare awaited them.

XXXIII

Deep in the bowels of the tangled jungle, a lone Indian fought desperately through the thick undergrowth of the dense tropical forest. His heart pounded in his chest as he frantically clawed his way through the impenetrable web of vines. It had been several hours since he escaped from the invaders. Now he could hear them a short distance away. Fearing capture, he sought a refuge in the thick maze, but there was none.

Being prey was a situation he had never known. As a young man, he had been the aggressor, a proud persecutor of the other tribes, especially his hated enemies in the Chol province. He was a feared and vicious captor, a fierce *Lancandon* warrior, ancestor of the ancient *Mayan* people.

This time it was different. The strange invaders with scales of armor had overwhelming supernatural powers. Some appeared to be half man and half beast upon their horses that far exceeded his speed. Their costumes were rock hard and shiny like the sun itself and deflected his poison darts. This suit of armor resisted blows from stone clubs and a rain of arrows. Many times in the past, he used his giant spear with its sharp obsidian blade to impale and mutilate his fiercest enemy with ease. But now his ancient weapons were no good against the white man whose strength and weapons were far superior.

The tall muscular man, dressed only in a light loincloth, turned his head. Sweat dripped from his brow. His long black hair fell loosely over his tattooed shoulders. He was surprised to see a large cavalry of soldiers descending upon him from all directions. He heard the thunderous blast

151

from the magical blowguns and thought, "Why have my gods forsaken me?" The remote jungles were supposed to be his haven and refuge.

He remembered stories from his kinsmen who had been captured and taken to the white man's village. They were guarded by soldiers and not allowed to leave. The white man told them it was for their protection, but they knew it was to prevent them from escaping and returning to their homes. Even when they did as the priests asked and discarded their stone idols and pagan customs, they were not allowed to go free.

The scared young warrior knew his fate was sealed. His way of life, living freely in the jungle, was approaching extinction. From the chronicles of his forebears, he knew many generations ago his tribesmen were attacked by the white men and made to leave their homes on the island of Lakan-Tum. They settled in the southern town that they called Sac-Bahian. There they fought bravely and resisted their enemies: the white man and a fierce tribe of cannibals. They were known for a ritual of consuming human flesh from their enemies and keeping their bones as trophies. Life was hard back then for his ancestors.

Random thoughts ran through his mind as he struggled through the underbrush. He could not be captured by these intruders! He had to find safety and escape as generations before him had done. At all cost, he must remain free, for if he was captured, he would die from their diseases. In their captivity, he would be an easy prey and suffer attacks from enemy tribes. No, he had to run; he had to hide; he could not be captured. His tribesmen were accustomed to living as wanderers to elude their enemies. That was his life. That was his defense. He needed his freedom. For several hours, he ran closely pursued by the soldiers. Finally, he fell to the ground. Breathing heavily, he tried to get up but could not. A heavy weight kept him down. Again, he tried to stand, but the coarse netting held him down. The more he fought, the more he became entangled. Finally, he got to his knees still fighting the unimaginable binding. With great effort, he stood and pulled hard on the web. He was a warrior and would never surrender. He had to fight for his freedom. All of a sudden, he felt the binding loosen, and knew freedom was near until a sharp blow knocked him to the ground. Blackness came over the brave young warrior.

When he regained consciousness, he found himself lying on the ground, his hands and feet bound. A Spanish halberd pointed at his chest. He felt helpless. With great despair, he knew he could no longer fight.

XXXIV

The *Lacandon* Indians lived in the remote jungles of Guatemala in a quaint village of a little over a hundred dwellings. Each one was made of thick wood with thatched roofs and a front door. There were two other buildings, one used for community services and a much larger one which served as a shrine to worship their gods. Lining the walls were stone statues of various sizes and strewn on the floor were dead animals and chickens. These things along with the lingering smell of incense were signs of a recent ritual.

Strangely, the entire village was empty. The Spanish soldiers could tell the Indians had departed quickly, leaving behind their animals and their possessions. They saw corn, beans, and cotton lying amid blowguns, pots, griddles, axes, adzes, chisels, and hand stones. Even their children's reed beds were empty and rocked in the wind. It was a ghost town, eerily quiet.

Three months had passed since President Barrios and his troops had left Guatemala. Now, the army was happily standing in the middle of the *Lacandon* Indians village, thanks to Fray Pedro de la Concepcion. The day before, he made contact with the Indians and advised them that the Spanish military was with him. Because of this warning, the Indians had scattered into the jungles.

In late April, the president of Guatemala, Father Margil and the troops entered the mythical town of Sac-Bahian which got its name from being rediscovered on the feast of Our Lady of Sorrows.

After a while, the *Lacandon* Indians began returning to their village.

Some had been convinced by the religious efforts of the priest, and some had been forced by the soldiers. The Indians were naked, covered only with a light noble loincloth which badly fulfilled its function. The men had long black hair and amber studded their pierced ears and noses.

Around the town, the governor's men built a wooden fortress and in its center raised a small structure to serve as the Church. Soon thereafter, President Barrios Leal returned to Guatemala with most of his troops. He died shortly afterwards.

President Barrios left a garrison of thirty soldiers and twenty Indian warriors under the orders of Captain Ignacio Solis in the town of Sac-Bahián. With them were Father Margil and friars from the Order of Our Lady of Mercy, including Father Blas Guillen and the Father Provincial Fray Diego de Rivas.

It was a long time before the indigenous inhabitants of the *Lacandon* region were reduced. Father Margil was pleased with the spiritual conversion of the newcomers but in his heart wondered if they would ever truly accept the new way of life. The Indians remained for a while in the town of Our Lady of Sorrows and were subsequently transferred to the town of Santa Catarina Retalhuleu, but epidemics and the climate change decimated their populations.

Father Margil stayed another two years performing his mission work among the Indians. While there, he took time to translate the Christian doctrine into the *Lacandon* language. However, his work among the natives was worrisome. He baptized more than two hundred Indians, but in secret they continued their idolatrous practices. He knew that given a chance any one of them would flee the village and return to the dense forest they knew so well. The *Lacandon* Indians were indomitable even after the reduction, and they continued to resist any further training.

It was at this village in March of 1697 that Father Margil received a communication from Commissioner General Father Manuel de Monzaval, informing him of his appointment to the guardian chair of the College of the Santa Cruz in Querétaro. He did not tell him that his first choice was Father Francisco de San Joseph, but when he failed to fulfill its mandate, the responsibility fell upon Father Margil.

In response to the mandate and following his promise of obedience, Father Margil left the land of the *Lacandon* to take over his new responsibility to Querétaro.

PART SIX: NEW PURSUITS AS GUARDIAN CHAIR

XXXV

𝕿he many years of humility and sacrifice were etched in Father Margil's weathered face as he slowly walked *El Camino Real* from México City to the checkpoint gate in Querétaro. Although he was tired and sunburned, he carried himself humbly in his tattered habit with the knotted rope reverently tied around his withered waist. The cinch was now frayed and dingy from the miles of travel. His large brimmed hat hung loosely on his back, exposing his bald head. His tattered brown habit was the same one he wore when he left Querétaro years ago. The only addition was a small skull hanging from one end of the cinch, which had served him well in his fiery sermons in the southern provinces.

As he anticipated, crowds awaiting his arrival began to form miles before he reached the gate. Even the benefactors of the College of the Santa Cruz had come to see the legendary man who had performed so many wondrous deeds. His brothers in habit were there eagerly awaiting the firsthand details of his missionary work in the faraway lands.

Stopping briefly to greet his followers, he continued walking toward the convent with the swarm of people following behind. As they neared the monastery, the church bells began to ring loudly to announce the arrival of the holy man who had converted thousands of indigenous souls in remote jungles. The bells prompted the worshippers to sing *Te Deum*, an early Christian hymn of praise.

As the tired new guardian entered the convent to the melodious chorus, he knelt in prayer. His body ached from the long journey, but he was so thankful for the goodness of Our Lord for his safe return. He asked His Lord and Savior to give him strength to continue his work as the guardian chair. He then turned, blessed the crowd, and told them the Lord had called him back home.

The beautiful town of Querétaro was the place of his beginning. It was here that he started on his great life mission. He was young and innocent to the ways of this harsh country back then. Now from years of experience in difficult situations and harsh landscapes, he was much wiser and a proficient religious.

Oh yes, he remembered now, there was unfinished business here. Before he left, he had promised to fight against the demons in the town, the intolerable vices of gambling, drunkenness, roosters, and street comedies. Now as Provincial Guardian, he would have time to lash out against those immoral practices. From what he learned, it was desperately needed now more than ever.

He said to himself, "They also needed an infirmary for the poor, a larger convent to train more missionaries, and hospitals for the sick. So much to do, so much to do."

XXXVI

Courtyard Comedy Theater
May 1697

𝕴n a crude theater nestled in downtown Querétaro, a handsome young man stood behind an imaginary gate of a makeshift balcony and sang to a lovely maiden standing with her back turned. The damsel twisted her body and smiled coyly at him. Her modest flirtatiousness was obviously false.

"Man is he devil," shouted the actor, "And if women are willing... the devil will take them!"

Just as he finished the sentence, he began to chase the damsel around the flimsy balcony. She emitted a faint cry of terror and half-heartedly tried to run away from the 'demon.' He caught her, took her in his arms, and gave her a passionate kiss.

The audience exploded in laughter at the jesting performance.

"I don't see why the religious can't enjoy a little fun every now and then," said a nobleman with a hearty laugh.

"The friars say this type of acting is falsely advertised as an art, but in reality it is a blatant display of lewdness, vulgarity, and lack of dignity," said his very serious companion.

"But it's just for fun. Look at how people laugh!" He answered.

They were in a courtyard comedy theater, known as *corral de comedias*, where the actors made jokes and performed satirical sketches for the purpose of making the audience laugh.

The outdoor theater was nothing more than a street corner adapted for the unsophisticated theatrical performances. The troupe built a wooden stage, about two steps high, with a backdrop. They lined several rows of

159

spectator benches in front and build a two story seating area for noblemen and special guests. These were sectioned off to allow for privacy to those who wanted to be discrete and out of the eyes of the commoners.

Regardless, all the spectators, some standing and others sitting, loved the follies of the crazy comedies. The audience had a rudimentary system of grading each performance. If it was bad, the patrons threw eggs or rotten fruit to assure a better performance next time. If the performance was good, the actors made an encore presentation by bowing to the applause of the crowd. Sometimes they were carried on the shoulders of the rowdy men. But more often, tempers flared and violence toward the actors erupted and spilled into the streets.

"But this is a literary work," replied the nobleman.

"Not to the friars! They think such frivolity is the work of the devil! They say that real literary works are their religious plays."

The nobleman and his partner sat hidden and unrecognizable in one of the boxes of the balcony. Here they felt secure and out of prying eyes. They could talk freely.

"The love of a poor man is like a dwarf rooster, always running, and never achieving," loudly bellowed one of the actors, as a minstrel sang and played his *vihuela* in the courtyard.

The laughter of the people was heard throughout the area. Even the nobleman on the balcony laughed aloud.

"The religious say that the kind of love shown in these comedies indicates the lack of religious values."

"Oh, c'mon, it's just an innocent farce!"

"They also say that these teachings are neither innocent nor harmless, and that these plays are praising insolence and dishonesty. They say that these works can only be described as the work of the devil."

On stage, a street vagrant looked longingly at the damsel who walked past ignoring him completely.

"When I saw you coming," muttered the vagrant, "I felt an irresistible desire to join your nice petticoats with my frayed pants."

The nobleman could not stop laughing. With a silk handkerchief, he wiped tears from his eyes. The play was finished, but the people continued to applaud the actors who returned and bowed graciously.

Exiting the balcony box, the nobleman and his friend continued their conversation about the holy priests.

"According to the friars, the puns used by actors in the comedies are lewd and cause evil thoughts. They say the actors ridicule love and courtship. They only provoke lust and unnecessarily inflame the hearts of people."

"It's just good fun! And fun is necessary for people to forget their daily worries."

"They say you can't call these productions healthy diversions. In fact, they have vowed to end them."

"Well, I can't believe this is happening!" angrily answered the nobleman as they walked down the street to board their carriage. He turned and said, "Especially that Father Margil! Since he arrived here, he has dedicated most of his preaching against these plays. Slowly, but surely, they are grinding to a halt."

The nobleman turned to his companion:

"Let me tell you, a few days ago, in front of this comedy house, Father Margil stood on a high table and started throwing not voices, but real thunder, toward the actors, whom he called `fakes.´ He said a legion of demons had entered Querétaro, and the Archangel Gabriel would soon come to exorcise them from the souls of those who participated in these performances."

"For God's sake, that sounds a bit harsh!"

"Things were quiet here for many years while Father Margil was gone to the border provinces, but now he has returned with renewed vengeance," said the nobleman. "Not only is he after the comedies, but he has castigated gambling, which he calls the 'father of blasphemy.' I heard people say that Father Margil even challenged players who bet their rosary beads. He made the cock fighters kill their prize birds, and bullfights and dances are suspended during the Passover."

"From what I understand, he has been appointed the new guardian of the College of the Santa Cruz for the next three years and will be preaching throughout our lands."

"Three years! He will certainly end all our fun pastimes!"

"People have already begun to notice the change, Your Excellency. I heard a traveler entering our city by El Camino Real at the Gate of Hacienda, was told: "Querétaro is no longer a fun town! It's sad and embarrassing to say we no longer have our doors wide open to those who want to openly celebrate and gamble.""

XXXV

As he did every night at eleven o'clock, Friar Antonio de Los Angeles Bustamante, doorman of the College of Santa Cruz of Miracles, went to Guardian Father Margil's room to awaken him. In silence, Father Margil left his cell and followed his brother to the temple. The doorman opened an old heavy book *The Mystical City of God* to the chapter that chronicled the life of the Blessed Virgin Mary. Father Margil read:

> *Thus the celestial spirits were instructed in regard to the will and the decree of the Almighty. The holy archangel Gabriel humbled himself before the throne of the most blessed Trinity, adoring and revering the divine Majesty in the manner which befits these most pure and spiritual substances. From the throne an intellectual voice preceded saying: 'Gabriel, enlighten, vivify and console Joachim and Anne, our servants, and tell them that their prayers have come to our presence and their petitions are heard in clemency. Promise them that by the favor of our right hand they will receive the Fruit of benediction, and that Anne shall conceive a Daughter to whom we give the name of Mary.*

The doorman listened attentively to the reading of the friar. When he finished, they bowed their heads and spent several minutes in meditation.

162

Then the doorman closed the book and sat in a nearby chair as if he was the teacher. Father Margil knelt in front of him as was the custom and confessed his sins.

When he finished listing his failings, his penance was to lie on the floor face up and say three creeds. Next, they quietly reversed roles. The doorman knelt before Father Margil, recounted his sins, and then lay on the floor to recite the same prayers as penance.

After the confessions, they continued praying in solitude until midnight when they were joined by the other friars. They prayed the Divine Office, recited psalms, sang hymns, and read writings from the fathers of the early Church in order to sanctify the life of the Christian community.

In the early hours of the morning, they continued in prayer. Father Margil then retreated to the quietness of his room to pray alone, read the Holy Scriptures, and rest for a few hours.

When dawn broke, Father Margil was still praying. He rose and drowsily began confessions until shortly before the noon mass. After he said Mass, he ate vegetable broth but only enough to sustain his strength, in accordance with his regimental fasting. Then he went back to the confessional and stayed until mid-afternoon. Without taking a nap, he continued praying until vespers, only taking time to read the moral conference and visit the sick. This was his daily routine, rarely changed and always performed willingly.

Friar Antonio de Los Angeles, the doorman of the convent, held Father Guardian in great esteem and credited him for his new conversion. Years earlier, he entered the convent as Don Miguel Antonio de la Hoz y Gonzalez Bustamante, a rich and handsome young man. He inherited from his family a large estate and much property, but he had a deep void in his life that money could not fill. At the age of thirty-one, he sold everything and entered the Convent of Santa Cruz as a lay brother, where he took the name of Friar Antonio de Los Angeles.

Ironically, Friar Antonio, a wealthy lord before, became a dedicated beggar on the streets of the city. His daily routine was to leave the convent and knock on doors begging for food and alms to feed his brothers at the convent.

In his later years, when he became aged and no longer able to walk long distances seeking alms, he was assigned to the chair of doormen at the convent, where he met Father Margil.

Together they made an offer of mortification, which included sleeping for only four hours a day; abstinence from meat and fruit, except on Sundays; continual fasting; and wearing only sackcloth clothing three days a week and every day during Advent. Throughout their time at the College of the Santa Cruz, they were joined together by the great understanding of their common dedication to their faith.

XXXVI

𝕵uan stumbled along the street losing his balance and falling against his drunken friend as he attempted to walk along Old Bridge Street to the privacy of the corner to urinate.

"I beggg... I beggg... your.... Parrrrdon," he said in a drunken slur. "I'm... I'm a little....unsteady for some reason."

His partner ignored his comments and concentrated on his own mug of *pulque*.

For hours, Juan had been drinking his favorite brew in the crude make-shift *pulquería*, a cantina open on three sides and covered by a blanket. In those hours, he had squandered his money on drinks for himself and his friends. He had nothing left from the sale of his goods at the *parian* market. Now a half day later, he was drunk, had not eaten a morsel, and could not even remember where he lived or if he had a family. The other patrons were in no better shape.

Every day the cantina was filled with intoxicated patrons hotly debating irrelevant issues, Often tempers flared and drunken brawls erupted. Ironically, the next day all was forgotten until a new argument broke out. They all knew their rhetoric was mere nonsense blowing in the wind.

Other patrons, oblivious to the quarrels around them, played cards on a *pulque* barrel and gambled their meager earnings.

The establishment was for men only, but on occasion bawdy women entered looking to make a quick *peso*. In the eyes of the drunken brawlers, the women from the dark streets were like beautiful, young, and unsoiled flowers. The bartender, known as the *sobresaliente,* monitored the happenings in the cantina. He knew if the Royal Guard was called for a violation the owner of the establishment could face stiff fines and license revocation. Worse, if a person was killed or wounded, they could possibly face stiff court penalties as restitution for the families of victims.

To discourage loitering in the open-air cantina, no food was served, seats were not provided, and no music or dancing was allowed. The patrons could only stand and drink during the time of operation, from dusk to dawn. However, as the day progressed, Juan and his friends, overcome by the devil spirits, passed out and slept awkwardly leaning against the walls or quietly in corners.

After walking only a few steps outside the cantina to urinate, Juan felt a blow to his head which caused him to stumble and fall. He tried to stand but in his condition could not. When he looked up to see who had hit him, he was surprised to see his angry wife.

"Look, at you!" snapped his wife.

"Oh, c'mon, I've had only one little drink, only one little *chinguirito.*"

"One *chinguirito,* you've had too many *chinguiritos*! Where is your money? Give me your money! I need it for our children," she said as she rifled his shirt pockets.

A drunken patron shouted from the rear of the cantina, "Get outta here and go home, nosey old woman!"

"Shut up, you ugly old goat!" she replied.

The woman, determined to get him home, helped him to his feet. Then acting as his crutch, they stumbled down the street. The patrons laughed at the impromptu show but almost immediately returned to their drinks. When Juan and his wife reached the corner, to their surprise, they encountered Father Margil. The woman's eyes quickly filled with tears as she kissed his hand and tried to explain why they were on the street so late at night.

"Father, look at my shameless husband!" she said between sobs.

"Do not weep, my dear lady," consoled Father Margil.

"He does not listen to me, Father! He drinks all our money away, every day! And now we have nothing to feed our children," she cried.

"Kind lady, take your husband home. When his head clears, I will speak to him," calmly reassured Father Margil.

"Now go in peace, with God's blessing!", said Father Margil.

XXXVII

Congregation of Guadalupe Church, Querétaro
June 1698

𝕿he newly constructed Church of the Congregation of Guadalupe was majestic and dominated almost the entire central square in Querétaro. Its pink stone facade was unique because it had two high towers on the outside with a shorter central tower and a baroque entrance dedicated to the Virgin of Guadalupe. Inside the sanctuary, it had elegant Doric columns and an unforgettable elaborate baroque altar.

The beautiful work was partially completed eighteen years earlier with the blessing of Bachelor Juan Caballero y Osio, the parish priest of Querétaro, who personally paid for most of the construction.

In 1688, a brotherhood was established between the Congregation of Secular Priests of St. Mary of Guadalupe and the newly formed Apostolic College of Propagation of the Faith of the Santa Cruz. The brotherhood was dedicated to prayer, mortification, community, and ministry as teachers. It was a tradition that the Brotherhood of the Franciscans held a Eucharistic celebration and preached from the pulpit of the Church of the Congregation on the Feast of Saints Peter and Paul. Then on the Feast of the Exaltation of the Holy Cross and the Three Jubilees of Forty Hours a celebration was held in the Franciscan church. The Brotherhood also worked together in administering the Holy Sacraments of the Church to the religious. Many times they heard confessions and held funerals for the priests.

On this day in June, the temple was beautifully decorated for the solemn Eucharistic Feasts of Saints Peter and Paul. As was established by the brotherhood, Father Margil from the Franciscan College was invited to preach, an honor he accepted.

All the members of the royal city council and the prelates of the various religious orders were present at this solemn Eucharist ceremony. High society men and women in their finest clothing awaited the words of Father Margil.

Perhaps the fathers of the Congregation expected a scholarly dissertation on the evangelical ministry of Saints Peter and Paul. Not so, instead Father Margil chose to make a public outcry about the importance of living God's word every day. From the pulpit, he strongly criticized the conduct of the high ranking authorities of Querétaro. To the amazement of the unnamed individuals, Father Margil spoke in great detail of their lurid conduct. He was very clear and open and showed no regard for their personal sentiments.

His allegations of rampant bribery and corruption in government were common knowledge to the general public. They all knew that everyone suffered mercilessly from the illegal acts of the authorities.

This was not the first time corruption had been denounced from pulpits in various parts of New Spain. Six years earlier in the cathedral in México City, serious riots were ignited by a powerful Easter sermon given by Father Antonio de Escaray, Preacher of His Majesty. The largely attended celebration included the Viceroy Don Gaspar de la Cerda y Sandoval, Conde de Galve, the Court, and the Councils.

Father Escaray's truth told from the pulpit was the origin of the melee. Ten thousand people participated in looting, rioting, and damages totaling more than three million *pesos*. During the fracas, parts of the Viceregal Palace and City Hall were burned.

It seems his sermon brought to light the plight of the common man who suffered from a monopoly of local merchants who sold their products at exorbitant prices and paid them little. This was all at the encouragement of the corrupt government authorities. The Franciscan's sermon publicly aired the issue which had been hidden from the people. The truth served to incite the frustration of the victims.

There had been disparities between the clergy and the authorities in New Spain before the riot. In 1624 there was a great dispute in México City between the Archbishop Juan Perez de la Serna and the Viceroy Diego Carrillo de Mendoza y Pimentel, Marquis of Gelves, which ended in a serious riot and the removal of Viceroy. Fifteen years later another conflict occurred between the Archbishop Juan de Manso and Viceroy Lope Díez de Armendáriz, Marquis of Cadereyta.

For these reasons, complaints from the pulpit were not unfamiliar in New Spain, but they were new to the people of Querétaro. Father Margil preached in this conservative city as no one had every dared to do before him. The authorities were not accustomed to anyone being identified in this manner, much less from the pulpit. For the officials of the city, it was a total humiliation. It was inconceivable that criticism was actually coming from the highest ecclesiastical forum.

Maybe this was not an opportune time or way to report these transgressions, but Father Margil felt the urgent need to make public what was secretly known by all. Without hesitation and in hopes of leading the transgressors back to the righteous path, he continued. Soon every person of authority was left to contemplate his own personal indiscretions.

"This is unbelievable! I've never before been humiliated like this!" said one of the officers who had just left the Eucharistic Mass.

"We cannot allow ourselves to be talked about like this!" replied one of the aldermen.

"We will have to report him to the Holy Inquisition!" concluded one of the attendees.

"It is blatant humiliation!" said another.

"No one has ever preached from the pulpit in this manner!" whispered one of the ecclesiastical authorities.

The scandal was enormous, and the authorities angrily complained about the outrageous accusations. They immediately went to the commissioner of the Holy Inquisition to report Father Margil's' audacity.

The commissioner, also the city's mayor, was a man of wisdom and exemplary behavior. All who knew him knew of his kindness and simplicity. Since taking his religious vows those qualities were further unfolded in his new work. He was of the religious; therefore, he was full of zeal for the holy faithful, so patient, and always ready to listen respectfully to the plaintiffs.

They presented themselves before him and gave a broad overview of Father Margil's behavior during his sermons. He listened quietly without comment. Then he excused the complainants with a promise to have a prompt decision on the grave matter.

The commissioner, charged with the functions of the Inquisitor, sought counsel from the leading prelates and theologians in the city before he proceeded to take action against Father Margil. He knew Father Margil well and was quite knowledgeable of his many virtues.

"Excellencies," commissioner said, "I must draw your attention to a serious matter that interests the greater service of God, the King, and the Inquisition. We must examine the behavior of the venerable Father Margil, barefoot religious of the Order of San Francisco and Seraphic Guardian of the Apostolic College of Propagation of the Faith of the Convent of Santa Cruz.

The commissioner set out the accusations of the authorities without adding or omitting any detail. After the commissioner's speech, he asked those present for their opinion. Almost all were in favor of a formal denunciation of Father Margil; however, some were more cautious and favored only a warning instead.

However, one of those present made known his displeasure with the complaints.

"Illustrious Fathers" he told them, "I think men like the holy Father Margil should not be measured by common rules. They speak more with the Spirit of God than from human prudence."

He paused for a second, and then continued.

"Father Margil could not be gentle on a topic for which he is concerned. Yes! He has spoken harshly but with transparency and, above all, with truth."

He turned to the other attendees.

"Truth is sometimes uncomfortable, but there is no sin in it."

After listening to the opinions of everyone in the room, the commissioner made a formal complaint of the matter to the Holy Tribunal of the Inquisition where it languished and died. A formal trial against Father Margil was never made.

Soon afterwards, Father Margil, guided by his virtue of humility, wrote to one of his Franciscan brothers:

"I have made a covenant with God that Father Margil does not speak, does not look. So in all other things, His Majesty preaches, talks, hears, confesses and does everything through me. What would the angels be without God? Nothing. What would Mary Most Holy be without God? Nothing. What would the humanity of Christ be without God? Nothing. Without God, in fact, all of us are nothing, nothing, nothing!"

XXXVIII

Garden of the Convent of the Santa Cruz
June 1700

As it was his custom every time he returned to the Convent of the Santa Cruz, Father Margil wedged his walking cane into the loose soil of the nearby garden. It was the same wooden staff he had used for years on his evangelization missions in the strange new provinces to the South. He had used it to climb lofty mountains and to clear tangled underbrush in dense jungles. It served him when he crossed rapid rivers and helped him ward off dangerous animals and snakes. At times it even served as his support for a short siesta on the many trails in far off lands. It was his constant companion and had been with him at his frequent fire and brimstone sermons and had witnessed infinite paths, hunger, and pain. Now the two old friends were home for a long needed rest.

For the next three years, the old dry bough rested peacefully planted in the serene garden of Santa Cruz. On the day Father Margil was to leave on a new assignment back in Guatemala, he went to the garden to get his trusted rod for the long journey south. To his surprise, it was tightly embedded in the ground. He tried to pull it free from the firm grip of 'mother earth' but to no avail. Father Margil made a final effort to dislodge his old companion but found the lifeless piece of wood had rooted itself into the ground. It now had a permanent home at the Convent of the Santa Cruz and would soon grow into a tree.

Father Margil smiled, and with great respect for the new life God had created, he lovingly resigned himself to find another staff and leave his trusted comrade. The following spring, the stick grew larger, added more branches and sprouted feather-like leaves. The greatest surprise to its spectators was that along the limbs, surrounded by leaves, grew ghastly clusters of *espinas*, thorns or spikes, just like the thorns in the crown placed on Jesus before his crucifixion. On a closer look they also noticed that some of the *espinas* formed a perfect cross. They had a long center spike with two smaller ones on each side, as if it represented the cross of the Passion of Our Lord Jesus Christ. Now the people truly believed the small tree recognized Father Margil's holy hands and instead of flowers and fruit, a perfect crucifix was made in his honor. For generations to come, the devout of México believed the miraculous tree, which was not found anywhere else in the region, grew only in this garden as a testament to Father Margil. When he returned years later and looked at the wonder, he recognized the thorns as the ones Father Lináz had offered him years earlier when he was invited to the New World.

XXXIX

College of Christ Crucified in Guatemala
September 1701

"Put it here, my brothers," Father Margil said to the group of Indians who carried a large piece of cut stone. "This one will be our first cornerstone."

He watched as they carefully placed the stone exactly where he pointed. Next, the friar stood near the stone, counted a predetermined number of steps, and then marked the spot with a rock. He turned and once again stepped and marked a spot, until all four sides were set. It made a perfect rectangle. He looked at the Indians and said:

"Now put a cornerstone at each place I marked with a rock."

The perplexed men placed the stones exactly as they were instructed and then watched him as he tied a rope between each one. "Now we have the boundaries, and the ropes will ensure the walls are straight," Father Margil said.

Next he placed a special stone in front of the new building. It was carved with "8th September 1701," the start date of construction. After that, the Provincial Father Jose Gonzalez, blessed the project, and Father Margil began the construction of the new College of Propagation of the Faith of Christ Crucified. The project was funded by Friar Pedro de la Concepcion who purchased the land in the city of Santiago de los Caballeros in Guatemala. He received an extra lot of land as a donation from a generous Indian benefactor.

Enthusiasm filled the air from the first day of construction, and cash donations flowed generously. It was a labor of love as every man, woman, and child volunteered to help. Some helped build, others cooked, and others carried supplies back and forth. So many donations of food and materials came in that it was hard to keep up with them. Others who were unable to perform physical tasks showed their happiness in celebration of the new college by organizing entertainment for the crowds. They decorated wagons and oxen with flowers and ribbons and marched in the streets singing and dancing.

Father Margil was both a teacher and a laborer as he humbly performed the dirtiest of tasks. Seeing him work, many distinguished citizens, who normally would have nothing to do with dirty work, followed his example.

It had been only a little over a year since the Royal Decree, dated 16 July 1700 from Madrid, had authorized Father Margil's return to Guatemala. In that short time, he had was sent by the commissioner general to carry out the establishment of the College of Propagation of the Faith in Guatemala. It was a miracle that he accomplished the task in such a short time.

The first part of his year had been spent in a single wooden room attached to the Calvary Hospice, where he and Friar Pedro de la Concepción, who was in charge, had made the plans for the new college. The rest of the year was spent building the college, which was completed and blessed on 13 June 1702, the feast of St. Anthony of Padua. The festivities included a procession from the cathedral, where people carried the Holy Sacrament, and bells rang throughout the town. The procession consisted of the councils, the religious orders, the nobility, and the poorest and most humble man of all, Father Margil.

Because of his great achievements the following year, by a clear majority of votes, the Chapter voted Father Margil to be the Chair and first Guardian of the College. Soon after the election, Father Margil wrote to Friar Antonio de Los Angeles, his brother door keeper of the College of Santa Cruz, "*It seems that our Lord wants me to be guardian here, as they have involved me as the guardian. The nothingness is nothing, and nothing can be, and in this way, be it he who may.*"

From that day forward, he referred to himself as *nothing* and signed his letters *La Misma Nada*, meaning *Nothingness Itself*.

After spending a short time at College of Propagation of the Faith of the Christ Crucified, to make sure it was on the right path to success, Father Margil left the college for a new assignment. This time he would travel to Nicaragua, where he and Father Rodrigo de Betancourt would preach in the land of the witches.

XL

As the scantily dressed Indian chief advanced slowly into the darkened cave, a cold wind chilled his body to the bone. He had met with *la bruja*, the witch, on several previous occasions, but this time he dreaded the encounter. The pungent smell of charred flesh and thick smoke lingered in the air. Lighting only a few steps in front of him, his torch flickered in the darkness of the deep dwelling. He had just enough light to see the animal carcasses and bones scattered on the filthy floor. In his mind, he knew that witches possessed magical powers and could turn people into animals who roamed the nights. His people believed you could gaze into the eyes of a wild beast and see a witch looking back at you. This was true of pumas, jaguars, tapirs, raccoons, eagles, and crocodiles. The vile temptress was specifically fond of taking the form of a snake to perform her evil deeds. The Christian fathers had told them the serpent was the embodiment of evil itself just like in the book they called *La Santa Biblia*.

Because her home was in a cave, La Cueva de Coyotepe had been very difficult to reach. To get there, the chief travelled up steep slopes and through narrow canyons along the valley of Sébaco in the Tologalpa provinces before finding the gloomy, almost impregnable hollow in the mountain.

From this point, it was still a good distance inside the cave before he came upon the old hag sitting in the back of the cave. Even though he had seen her before, he was still startled by her unkempt appearance and her foul smell. Her countless years showed on her black, wrinkled, naked

175

body and in her limp breasts that hung down to her navel. Her piercing eyes were sunk into her skinny head, and her animal-like yellow teeth barely showed under her long pointed nose. Her thin scruffy hair, her long claw-like fingers, and black fingernails gave her the look of a wild beast. The appearance of this evil creature was seared in the chief's mind and produced a shocking, diabolical sensation all over this body.

"Why do you come?" she angrily screeched.

"I come about our harvest. I want to know if we will have a favorable rainy season and a good harvest of corn this year," answered the chief.

He was not the first chief to visit the old woman in the cave. It was a tradition among the chieftains of the region to consult with her and the other witches who lived in nearby. Since the beginning of time, their forefathers had sought predictions from the *brujas* in matters of war, crops, and in most aspects affecting their villages.

"Have you done your duty? You know, you are not to come unless you have done your duty," screeched the old woman.

"Indeed, as you desired, we have killed eight people, including men, women, and children. Two days ago we offered their blood to our idols and their bodies were placed at the entrance of your cave," humbly said the chief.

"I know!" laughed the old woman, and in a course voice she said, "They were very tasty, especially the little ones!"

"But what have I not done, my sorceress?" asked the chief.

"You have not driven away the white men! You have not required the invaders to go away from these lands. You know they only bring disaster to our lands. You must drive them away forever. You must banish the evil ones permanently!" shouted the witch.

"We have tried, but the white men keep coming, more and more of them, and now they are supported by soldiers and their holy men," pleaded the chief.

"Until they go, we can't live in peace. My powers are hampered by the practices of those coming from overseas. The fathers, above all, are causing us many disasters, especially to our long traditions and beliefs. They have broken and burned our statues of our gods and goddesses in the streets," fiercely replied the old woman.

"They have reached the main towns. There they try to convert us into their religion. But we always secretly resist and continue our own rituals in private. Every time they anoint the chrism on our forehead, we wash it off as soon as they turn their heads."

"You cannot fool them. The friars are not as stupid as they seem, it will not be long before they reach us here. Then they will force their way into my sacred cave!" cried the witch.

"I will make sure that does not happen," the chief responded.

"They are devoting themselves to the destruction of our sacred images. I've been told that on the main square they pile them up and set fire to them," cried the woman.

"Unfortunately, it is true, venerable lady. We tried to stop it, but the soldiers would not allow us to save our magical stones or our idols," said the chief with sadness.

"I was also told that one of our most venerable elders, a wise sorcerer and chief soothsayer among us, has been arrested in his shrine by white men and sent to distant lands where they locked him up for the rest of his life. As long as the friars remain here, I don't wish to be seen by you or by any of the others," said the witch.

"I beg you not to abandon us, your highness. We need your knowledge and your good wishes as we consult with you every week. We will offer more human sacrifices if it pleases you," pleaded the chief.

"You have heard me. Until you banish those bastards, you can never see me again!" said the old woman as she turned her back to him. To his shock and disbelief, she disappeared into the bowels of the cave right before his incredulous eyes.

XLI

𝕱ather Margil stood at the bedside of an emaciated old man. He made the sign of the cross and began the holy sacrament of Extreme Unction. "By this holy anointing and by his most tender mercy may the Lord forgive thee whatever thou hast done amiss by thy sight, hearing, smell, speech, taste, touch, and walk."

In a whisper the Indian man responded, "Father, I have already confessed my sins to our chief priest. He told me not to confess to the priests of the new religion."

Father Margil and Friar Tomás Delgado had travelled through many towns: San Pablo, San Francisco Zapotitlan, Santos Reyes de Cuyotenango, San Bartolomé Mazatenango, San Martin Zapotitlan, San Antonio Suchiltepequez, Zamayaque, San Gabriel Mazatenango, and San Antonio Retalhuleu. In most of them, he heard these same words from the sick and dying.

These were the lands known for a multitude of sorcerers, witches and ministers of the devil. At one time during his travels, Father Margil recorded over six hundred Indian warlocks in one province alone. In the town of Zamayaque, the seat of the supreme authority of the idol worshipers, he counted a staggering one hundred and twenty witches and warlocks.

When the chief priests visited the sick, they fumigated the room with fragrant resin, lit a candle, and gave it to the bereaved. Then they listened to the confessions. If the confessor was married, he was required to tell his sins in front of his wife. If the confessor was a female, she was made to loudly proclaim her sins, without reservation, to her husband. If the confessor was single, the priest ceremonially collected the candle wax and took it with him after the ritual. Each time the Christian priests arrived for confessions, they were told of these rituals and that their services were not needed.

In most of the Indians' villages, idol worship had been passed down from generation to generation, and their stone gods were heirlooms passed from father to father. They were old and worn but precious in the eyes of their owners who displayed them proudly in their homes. The priests often heard of the warlocks and witches and their diabolical rituals to ward off evil spirits, which included the religious. They used herbs and spells to transform themselves into wild animals, and they decorated trees around the village with demon-like images in hopes of scaring the priests.

On the banks of rivers, where the people fished for *acamayas,* river shrimp, it was customary for the evil witches to leave finely decorated baskets and scented nets as an offering for the goddess of the waters. They asked her to take care of their fishing nets and were pleased when she appeared in the form of a snake.

The most common objects used by the witches were the velvety green diaphanous stones. These pagan stones allowed the witch to shape-shift into an animal and actually become the animal's spirit, which they called *nahual.* It was during these rituals that they usually sacrificed a child's life to their demons and evil spirits.

In one region, the priests discovered a beautiful round altar stone, about two yards in diameter and imprinted with the image of an imperial eagle. Laying on it was a small idol of stone made into the shape of a human. Nearby were three large mounds of dirt like volcanoes and covered with spears and lances. They learned the crude weapons were placed there and used to torment the mourners and families of the sacrificed children. This wicked place was dedicated to the god of hunters and healers.

In these evil new lands, Father Margil prayed that the hearts of the people would be opened by the Holy Spirit and that they would be willing to accept the one true God, Our Lord and Savior Jesus Christ. He knew the overwhelming task at hand was to fight against these false gods, witches, warlocks, and the devil himself.

No matter how difficult the task, he felt the hand of God would guide him, and with this he found renewed strength. He began his mission with the most powerful sermons of his lifetime. His oration was so powerful that many of the indigenous people immediately accepted the Gospel and gave up their pagan idols. Such was the success of his mission in Suchitepéquez, that those who had not heard his preaching believed his success was from threats of punishment. In time, these allegations were proven false.

Father Margil's mission work in Guatemala was deemed a huge success because he had reduced to ashes countless idols, undid diabolical pacts, converted witches, and united barbarians and gentiles alike to Christ. In a report to the Royal Audience of Guatemala, Captain James Beard stated that due to the evangelization of Father Margil many lost souls had been saved, and everywhere Father Margil went, the number of Church marriages increased twofold. In the middle of 1706, Father Margil received a new assignment from the commissioner general of the Franciscan Order to establish another college. This time it was the Apostolic College of Propagation of the Faith in the Hospice of Guadalupe in the far-away city of Zacatecas.

XLII

As the traveler stood looking down upon the City of Our Lady of Zacatecas, he saw only a few hundred simple houses nestled in the nooks and crannies of the hillside and along the cobble stone road meandering into the canyon city below. The beautiful slopes of Bufa and Grillo were rough and not easily traversed but held great treasures below the surface. Often in the early morning hours, a thick fog covered the city and the rugged mountains, but today it was clear and dry with no fog; only the piercing north wind blew, which numbed his extremities. No winter frost or snow blanketed the ground. The dryness and lack of vegetation in the area was largely due to silver mining in Our Lady of Guadalupe Vetagrande, approximately two miles to the north.

Although the city was arid and lacked vegetation, its edifying religious point of view made up for these shortcomings. According to the voice of one reporter, the development of Christian morality was at its peak there. Most residents of the city had repented and set aside their old customs and ways. Now they lived together amiably and openly displayed great charity to one another. These new ways were largely due to the work of the Franciscan Fathers who had ministered to them for many years. The friars had actually become an integral part of the original founding of the City of Zacatecas.

Father Antonio Margil, Father Jose Castro and other religious from the College of the Santa Cruz arrived in this prophetic city on the 12th of January in the year of 1707.

Upon entering the city, they went directly to the Convent of San Francisco and presented themselves before the Provincial Father Friar Hermoso de Celis.

"With your blessing Father Celis," said Father Margil. "We would like to establish the Apostolic College of Propagation of the Faith in the Hospice of Guadalupe."

With a scowl on his face, the Provincial Father immediately said, 'No!' A feeling of *déjà vu* came over Father Margil as he remembered being rejected the first time he tried to establish the college in Querétaro. Now he prayed for the same outcome. After a short review of the documents submitted by Father Margil and the records showing the support from Friar Francisco Estevez, the Commissioner and Prefect of Missions, the Provincial Father reluctantly accepted the proposal.

With this first step behind him, Father Margil walked to the cathedral located in the central plaza. There he relaxed and admired the majestic old house of worship with its stone carvings: three images of the Eternal Father, Jesus and the Twelve Apostles, angels, and many more. He was especially struck by the image of the Holy Eucharist, reflected in the stained glass window of the choir loft. When he entered through the access gate, he saw the image of the Blessed Virgin Mary in the center of the courtyard. He immediately knelt and prayed for success, protection, and shelter for this most important undertaking.

Before construction could begin, he was required to present the college's foundation certificate to the civil authorities. Expecting setbacks, he was pleasantly surprised when they approved and signed it without question.

Now it was time for him and his companions to travel to the Hospice of Guadalupe, only one league south of the city of Zacatecas. When they arrived, they were warmly welcomed by Father Jose Guerra, the Superior.

While walking through the Hospice corridors, Father Joseph said to Father Margil:

"This place was established by Friar Francisco Estevez, Friar Antonio de Escaray, and Friar Francisco Hidalgo about twenty years ago. Because their preaching made such an impact on the townspeople, they asked to establish this hospice on donated land."

They entered through a door and Father Joseph continued:

"I don't need to repeat that we welcome you, Father Margil. We are honored that you are the founder of our College of Propagation of the Faith."

"Well, I must confess that I was not their first choice," said Father Margil. "The venerable Father Friar Pedro de la Concepción was to have the honor, but to his misfortune, pirates attacked his ship as he left Cadiz, and the whole crew was stranded on the beaches of Portugal."

"Good lord!" exclaimed Father Joseph, "what happened to them?"

"Father Pedro walked to Madrid and presented himself before his Majesty who decided to appoint him Bishop of Puerto Rico instead of sending him here. Father Pedro very kindly suggested me for this position to the Commissioner General of the Indies, and, as you see, here I am. Undeserving but eager to work."

"Undeserving? Father Margil, your fame precedes you in every corner of New Spain!"

"Fame is a bad thing, Father Joseph, a very bad thing!" said Father Margil, shaking his head. "Many times I have repeated to myself: 'Do not forget your nothingness, no matter what others may do to you. Do not fear so long as you live, Antonio, any demon greater than that called 'I.'"

"I do not mean to flatter you, Father Margil. I simply repeat what is known in these regions," said Father Joseph.

"Well, I think we have had enough talk for this day. It is time to begin our work, for we have much to do."

XLIII

College of Propagation of the Faith of Guadalupe
February 1710

𝔄 young friar, studying at the College of the Propagation of Faith of Guadalupe, dipped his quill into an inkwell and wrote the following words in a letter:

Dear Brother in Christ, May the Lord give you peace!

I was overjoyed to hear from you and am happy you are in good health. May God and the Blessed Virgin Mary continue to save and protect you for a very long time.

In your letter, you asked me how my first years of school have been and, in particular, about my experience working with the venerable Father Margil.

My brother, I must say that the last three years have been incredible and a most pleasant experience. I thank our Lord every day for allowing me to be here and be a part of the founding of the College.

Father Margil is an extraordinary man. I could almost say he is a saint, but claiming this would preclude the judgment of the Holy Church, who decides the sanctity of these matters.

Nevertheless, I can say that with his great enthusiasm and tireless ability to labor and toil in these lands, he alone can achieve more than many men combined.

From the beginning, he engulfed himself into the project of enlarging the College building, which was formerly the Hospice. The expansion has now increased the number of rooms and has expanded the overall size of the temple. When the building was complete, he alone beautifully decorated the chapel and worked our garden into a lush and productive source of food. He even made arrangements for a beautiful flute organ and many library books to be delivered to us from Spain. It's unbelievable how much money he has collected to be able to provide us with these luxuries, which unfortunately are extremely expensive. He does these things gladly, never wanting praise, for he knows they are for our benefit, and we will take care of these precious commodities.

While doing all of this, he still had time to establish new rules and regulations for the College. They are very strict but needed and useful to us. Everyone tries very hard to follow them; for that reason, they must be read and studied continuously.

Now, let me tell you about his missions and pilgrimages. He arrived here at the College, three years ago, but before the end of the first year, he went to the province of Nueva Galicia. He spent the first three months doing mission work in Guadalajara, and at the end of the year, he came back to Zacatecas. Then at Easter, he went back to Guadalajara once again where he spent about five months. He next went to Durango before returning to Zacatecas. A month later, he was on his way to México City to meet Very Reverend Father Fray Juan de la Cruz, the Commissioner General.

When he arrived in México City, the Commissioner asked Father Margil to take charge of the Provincial Chapter that was to be held in San Luis Potosi. For this reason, our holy man headed to the city to launch the call for the Chapter. You know organizing an event of this magnitude is not easy, but he undertook the assignment with great energy and enthusiasm.

As we all know, the venerable Father Margil can't rest for long, so until the start of the Provincial Chapter, he took up mission work at Santa Maria de los Lagos.

When time came, he returned to San Luis Potosí for the Chapter meeting and afterwards went to Querétaro to submit his report. He then returned to Zacatecas. This has been the most recent journey of our venerable Guardian. Unbelievably and unimaginably, my brother, through all his voyages he walked barefoot and only wore a worn-out pair of sandals when the terrain warranted.

Just thinking about the hardships he has endured, I am more exhausted than he ever appeared to be.

His preaching is unbelievable as well. Recently while on the pulpit in our convent, he stripped his habit to his waist and beat his back with a dog chain. He ignited so much love in the people that many burst into tears and *immediately repented of their sins. I tell you, my brother, the Father Guardian did not do this to solicit applause or garnish indecent thoughts. He did it with the firm intention to save souls and soften hearts.*

This writing is only a small sample of his wondrous deeds and only gives you an idea of the strength and temperament of our Holy Father Margil.

With this, I close my letter to you. Thank you again for your kind, but undeserved, words of affection in your most recent letter. I look forward to your response, and as always, I hope my letter finds you and your fraternity in good health.

Your brother in Christ

PART SEVEN:
NORTHERN KINGDOMS

XLIV

The young Indian man picked up an ear of charred corn, cut away the soot, and placed it in a small bowl. He then mixed the soot with a small amount of water to produce a black paint used to cover his entire body and face. Next, he mixed a bit of red ocher, made from river clay, with water and painted red stripes around his body. A small waistcloth covered his manliness, the only place on his body not painted. He placed a wooden lion-like mask over his face and grabbed his spear. He walked proudly to the center of the small town square where the other Indians awaited the arrival of their fierce looking comrade.

The rhythmic beat of drums filled the air. To begin the ceremony, the men chewed bulbous buttons from a small spineless cactus the Coras Indians called *hualari*. When the hallucinogenic magic of the divine plant activated their senses, they began to dance around the fire and chanted to the drum beats. As they continued to eat the bulbs and dance, their minds began to experience a sense of well-being, a feeling of calmness and harmony with nature. Myth and reality were indistinguishable as their visions took on new reality.

One after the other, they danced in a ring marking rhythm with their feet. Their intoxication from the sacred medicine increased with each beat of the drum. After some time, when all participants were deeply under the influence of the psychedelic drug, the ritual began.

The men who could still stand began to run. They seemed to fly in all directions, on and on and on. At one point, the largest group stopped, but a cry from their leader urged the race to begin anew. After a while they stopped again, but soon they resumed in a different direction. Some ran in straight lines, others in circles, and still others aimlessly. The ritual continued until the next morning when the last man could run no more and fell to the ground. The effect of the *hualari* bulbs was the only thing that kept them going all night. The plant was an inexhaustible source of energy for the Indians, who saw it as a gift from the Great Spirit. It took away their hunger, thirst, sleep, and gave them courage to fight. It allowed them to purify themselves and gave them the ability to absorb the power of their divine gods.

The ceremonial ritual involved only the men. The women were there only to prepare the food consumed by the participants during their hallucinogenic state.

The cloud of dust rose from the endless race like a fog that limited their visibility to a short distance. To a stranger, the chaotic dance had no order or reason. That is why the celebrations became known to foreigners as *mitotes*, crazy feasts without rules or goals. But in fact, very few outsiders had witnessed the rituals and lived to tell their stories; and virtually no white man had ever entered the sacred circle. Although a few had secretly tried, the lucky ones were expelled, but the unlucky ones were killed.

At nightfall, in the light of torches, the ritual to the god Tayaó invoked the hunting of a deer and its sacrificial offering. The appearance of these warriors was terrifying to anyone who was not a villager. Some of the warriors were fully tattooed with grayish white, black, and red paint. Others were decorated in black with white or yellow spots. All wore fierce looking animal masks and held spears and clubs in their hands.

These rituals took place in the remote village of the *Coras*, located in western central México about four hundred miles west of Querétaro. This was a place that had remained unaltered, autonomous, and rebellious for centuries. It was a place where the people were proud of their traditions and independence, and they wanted no strangers coming near their village, regardless of where they were from. They chose to keep it this way. The warriors who fought to keep strangers away called themselves *nayarites*, meaning warriors fighting and persevering, and they were honored to carry the noble name.

Their villages, several days walk from the nearest town, were virtually impregnable and inaccessible. They were located amid the rugged and endless Sierra de Nayarit Mountains in the land of Nayar. Very little grows there, only cacti and thorn bushes called *acacias*. But the inhospitable geography was nothing compared to the protection given by the fierce *nayarites* who stood at the gates like Trojan warriors ready to kill anyone who dared to enter.

XLV

𝕱ather Margil fell to his knees and spread his arms to form a cross as he lay prone on the rugged ground. Father Luis did the same a few feet behind him. Praying to themselves, they awaited the blows that would surely come next. The Indians surrounded them and taunted them with their arrows and machetes but did not strike. Listening to the shouts of impending death, the defenseless friars lay quietly. Detecting no mercy in the tone of their adversaries, they felt their end was near. Their two Indian guides cowered nearby and raised the holy cross as if to shield their bodies.

Amazed and confused by the attitude of the friars, the angry Indians dropped their weapons and motioned for Father Margil to stand. He rose and immediately embraced the Indian leader in a display of love and friendship. He then turned to one of the guides and asked him to interpret his message of peace to the Indian warriors.

"Do not waste your time," uttered the belligerent Indian. "We are warriors sent by our leaders to ensure that no one enters our sacred lands. We do not want strangers here. You must leave now or suffer the consequences of death."

Father Margil and Friar Luis had been sent to the Sierra del Nayar region at the request of the Royal Audience of Guadalajara, who wanted to reduce the *Coras* Indians. They had tried several times but were repelled each time by the mighty warriors. Knowing that it was important to rid the region of rebellion and idolatry, the Indian Council decided to try once more. This time they appointed Father Margil as an evangelist for the region by a decree dated the 31st July 1709.

Father Margil, who was still in Zacatecas, received the news of his appointment at the end of 1710 and immediately left for the capital of Nueva Galicia. He appeared before their court and requested that the reduction of the Indians be made by peaceful resolution.

"Holy Father Margil," said one of the judges. "I do not want to contradict your opinion, but do you realize that these Indians have already killed many of our Spanish citizens, including several Franciscan brothers?"

"Well I know, Your Honor," Father Margil answered. "But I ask you, in order to have peace in the area, to forgive them for the deaths they have caused and other crimes."

"Then, how do you expect our mayors to actually exercise authority there?" said one of the judges.

"What I ask you is that once the Indians have been reduced, they be allowed to appoint their own mayor from among their people."

"I think your view is too optimistic, Father Margil. But we have to trust you. This court grants you the necessary authority to carry on with this mission. When finished please inform us of your results. If they are negative, we will respond with relevant military actions."

Satisfied with the response of the courts decisions, Father Margil, along with Friar Luis Cervantes Delgado, from the College of Guadalupe, a guide from the village of San Nicolas de Acuña, and another from the village of Colotlán began their trek into the mountains of Nayarit.

Upon reaching Guazamota, gateway to the highlands, Father Margil sent out two ambassadors, one of whom spoke the *Coras* language. The ambassadors carried with them a copy of the Royal Decree, which authorized their expedition into the Nayar region and afforded those who chose the Catholic faith the protection of the Crown. Along with the decree, Father Margil personally wrote a letter explaining that his interest was in saving their souls from the hands of the devil. He included a crucifix and a rosary as part of the welcome package.

Not knowing what to expect in the land of the *Coras*, the ambassadors reluctantly began their mission. When they were halfway into the journey, near the Coaxata ranch, they were intercepted by a small group of warriors.

"Where are you going?" said one warrior with his spear pointed directly at the heart of one ambassador.

"We bring a message to your chief, the *hueytacatl,* " he said.

"Your message is not of interest to us! We do not want to be Christians! Our chief has sent us to tell you to not waste your time. We are at peace with our lives, without your religion, and we will die before we accept your ways!"

Losing the battle, the ambassadors returned to where the missionaries awaited and hung their heads as they delivered the sad news of the disdain the warriors had for their Christian faith. Politely, Father Margil listened, then stood and said, "It is time for us to go to the village of the *Coras*."

Early the next morning, Father Margil, Friar Luis, and the two guides headed for the mountains. After several days on the trail, they were intercepted by an Indian warrior whose body was entirely painted black and red. When he learned the friars were unarmed and only wore crucifixes around their necks, he let them go.

A half a day later, they were ambushed and surrounded by thirty heavily armed warriors. Father Margil knew this was the time to begin the conversion process. He said, "We come with the love of our Lord and Savior Jesus Christ!"

The Indians looked at him bewildered by his words. For a very long time, he continued to preach to them by way of an interpreter, but all his arguments fell on deaf ears. Getting nowhere, he soon realized it was useless and that he spoke in vain.

With a warning from them not to proceed further, the Indians filed past them and began climbing up the mountain. From a ledge above, one threw a dead fox stuffed with straw, and it landed near the friars. Laughing, the warrior shouted:

"Take it home for dinner tonight."

Quickly, he disappeared into the mountains.

In one last attempt, Pablo, one of the guides, ran quickly up the hill to talk with the one who appeared to be the leader of the group.

"Tell the fathers that we are former Christians and are now reluctant," said rebel leader to Pablo. "Our elders have told us not to allow you to cross the Nayarit border, so we can't let you pass from this side of the river. They have instructed us to kill you or they will kill you as rebels and us as traitors. "

Then he whispered to Pablo, "Give this message to the fathers for me, but do it secretly."

Turning his head to make sure nobody could hear him, he continued whispering; "Tell them we are at the border. Although we are reluctant right now, as soon as the soldiers come, we will join them. All the tribes in the border will join them, so the Christians can come freely without fear of being killed by the barbarians of Nayarit. When the soldiers come, we will assist them as guides, armed or unarmed. Until the friars return accompanied by soldiers, tell them not return. As protectors, we will be obligated to kill them. If we fail, we will all die."

Pablo, convinced they could go no further, returned to Father Margil and revealed the secret conversation he had with the leader of the warriors.

"They're determined not to let us pass, Father Margil. I've seen it in their eyes. If we try to pass, they will kill us. Plain and simple, it will be our lives if we go further."

Defeated and sad, Father Margil, Fray Luis, and their guides returned and gave their negative report to the Court. But they found the Viceroy had other expeditions on his mind, like the ones into Guadalajara and México City, which were both being sponsored by the Viceroy Duke of Linares. Also a conflict in San Juan de Ulúa had his attention. During all these distractions and delays, the return expedition to the Nayar waned and after a while fell into oblivion.

XLVI

"At last, we have built our first mission since the founding of the College of Propagation of the Faith of Guadalupe in Zacatecas seven years ago," lamented Father Margil. "But only God knows the great work we have done in his name during those seven years."

Admiring the simple adobe and wood structure, he added:

"Now we will honor Our Holy Mother by naming it Our Lady of Guadalupe."

The tiny mission building stood on the banks of the *Sabinas* River, about one hundred seventy miles from Monterrey and seven miles from the *Mission San Miguel Archangel.* It had been founded by Friar José Díez and Fray Pedro Muñoz from the Apostolic College of Santa Cruz.

In this isolated region getting the supplies to build the mission and gaining the confidence of the local people had not been an easy task for Father Margil. During that time, the aging friar extended himself to great limits doing God's work every day. Now, his extraordinary life journey was apparent in the lines and wrinkles on his face and tired body. The many years of fasting and penance, coupled with the stress from dangerous situations, the long walks, and the many nights that he slept outside exposed to the elements, had left their indelible marks. He was just shy of sixty years of age and completely bald. His once proud shoulders were now slumped. He walked slightly stooped with his head bent downwards. His feet, battered from years of walking with only meager leather sandals over rugged terrain, were encrusted, blackened by the soil, and gnarled with age. His gait was slow and he gave a squalid appearance. Twenty years earlier, he could walk faster than a horse, and he seemed to fly from town to town leaving behind most of his companions. Now, he shuffled along as though in pain. Even with all the changes that had affected his body, his heart was still strong and was still filled with joy and love for his mission in the Church.

Earlier in the year, Father Margil and Brother Mathias Sanz left Zacatecas and travelled the nearly three hundred miles to where they were in the province of Nueva Extremadura. It was here they founded the new mission along the Sabinas River.

One year later in August of 1715, they founded a second mission on the banks of the Salado River under the same name of *Our Lady of Guadalupe*. Despite his toils and sacrifices, he soon realized it was impossible to keep both missions open in the hostile environment with the aggressive Indians constantly nipping at their heels. Showing no mercy to anyone in their war path and refusing to allow the priest and the missions to flourish, the fierce warriors ravaged the entire region.

Just three months after the founding of the first mission of *Our Lady of Guadalupe*, the *Tobosos* Indians attacked the neighboring mission of *San Miguel* and killed a woman and wounded a shepherd boy. The church was ravaged and the sacred vessels stolen. Father Pedro Muñoz miraculously escaped with his life. Fearing another Indian attack, soldiers escorted Father Margil and Fray Matías to the safety of the mission of *Our Lady of Sorrows*. While there, neighboring Indians attacked the missions of *San Juan Bautista del Rio Grande* and *San Bernardo*. Luckily, Fray Pedro Muñoz Alonso Gonzalez escaped unharmed. Soon Father Margil learned their second mission dedicated to the Holy Mother had suffered the same fate as its namesake. It was lost.

Father Margil's spirits were not dampened by the loss of his first two missions. He travelled to Boca de Leones, where with the travel license of the Bishop of Guadalajara and the support of the Governor of Nuevo Leon, he founded a hospice to serve as a resting place for the missionaries travelling from the College of Guadalupe to the northern provinces of New Spain. The hospice was simple and made of adobe and had the full support of the people in the town of Saltillo. Ironically, it would be the only work of Father Margil to survive through the years and claim a place in the long rich history of the region.

Father Margil faced many adversities in his work, but he continued to work tirelessly with the many indigenous populations. His fame in the territories always preceded him, as he carried the word of God to places like New Extremadura, New Kingdom of Leon, New Vizcaya, and the towns of Cadereyta, Village el Pilón, San Cristóbal, Linares, Valle de Huanuco, Mota, and others.

While at the new hospice, he heard stories of the Indians in the northern reaches of New Spain from the first Spanish missionaries who returned from those lands. From this, a seed was planted in his mind. As he made his rounds through the provinces around Boca de Leones, he prayed that God would soon send him to the land called *Tejas*. In an answer to his prayers, a few months later, he was appointed Vice Commissioner of Missions of New Spain and given permission to travel with Captain Domingo Ramon to establish missions in the most eastern provinces.

His answer to the assignment was, "The Indians are awaiting us in this new land. We still have much work to do in God's name to bring Christianity to Texas."

PART EIGHT: THE NEW PHILLIPINES

XLVII

"In the name of the most high, mighty, invincible, and victorious Prince, Louis the Great, by the Grace of God, King of France and of Navarre, Fourteenth of that name, we declare these lands as possession of the French Crown, King Louis XIV. Thereafter, this place will be called La Louisiane in honor of His Serene Highness."

This solemn declaration was made by Robert Cavalier de La Salle, commander of the French expedition, standing at the mouth of the mighty River Colbert, later named the Mississippi River. After the brief ceremony, which included the burying of a lead plate engraved with the arms of France, erecting a holy cross, and chanting the hymns *Te Deum and Vexilla Regis,* they fired their guns and shouted "Long Live the King." La Salle then took a reading with his astrolabe of the latitude of the river in hopes that the King would later allow him to return. This information he kept secret from the rest of the party.

With a drum roll and salute of the French flag, the actions of Monsieur De La Salle on this day served as stimulus for Spain to begin protecting the territories they had previously claimed in the New World. They abhorred the French and felt they needed to be extricated from the Spanish-claimed lands.

Proud of his accomplishment, La Salle returned to France and asked the King for permission to establish a French base for the purpose of conquest and colonization on the newly discovered La Louisiane.

In July 1684, Louis XIV awarded him a 36-gun warship, *Le Joly,* and a smaller frigate *La Belle,* and two additional ships, the *L'Aimable* and the *Saint François.* The four ships were needed to transport the three hundred crew, settlers, and soldiers and the supplies and munitions for the new colony. The expedition was doomed from the beginning when La Salle and Captain Sieur de Beaujeu of the Royal French Navy became embroiled in a bitter feud. When they neared Santo Domingo, the *Saint François* and its precious cargo of provisions were lost to pirates near La Española Island. Then illness, navigational errors, and desertion of several men to the pirates further beleaguered La Salle's dream voyage. When they failed to locate the entrance of the river and ended up four hundred miles west of their original destination, La Salle and Beaujeu blamed each other.

Their only choice then was to enter the coastline along an inlet they named Matagorda Bay. Immediately the *Aimable* ran aground and lost most of its cargo. From there, La Salle travelled up a small bluff overlooking Rivìere aux Boeufs, later named Garcitas Creek, and established his colony. Not named at first, it later became Fort Saint Louis. From the meager outpost, La Salle continued to search for his coveted Mississippi River, but his bad luck continued due to the rough terrain. Finally making amends with Beaujeu, they agreed that they were in dire need of supplies. As a result, La Salle and sixteen men made an attempt at an overland excursion to Canada; however, the mission failed.

La Belle was lost in a storm in another failed attempt. With the settlers dying from the need of food and medicine, La Salle agreed that their only hope for supplies was a voyage to France. When Beaujeu and one hundred twenty people left on the *Le Joly,* it was a sad departure. He promised to return quickly, but he never did. Even if he had, it would have been too late to help the beleaguered settlers. On La Salle's fourth attempt to find the Mississippi, he was murdered in a conspiracy by his own men. On Christmas Day the next year, the last twenty settlers were killed by the *Karankawa* Indians, and five children were taken captive. Thus, La Salle's ill-fated excursion ended.

Hearing the news of the French incursion from a deserter of La Salle's expedition, the Spanish immediately jumped into action. Not knowing where the French had settled, they theorized that they were building somewhere near where the big river emptied into the gulf. It was a vast territory, but their fear of a French settlement on the property of the Spanish Crown was frightening to the authorities.

They decided to send an expedition in search of the Frenchman LaSalle. After a lapse of over a hundred years, the Spanish had almost forgotten the routes north and had lost many of the maps from the earlier expeditions. Now with renewed interest, they sent five maritime expeditions through the Gulf of México and six land expeditions, which they called *entradas,* to form permanent settlements in the *Nuevas Filipinas,* the New Kingdom of the Phillipines. This territory, along the Medina River, was commonly called Texas throughout the Spanish colonial period.

XLVIII

𝕬 young Indian boy, perched high in the branches of a majestic oak tree, waited patiently for the grazing herd of buffalo to approach. As the wooly beasts neared, he mimicked a whip-poor-will and listened for its echo in the valley below. This was the signal to his brother hunters, camouflaged with leafy branches, to move slowly and surround the buffalo on three sides. When in position, they methodically set fire to the bushes. When the fire raged, the Indians threw down their weapons, ran wildly toward the buffalo shouting and waving their arms, and began throwing rocks at the animals. Surrounded by fire, commotion, and chaos, the strongest bull led the stampede through the escape route earlier prepared by the hunters. The warriors waiting for the charge of brown beasts were heavily armed with bows and arrows, stones, and spears. The ground shook under the weight of the huge animals and the roar of their hooves was deafening. When the resulting dust cloud neared, the hunters fired into the teaming mass hoping their arrows found their mark.

When the last beast passed, the exhausted young hunters shouted with joy at the sight of the dozens of dead animals lying in the valley. They approached cautiously because they were not out of danger yet. Several wounded buffalo bulls pawed the ground, snorted wildly, and glared at the approaching Indians with their fiery black eyes. Carefully advancing with readied weapons, the hunters finished them off one by one. Today was a good day. No one had been mangled or maimed in the battle. The next days were devoted to butchering the coveted animal, preparing its meat, and tanning its hides. They respected these sacred animals that provided them with food, clothing and shelter. They knew they survived only because of them.

The *Lipan, Comanche, Kiowa, Apache*, and *Tonkawa* all hunted buffalo in this method. Although they were related and often shared a common language, the tribes lived many miles apart scattered throughout Texas. Relationships between tribes were usually warlike, and rarely did they allow marriages between different tribe members.

The Indian nations located in the far Eastern reaches of New Spain included four main confederations of the *Hasinai, Kadohadacho, Natchitoches, Adai,* and *Ayish* Indians. Each nation had many tribes within.

Father Isidro Félix de Espinosa explained to the priests, "These Indians are called the *Tejas* because the Indian word means *friends*."

"Yes, *Tejas* will be a good name for these industrious and docile people," Father Margil replied. "I like the way they live in communal villages with beehive shaped houses that are covered by grass. They are so calm and peaceful, and they don't rove like many tribes I have been with before. They tell me the thatched dwellings are warm in the winter and cool in the summer and that up to forty family members can live peacefully in the same house."

Father Espinosa continued, "The women are beautiful in their clothing made of woven fabric and deerskin, decorated with colored thread, and stones. The season determines whether they wear moccasins when they cultivate the fertile red soil that produces so much corn, pumpkins, melons, squash, and beans. They also gather nuts, seeds, acorns, grapes, and berries from the surrounding forests and cook for the entire village. They make delicious meat, bread, stew, tamales, and mush, as you already know."

The Spaniards were surprised to find that the *Tejas* Indian men, who were the hunters and protectors, did little else. When they brought home their kill for the day, the women took over and prepared it for the village. They wore very little clothing except for a long rectangular piece of tanned deerskin or animal fur, which they called a breechcloth. It was worn between their legs and tucked over a belt so that the flaps fell down in front and back. Usually, they wore stone and shell necklaces and brightly colored bird feathers as decorations. Their bodies were covered in tattoos to indicate their tribe, and their heads were shaved with a strip of hair down the middle.

Father Margil was not surprised that the Indian women possessed extraordinary strength. As he had seen in the southern jungles, the pregnant woman gave birth in seclusion in a hut built by her husband near a river or stream. In the same manner, she prepared a mat and coverings and awaited the arrival. When the time came, she held onto a stake driven in the middle of the hut until the child arrived. After the birth, she took the baby to a nearby river and they bathed. This ancient ritual was no different than the other tribes he had seen before. Rarely did the mother or the child suffer any consequences.

The *Tejas* Indians, as they were often called, were of medium height, and excellent runners, a gift which was especially useful in hunting and war. Their rivals were the *Comanche* and *Apache*, more warlike tribes, accustomed to a nomadic life. They often came to the *Tejas* villages to pilfer and steal and on numerous occasions, burned their houses and killed their defenseless inhabitants. The extraordinary mobility of the barbaric warriors made them a nuisance to all.

In 1689, when the viceroy heard that the French had established a fort in Texas, they were incensed that they dared encroach unto Spanish territory. They responded by sending Alonso de Leon with a small expedition to locate the Frenchman LaSalle. When his troops found the remnants of a French settlement, Fort Saint Louis, they also met friendly Indians from the Hasinai Confederacy. The Indians who lived between the Trinity and the Red Rivers, expressed an interest in learning about Christianity, and the Spanish believed they were suitable subjects for conversion. With the approval of the viceroy, the following year, De León led an excursion of soldiers and Franciscan missionaries to the borderlands to find their village.

It was this expedition that brought the seeds of Christianity to the land of the *Tejas*. They arrived in May 1690 and established the first mission near the Hasinai village of Nabedache. The Franciscan priests Father Damian Massanet and Father Francisco Hidalgo were there to witness the historic event. On the first day of June, they dedicated the *Mission San Francisco de los Tejas* by inviting the Indians to attend their holy Mass.

Frustrated with the Indians refusal to live at the missions and give up their old ways of life, some of the more impatient priests decided this mission was too difficult and decided to leave the mission. Even the urgings of the other Franciscans did not change their minds. When they left, Father Massanet and Father Hidalgo labored alone at the tiny *Mission San Francisco*. Hearing about the failure of the unprotected mission, the viceroy and his advisors decided to close the mission after a meager three years.

XLIX

Presidio of San Juan Bautista, Gateway to Texas
January 1715

𝕴n the quiet morning hours of a cold winter day in January, the inhabitants of the *Presidio of San Juan Baustista*, located on the crossroads leading into Texas and just five miles from the Rio Grande, were awakened by the cry from a sentry:

"The French are coming! The French are coming!"

The sleepy soldiers mustered frantically to the sound of a bugle and took defensive positions along the outside wall of the presidio. Never had their French enemies dared to venture so far into Spanish-owned territories. And now, a small band of Frenchmen and their *Tejas* Indian guides were boldly approaching the presidio and mission.

The foreigners signaled with a white flag and shouted, "We are on a mission for Monsieur LaMothe de Cadillac, Governor of Louisiana! We are looking for the Spanish priest named Father Hidalgo! He wrote a letter to our governor requesting French help for the *Tejas* Indians living in your eastern regions!"

The party of four Frenchmen, led by Monsieur Louis de St. Denis, was accompanied by *Hasinai* Chief Bernadino and three young Indians from his tribe.

St. Denis yelled as he approached, "Father Hidalgo is the friar who first came and evangelized the Indians in the *Hasinai* village some years ago!"

With this introduction and mention of the well-respected Father Hidalgo, Captain Don Diego Ramón, commander of the presidio, reluctantly opened the gates for their French visitors.

Not knowing what to do with the presumptuous foreigner and his companions, Ramon decided to detain them under house-arrest until he received orders from the viceroy in México City. Since this communication would take months to reach the capital and return, Ramon decided to incarcerate St. Denis in his own home where he could keep a close watch over him. As time went by, the romantic St. Denis became smitten with Ramon's seventeen year old step-granddaughter, Doña Manuela Sanchez Navarro. Ramon and his wife were horrified at the fact that the girl, half his age, was love-struck as well.

A few months later, the viceroy's order finally arrived and commanded the Frenchmen be escorted to México City. Professing his love for the maiden, St. Denis asked Captain Ramon for Manuela's hand in marriage. Although disgusted with the Frenchman, Ramon reluctantly agreed because he silently doubted that he would ever return from the capital.

When the smooth-talking St. Denis arrived at the viceroy's palace, he met with the War Council and managed to convince them to re-occupy eastern Texas and reestablish the missions there. He told them it was critical for the Indians to become Christianized, but, most importantly, the occupation of their own lands would prevent further French intrusion.

The viceroy and his council liked what he said and soon voted to approve an *entrada* to establish six missions and presidios in the province of Texas. It would consist of a convoy of seventy five people: twenty-five soldiers and their families, six missionaries from Querétaro, two missionaries from Zacatecas, and two lay brothers. Capitan Domingo Ramon, son of Captain Diego, would be in charge of the expedition, Father Isidro Felix de Espinosa from the College of Propagation of Faith of Querétaro, and Fray Antonio Margil de Jesús, from the College of Zacatecas, would be the religious in charge of the four missions.

"By the order of his Excellency, Duque de Linares, viceroy and captain general of this region of New Spain, I have been made Commander-in-Chief to enter the province of Texas for the protection and custody of establishing missions. This is a great honor but also a grave responsibility," proclaimed Captain Domingo Ramon to the small party of soldiers who would journey with him to Texas.

After many months of delay, Ramon's expedition left the town of Saltillo with a diverse group of travelers headed north to the Rio Grande. The caravan of travelers, which stretched for miles as it slowly snaked its way up *El Camino Real*, consisted of soldiers, women, and children riding in carts, animals, and wagons loaded with supplies, seeds, tools, and gifts for the Indians. The humble friars walked alongside the wagons in their brown cassocks and meager sandals aided only by a walking stick.

Every day there were challenges for the rag-tag group of travelers: desertion of soldiers, sickness, straying livestock, Indian raids, and, of course, the constant need for food and water. It took them two months to finally reach the *Mission San Juan Bautista del Rio Grande.* When they arrived, they were exhausted but happy. Friar Espinosa, president of the Rio Grande missions, celebrated with a Mass to thank God for their safe arrival, and afterwards they feasted with exaltations, prayers, festivities, and good food.

Returning with the group was the Frenchman St. Denis, who with the confidence of the viceroy now carried the title of Second-in-Command and Supply Officer. Hastily, he approached Captain Ramon who was surprised at his reappearance, for his permission to marry Doña Manuela. True to his word, the hesitant Captain Ramon gave his blessing for the marriage. After the normal Catholic bands of matrimony were posted, the suave cavalier and the young maiden were married in a grand social event.

For the next several months they made their home in the mission that was the richest and most prosperous of the region along the Rio Grande. The surrounding pastures were cultivated and the fertile lands were encircled with homes closely guarded by the presidio soldiers. Nearby, stood the missions of *San Bernardo* and *San Francisco Solano*, which along with the *San Juan Bautista*, were logistically set at the entrance to the northern part of the territory and served as a solid base against Indian raids.

It took a few months for Captain Domingo Ramon and his caravan to complete preparations to make their push north along *El Camino Real* into the province of Texas. When they were ready to leave, they were missing Father Margil, who was last seen a month earlier in El Potrero where he provided the caravan with some horses, goats, and oxen.

They waited a few more days, and when they had almost given up hope, they saw someone running toward the presidio.

"Come quickly the padre is dying! Said the young shepherd boy. "He is gravely ill about thirty miles from here along the river! Come quickly, I fear that he will die without your help!"

L

Although nearing sixty, Father Margil was undaunted and could hardly wait for his new assignment in the province of Texas. In April when he completed his work at the Boca de Leones hospice, he began his journey to rendezvous with his companions at the Presidio of Rio Grande. But first, he had to cross the torturous barren plains of the Coahuila Desert. The elderly priest was still able to travel many miles a day, but his age had slowed his gait considerably. Now with every step, he felt pain throughout in his aging body.

He travelled a few days before the hot sand-laden winds began to blow. It was all he could do to keep his legs moving forward. With his head scorched by the relentless rays of the sun and his feet burned by the hot desert sands, he began to hallucinate and talk to himself.

"I must go on! I must continue! My brothers are waiting for me! Sweet Jesus, help me! My mind is willing, but my body is weak."

His recent bouts of high fever had returned and intensified with the boiling heat of the desert sun. His thirst was unbearable as he imagined cool droplets of water falling on his tongue. The friar tried to distinguish passing landmarks but they were only a blur. He was delirious with fever and thirst, and his mind was playing tricks on him.

He lost count of the days that passed, and when he was only a few miles from his destination, he could go no further. With much difficulty, stumbling and incoherent, he tried to cross the Arroyo de Juanes but was unable to do so. A young shepherd boy found him lying under a tree near the river, and ran to the nearby mission for help. Father Isidro Félix de Espinosa, two missionaries from Zacatecas, and two soldiers immediately went to his aid. When they arrived, Father Margil was pale and shaking and barely able to speak. They immediately took him to the nearby presidio for care.

There he stayed in bed for days with a raging fever. He was so sick that Father Espinosa, with tears in his eyes, gave him his last sacraments. He immediately fell into a deep sleep and felt the inner peace that comes with knowing that you are ready to enter the gates of Heaven.

By this time, Captain Ramon had completed all his preparations and was ready to begin their journey north into the borderlands of Texas. But, in deference for Father Margil, he waited six more days to see if he would regain his strength. The condition of the aging priest only worsened. On the seventh day, still in declining health, Father Margil gathered his companions around his bedside.

"Please leave today without me. When I am better, I will catch up to you, if it is God's will," Father Margil whispered. Everyone in his presence cried because they thought the end had come for the holy man who had done so many wondrous deeds in New Spain.

"Go in God's grace. I wish you well in this glorious challenge," Father Margil said as he embraced each one like a loving father.

Reluctantly but heeding Father Margil's wishes, the Ramon party left the Rio Grande on the 27th day of April 1716. Father Mathias and Father Isidro volunteered to stay behind with Father Margil and keep vigil over him for one more day. All day and night, they prayed and beseeched God for mercy for the dying priest. When his condition did not improve the next day, they decided to leave him in the care of friends and catch up to the caravan. Once again they bid him farewell. Before leaving, they helped him stand, as best he could in his weakened state, and they joined him in a fraternal embrace. Father Margil placed his right hand on the head of each one of his brothers, just as Jacob had done to St. Francis of Assisi many years before, and gave them a blessing. Then he renewed his sacred vows, and Father Espinoza gave him God's final blessing. With great sorrow and pain, they left him to die.

For the next several weeks, Father Margil fought valiantly for his life, tossing and turning, going from periods of quietness to fits of hallucination. One morning, in the second month, when the sun shone bright through the open window, he opened his eyes and looked around in amazement. For the next few days, he continued to recover from his life-threatening illness. When he was able to stand and eat a little, his thoughts immediately turned to the land of the *Tejas* Indians and his friends traveling northward.

Even before he had completely regained his strength, he packed his bags for departure. The friars aiding him urged him to rest a few more days, but their appeals fell upon deaf ears. He was determined not to miss another day of what was his biggest and most important assignment of his lifetime.

"I must catch up as fast as I can! Please Lord, allow me the speed of my youth," he prayed.

LI

Mission Nuestra Señora de Guadalupe
June 1716

Ｗith the sun slowly rising in the distance, Father Antonio Margil de Jesús stood on the banks of the Rio Grande River gazing across at the trail that disappeared into the horizon. The deep ruts left behind by Ramon's caravan of carts and livestock were still visible in the road. This path would serve as his road north.

"It's a good day to travel, on this the Feast of St. Anthony of Padua. Thank you, dear Lord, for allowing me the strength to journey into the land of the Tejas, where there are souls crying out for your love and redemption," prayed Father Margil.

He was weak from his recent illness, so for the first time in his life, he was forced to ride a mule on the journey. The commandant, refusing to allow him to travel alone, sent two soldiers to help him gather food and provide shelter along the dangerous *El Camino Real*. Although the heat was much more intense now than when Ramon left, the small party was able to travel much faster than the Ramon party. On good days they traveled about twenty miles, on bad much less.

With a blessing and the sign of the cross, the three travelers headed north on the dusty road. They were fortunate that the spring rains had left pockets of green pastures along the plains allowing for an abundance of small animals for food. In a little less than a week, they reached the foot hills of the Nueces River which they found almost dry. The earlier Spanish explorers had named the river after the numerous pecan trees along its banks. It had deep *arroyos* that taxed the pack mules and the sure footed horses. Its banks were trampled by wild beasts searching for water. Father Margil and his companions dug shallow holes in the sand and filled a small rawhide pouch with water which seeped from below. They travelled onward and soon came upon the spring-fed Frio River, ice cold and surrounded by undulating plains.

"Quiet! I hear something!" cautioned one of the tired soldiers. Surveying the countryside, he saw in a tree only a few yards from the river a flock of turkeys flying into their roost for the night. Patiently, the soldiers waited for the darkness of the night before slipping up to the tree. Not having an exact target, they shot their *harquebuses* into the tree top. They could hear the turkeys flying in all directions.

"Look, we got three!" a soldier loudly proclaimed. "We will eat good tonight!

The next day, with a full stomach and dried turkey in their pouches, they continued their journey down the dusty trail. It was a good day because they had food and water. All too often they did not know where their next meal would come or if they would find a fresh watering hole. A few days later they came to the Medina River where they rested. Here they caught an ample supply of fish and gathered grapes from the vines tangled in the spreading oaks.

When they arrived at the Guadalupe River, where it joins the San Marcus River, they were blessed by an abundance of grapes, walnuts, wild turkey, and fish.

When they were half way through their journey, the land began to change from hills and rocks. Now the terrain consisted of many groves of big trees, plentiful springs, deep meadows, and only a few rocks. One night just before dark, they heard the bellow of a calf in the distance. When they walked to the top of the nearby hill, they were amazed to see three buffalos grazing in the meadow below with their newborn calves, partially hidden by the shadows of the trees. Father Margil was amazed. In all his travels, he had not seen such a beast. It was much larger than an ox, with short black horns that curved downward. Their necks appeared to be misshapen; they had tails like pigs; and they grunted instead of bellowing like a cow. The soldiers wanted to kill one of the strange beasts, but Father Margil would not allow it because they would not be able to process and carry all the meat with them. Instead, Father Margil spent the rest of the night in meditation and evening prayers. He thanked God for the beautiful wild land and for all of its strange creatures.

When they reached the Trinity River, the waters were swollen and overflowing their banks, and they were unable to cross. While waiting nearby for the waters to recede, they met five Indians from the *Ervipiame* tribe. The Indians expected gifts like they had received from the Ramon party but were not pleased when they only received a blessing from a strange god and a few meager supplies.

Father Margil and his companions continued on their journey and traveled further into the area of the borderlands marked by stately oaks and towering pine trees. They crossed a wide river called the Angelina and arrived at a hilltop overlooking Ramon's encampment surrounding the new mission. They had been travelling for forty days and it was now the middle of July. They slowly walked down the hill toward the mission.

"Look over there, I see a vision of Father Margil riding a mule!" a man working along the tree line cried loudly.

Looking up, another exclaimed, "Our eyes are playing tricks on us!"

"It's really him! Praise God! The saintly old priest is alive and has joined us on this glorious occasion!" a woman shouted.

After a warm welcome, Captain Ramon, excitedly informed him:

"Since we arrived in the land of the *Tejas,* we have built four missions. The first being *Mission Nuestro Padre San Francisco de los Tejas,* of which Father Hidalgo was put in charge since he had been with the original party that founded it years ago. The second mission is located about thirty miles northeast of the first, at the village of the *Hasinai* Indians, along a high river and named *Mission Nuestra Señora de la Purísima Concepción de Asís.* It was also assigned to Father Hidalgo and Fray Espinosa."

He continued, "The third and largest mission is *Nuestra Senora de Guadalupe,* located in the land of the *Nacogdoche* and *Nacao* Indians, about twenty five miles southeast of Concepción. Priests from your college were put in charge there. Lastly, *Mission San Jose de los Nazonis,* located about twenty miles northeast of Concepción was assigned to the priests from Querétaro. In total, the Franciscans from the college of Querétaro were assigned three missions, and the Franciscans from the college of Zacatecas were assigned one."

"You, Father Margil may join your brothers from the College of Zacatecas at the largest mission located in the village of the *Nacogdoche* Indians."

Los Ojos de Padre Margil

LII

𝕿here was great enthusiasm throughout the province of Texas over the successful establishment of the missions and presidios in the borderlands. The Indians were kind and generous and overjoyed to teach their language to the padres. It was not long before Father Margil heard of the establishment of a French post a short distance to the east. As he was accustomed to traveling in enemy territory, he was unafraid to venture across the Red River to Natchitoches. He knew the French Catholics there would welcome him. When he arrived, he was greeted warmly, and with an interpreter, he administered sacraments to many who were happy to return to God's graces.

Although the French were welcoming and open to his blessings, the *Tejas* Indians were not. They were friendly but different from the other Indians he had encountered in his earlier travels. They were welcoming, but fiercely independent. They openly told the missionaries they did not want a new religion and wanted to maintain their customs and rituals. Father Margil and the others were challenged trying to bring these souls to God.

"We are friends with your Holy Father, but we don't want to change our lives; we like how we live. We have our own villages, our own crops, and we are accustomed to trading with the Frenchmen who come from the east. Many of them are our family members because they have married our daughters. They are part of our nation," said the old *Tejas* Indian chief.

It was this reason, along with the lack of supplies, that postponed the founding of the last two missions planned by the Royal Council. It was not until January of the following year before Captain Ramon was ready to start the *Mission San Miguel de Linares de los Adaes,* just twenty miles west of the French fort of Natchitoches. The last mission was personally founded by Father Margil, who was pushed by his missionary zeal. It was named *Nuestra Señora de los Dolores de los Ays,* also known as *Our Lady of Sorrows,* and was located thirty miles west of *Our Lady of Guadalupe* in Nacogdoches. Both of these missions were under the stewardship of Father Margil and his friars from the College of Zacatecas.

While toiling at the mission of *Our Lady of Sorrows,* tragedy befell Father Margil when his lay brother Francisco de San Diego died unexpectedly. He was the only religious from the College of Zacatecas that had accompanied him to the distant lands of the *Ays* Indians to locate the new mission. The rest of the friars, soldiers, and their families had remained at the other missions further west.

With no one else around, Father Margil prayed for his distinguished and virtuous brother who lay dying, but he knew death was near for his brother made no response except for an occasional gasp for air. His body was pale and lifeless; his eyes were withered; and his lips parched. He removed the sacred chrism from his leather pouch and praying in Latin, he anointed the forehead, hands, lips, chest, feet, eyes, and ears of the dying man and began the ancient sacrament of Extreme Unction.

Father Margil had never felt such quiet loneliness. The only other person at the mission had left to deliver the news of Friar Francisco's illness and impending death to the nearby missions. The few Indians who lived in the mission had left in search of food. Now in this dark place with only a dim candle flickering, Father Margil was alone when the hand of God reached out and took the soul of his servant.

When it happened, Father Margil was somewhat startled. He had seen so much death in his many years, but for some reason this one was different because he was a close friend. He was just like Father Melchor who had gone to rest some years earlier. Now he would have two good friends in Heaven to watch over him and his missions.

Since there was no one to help him, Father Margil took a shovel and with his own hands dug the grave for his lay brother. With tears in his eyes, he placed the lifeless body at the bottom of the pit and slowly covered it with soil. He then knelt in prayer for the rest of the night.

Our Lady of Sorrows was the mission where Father Margil spent most of his time. Times were hard then as the years of drought plagued the lands and caused the crops to fail and the wildlife to move to more abundant grounds. To make conditions worse, the usually mild winters of the area had turned extremely harsh. The success of the missions languished because the Indians only came into the missions when they needed supplies or medicine. There was no wheat or grain, and most of their precious supply of fresh water had dried up. By the end of the year, many of the inhabitants, horses, oxen, and livestock had died of starvation. Desperate for food and water, Father Margil told his brother priests that it was time to resort to eating what was abundant— the black crows.

At first they all turned away, but he told his brother priests, "To the one who is clean at heart even the foul tasting bird is clean. We must do whatever is necessary in these desperate times to survive. God has put this challenge before us, and we must accept it."

Every day and night, Father Margil prayed for the charity of divine grace to bring the much needed rain for their crops. One night while in prayer in Nacogdoches, he had a divine vision. At sunrise he went to the dry bed of the Lanana Creek, accompanied by a small band of the mission Indians. There he prayed a morning prayer and placed himself in God's hands. As he stood on the banks at the source of the creek he struck a large rock two times with his staff. Instantly, water rushed forth and cascaded down the side of the rocks onto the dry creek bed and formed a pool of crystal clear water. The surprised Indians immediately fell to their knees to thank their new God for bringing them water.

When the rest of the inhabitants of the nearby missions heard about what happened, they were overjoyed and called it a miracle. From that day forward, the skies opened and rains came. The drought was over. Now with renewed hope, the Indians and the religious irrigated their fields and produced abundant crops. The little spring they called *Los Ojos de Padre Margil*, the eyes of Father Margil, never went dry again.

Throughout the hardships at the new missions, Father Margil seemed to suffer less than the rest of his brothers. He was always consumed by prayer and felt he had been led to this place of glory. All the hardships were really no trouble at all but only glory for he had suffered far worse in his early years. Now, in the quietness of the piney wood forests, the birds and wild game soothed his soul. One observer kindly remarked of him, "He spends the days, weeks, and months absorbed in God, growing old gently."

LIII

The missions were blessed the next year with rain that brought a good harvest and much relief from the menacing drought. But Father Margil found that establishing the missions along the borderlands between Spain and France was a challenge in the current political atmosphere. As the news of the struggle between France and Spain drifted from Los Adaes along *El Camino Real* to San Antonio, the stories of impending war caused upheaval along the way. The Indians, pawns to both the French and the Spanish, were caught in the middle.

Finally in the fall of 1719, when France declared war on Spain, the French in Natchitoches made a feeble attack on the *Mission San Miguel de Linares de los Adaes.* Reports of the attack grew larger as the word spread to the missions and caused terror among the families, soldiers, and some religious in the other five East Texas missions.

Fearing an imminent invasion, Captain Ramón gave orders to his soldiers, "Gather our people from all the missions and get them ready to begin an immediate withdrawal!"

Father Margil, who had heard the rumors of invasion were untrue, openly confronted the Captain. He said, "Our friendly Indians have offered to put out spies to warn us of a French advance. They tell me the French soldiers are far away and may never invade us."

"I'll have a mutiny if we don't get away from here soon," Captain

221

Ramón replied.

"I've already had eight families from the presidio tell me they have gathered their families and are leaving without the rest of us. All they want is two soldiers to protect them from Indian attacks and the dangers of the wilds."

Despite Father Margil's pleas to wait for further developments, he was outnumbered by frightened soldiers, families, and some religious. When the order came to abandon the missions, he had no harsh words to say about the departure despite all the hard work the missionaries had put forth in the new missions.

Hurriedly, Father Margil asked two Indians to help him bury his iron tools and implements. He gathered his holy ornaments and began the trip west with the rest of the group. The first night they spent at the *Mission San Francisco*, east of the Neches. The Indians followed to try to convince them to stay. Only after reassuring them they would soon return did the disappointed Indians return to their village.

For the next three months they slowly made their way to the safety of the much larger settlement of San Antonio. Even in the weariness of their hasty travel, the splendor of late spring was visible all around the beleaguered travelers. The vast plains and valleys were covered with majestic wild flowers and was the most stunning sight Father Margil had ever witnessed. The colorful blanket of blue-and-white, blazing orange, and yellow was abundantly populated with wildlife of all kinds. For a change, food and fresh water were never a problem during their retreat. Father Margil knew these were God's beautiful creations and were actually signs of renewed hope for the future.

When they arrived at the *Mission San Antonio de Valero*, better known today as the *Alamo*, they built straw huts and waited for further instructions. For the first year, the Spanish authorities promised Father Margil a quick return to his beloved *Tejas* Indians and the needed supplies and soldiers for the lost missions, but it did not come.

Father Margil and the other religious busied themselves as best they could by building another mission under the patronage of the Marquis de San Miguel de Aguayo, the new governor of Coahuila and Texas.

"Why do we want to build another mission so close to the others, Father Margil?" asked one of the young Indian boys.

"My son, we must have a strong mission system to resist attacks from those who wish to harm us, like the French and hostile Indians!" said Father Margil."

"You are right, the new *Mission San José y San Miguel de Aguayo* will be the strongest of all," the Indian said realizing the old priest always had the right answer.

"Yes, my son," said Father Margil, "I have built many missions, but this one will be magnificent, very large, and very secure. Here let me draw you a simple sketch on the ground. My plans call for the mission to be six hundred feet on each side."

"Oh, for sure, it will be the grandest ever, Father Margil," said the young boy.

"At night, I close my eyes and I can see it in my head. It will have high walls to defend us from attackers. In each corner there will be a door that can be sealed off in case of a breech. We will have portholes above the bulwarks where riflemen can fire at the enemy but still be protected. The front door will open into the center of the church yard. From all directions, you will be able to see travelers as they near the mission," said Father Margil with a look of satisfaction.

"And what if the enemy surrounds the mission?" asked the Indian.

"Well, the granaries of the mission will have enough food to last us an entire year, and our wells will supply the necessary water for even longer," he said.

"I see the greatness of your plans!"

"Now, I understand why you want to build this mission dedicated to Saint Joseph. It will be the largest and most beautiful."

"Now that you understand what we want it's time to go to work," Father Margil said as he shook his finger at the child.

As always, Father Margil worked enthusiastically and put all his efforts into their new project. The mission, located just four miles from the mission and presidio of *San Antonio de Valero*, grew and prospered while he was there. *Mission San José y San Miguel de Aguayo* later became known as a lasting symbol of the Spanish missionary frontier and often called the "Queen of the Missions."

Regardless of his new fame in the San Antonio area, Father Margil never forgot about his lost missions in the borderlands. Every day he meditated and prayed that God would take him back home so he could watch over his Indian friends.

LIV

𝕴n April 1721, the Spanish answered the French attack on the desolate missions when they appointed the Marquis de San Miguel de Aguayo to command a strong expedition of more than five hundred soldiers into the land of the *Tejas*. Filled with ambition and a need to be recognized, the Marquis graciously offered "his life, his sword, and his property" to the King of Spain. In just three months under his command, the troops banished the French soldiers from the Spanish owned lands and restored control of the Spanish territories and the abandoned missions.

With great excitement, Father Margil and his companions followed. Upon inspection of the missions, they found the *Mission of San Miguel de los Adaes* was the only one of the six that had not been completely destroyed during the three years of abandonment. It was quickly rebuilt with the assistance of the Indians who remained in the area.

Father Margil was humbly assigned to *Los Adaes*, the most active of the missions. It later became the capital of Texas, an honor it held for nearly a half century. While there, Father Margil patiently devoted himself to gathering the natives back into the missions, planting crops, and ministering to the needs of the people. Spiritually he tended not only to the Indians, soldiers, and their families of his mission and presidio but also to the people in the nearby Spanish missions of *Nuestra Señora del Pilar* and *San Francisco de los Dolores*. Once again, he ventured to the nearby French town of Natchitoches where he said Mass and heard confessions. He accepted that they were of one Catholic faith although under distinctly different crowns.

Father Margil smiled at the eloquence of the young Indian, who in a loud voice repeated the prayers he had been taught. As they did every morning, the Indians gathered in the Chapel of the *Mission Los Adaes* and prayed for rain and a good harvest.

After participating in the Holy Eucharist, Father Margil continued by giving the young children religious lessons. All morning long, the Indians repeated in chorus the Ten Commandments, the Sacraments, and other teachings of the Church. When it was time for the Indians to go to work, they were each assigned a job by Father Margil according to their God given talents.

"You will work in the field, my brothers, as you have expert skills for planting and harvesting," said Father Margil to a small group of Indians.

"You will take care of herds," he told another group. "As you are swift and not a single animal can run from you."

"Today, you will help me work on the mission," he told a few others. "You've proven your skills with making adobe stones."

To a group of young women, he said. "You are responsible for combing and spinning cotton for our cloth vestments."

"And what about us?" asked a group of little girls.

"You will help around the house," Father Margil said with a smile. "You are still very young and we will make your work into a fun game."

"Gracias, gracias, Padre!" the girls shouted in chorus as they ran into the mission. With smiles and songs, they began to sweep the floors and to clean the furniture.

At the end of their work day, Father Margil rewarded them for their hard work, by distributing the harvest from the gardens: beans, corn, pumpkins, and watermelons. With a prayer of thanksgiving, they sat and ate a meal of baked lamb and tortillas.

The nearby presidio had been rebuilt as well and was now surrounded by a strong wooden palisade which made it impenetrable. This strong defense, along with its high walls, made for a safe home for the military and their families, but the Indians remained steadfast and refused to live in the missions

Father Margil was very happy living in the newly rebuilt mission.

One day, Father Margil, with much surprise, received a letter asking him to come to Zacatecas as soon as possible because he had recently been appointed to a three year term as the father guardian of the College of

Guadalupe. He was sad, for he did not want to leave his new home where he was making so much progress with the reluctant Indians. He decided to wait for further instructions.

A few months later, he received another letter notifying him of the death of Fray Francisco Estévez, second prefect of missions of propaganda of faith of the West Indies. The letter also informed him of his appointment as the interim Prefect of the Missions.

This time, he knew he had to leave the solitude and silence of his beloved forests of walnuts, pines, oaks, and the lifesaving crows. In his old age, he longed for silence and solitude but knew it was out of reach.

That night he meditated one last time along a river bank; he thought how he would have liked to have surrendered his soul to his Creator in some corner of Texas. Nevertheless, he knew he had taken the vow of obedience long ago, and it had never been broken. As he looked to the heavens for solace, he saw, along the river bank, the lowly locust tree with its spiny thorns called *Espinas*. It brought back memories of the tree that miraculously grew from his staff in the garden at Querétaro. The thorns of both trees reminded him that his life too had been full of thorns, just as Father Linaz had told him it would be, many years ago, at the beginning of his great mission. Slowly he rose from his knees. It was time for him to begin his journey to see the viceroy and ask for aid for his beloved missions.

Sadly, he called together the Christian Indians who lived near the mission and spoke to them haltingly in their own language. He told them of his great responsibility in his homeland and that they would always be in his heart. He promised to return someday with the much needed supplies.

On his last day in the small mission, he gathered everyone to celebrate the Mass and to eat together as a community. The next morning, when the padre walked away from the mission, the Indians silently mourned their loss, but promised to keep his memory alive by repeating the story of the miracle of *Los Ojos de Padre Margil* over their camp fires for ages to come.

PART TEN:
HIS FINAL JOURNEY

LV

Once again Father Margil traveled the hundreds of miles across the vast expanse of the province of Texas obediently bending to the will of God to serve as the guardian at the Convent of Zacatecas. One day while preaching there, he was overcome by a severe pain and was consumed by high fever. His doctor told him he had an abscessed liver and his death was imminent and he needed to rest. As he lay inside recovering, the courtyard of the convent was filled with his distraught brothers from Querétaro and Zacatecas. They held prayer vigils asking for the intervention of Our Lord to improve his health and to redeem his soul. Their petitions were heard because the aging priest soon returned from the verge of death.

Although able to travel short distances and preach in the surrounding churches, his health continued to decline over the next three years, but his fame continued to grow. His preaching now was disbursed with periods of rest, and the periods of rest seemed to grow longer and more frequent. He grew fatigued while walking and often fainted while fasting.

When his three year term at Zacatecas was over, he made a month long retreat before journeying to the parishes surrounding Guadalajara and Valladolid. While on the last leg of the memorable mission trip while in the capital of Valladolid, he became exhausted and extremely ill. He was forced to stay in bed for seven days with extreme bouts of relentless high fever. When he left Valladolid, he was weak but said goodbye to his brethren in his usual reverent manner promising to come back soon. They fell on their knees and wished him well but secretly feared it would be their last moments with the holy priest.

Gravely ill, Father Margil did not want to give into his illness, but this time, against his will, his Franciscan brothers took him to Querétaro to recuperate. Two months later, with his health waning, his doctors advised that he needed to be moved to the infirmary in México City.

On his way there, he and his attendants stopped at the Church of St. Francis of Assisi where he asked to celebrate Mass in the little white church with large wooden doors framed in pink stone. A large quarry size image of the Seraphic Father stood at the front entrance of the church with the name of the patron saint he admired so much in his youth. He had arrived in the town one day earlier, in the rain and cold which had caused his fever to rage. Now he was totally consumed with chills and shook violently

When he prepared the Holy Eucharist, Father Margil noticed a white glow in the little church but assumed it was his fever playing tricks on him. What he did not know was that this Holy Mass would be his last. After the thanksgiving, he collapsed before the altar. With a sense of helplessness, his brothers placed him on a horse and continued their trip to the infirmary of the Convent of San Francisco in México City.

Although it was his custom to walk, he was no longer able to even ride a horse. When he arrived at Cuautitlán, they put him in a small carriage for the remainder of the trip.

It was in the afternoon on the Feast of the Indulgence of the Porciúncula when they arrived at the gates of the convent. With great difficulty, his brothers lifted him from the carriage and took him up the stairs to the upper cloister and into the infirmary. For the next four days he languished in the care of his Franciscan brothers.

On the 6th of August 1726, he gave his spirit to the Lord, embraced in the image of the crucifix with such soft respiration as a sigh. Thus the life of Father Friar Antonio Margil de Jesús, the Apostle of Texas, the friar with winged feet, came to a quiet end. He was twelve days short of his sixty-ninth birthday.

When his brothers reflected on his life, it was noted that he had served forty-three years wandering around New Spain, baptized more than eighty thousand faithful, walked thousands of miles in foreign lands, founded three colleges to serve new missionaries, and had established dozens of Franciscan missions. He did all of this as he lived a life full of thorns while he carried the Gospel of Our Lord to the far reaching ends of the new kingdom of Spain.

Sacristy of the Convent of San Francisco
August 1726

LVI

The Sacristy of the Convent of San Francisco in México City was magnificent and was larger than most of the temples and shrines in the city. It was more than thirty-six feet by sixty feet long. Inside it was beautifully decorated with colorful and ornate furnishings from the Indies and large paintings in gilded frames. One beautiful painting represented attributes of Mary, beautifully painted by the artistic lay brother Fray Diego Becerra. Other canvases depicted scenes from the Scriptures: the Garden of Eden, Jacob's ladder, by which angels ascended to heaven, the victory of Judith over Holofernes, Jael upon Sisera, and the water that Rebecca gave for drink.

On the front wall was a beautiful wooden altar dedicated to the Blessed Virgin Mary, with the name of the Immaculate Conception. In the corners, along the side walls, there were sculptures of Saint Joachim and Saint Anne, parents of the Virgin Mary, and a smaller image of Santo Domingo de Guzman. Above the large elliptical wooden table, in the center of the vestry, was a shrine to the Holy Christ. On the floor in front of the table, was the tomb of the Count of Santiago, covered with bronze inscriptions. The ceiling was a stunning golden coffer, and the sacristy had a beautiful tile border embedded in the wall and had sixty-six large wooden drawers to hold the ornaments for the Holy Eucharist.

There among the majesty of the old convent, in the glow of the sunlight that filtered through the large stained glass windows, was the body of Father Antonio Margil de Jesús. He lay on a black velvet catafalque in his simple brown robe with the white rope sash. Near the catafalque were three wooden candlesticks and a crucifix. The chapel was magnificently set and carefully prepared. The center table was removed to make room for the many mourners who would soon file past. Flowers filled every crevice and corner of the church.

Precisely at three o' clock sharp, the convent bells rang to announce the death of the venerable messenger of God. As the chimes drifted through the air, they were joined by the bronze bells of the cathedral and replicated in all the temples and monasteries throughout the city. Throughout the city, the melodious music from the chapel choir, acolytes, choral chaplains, and priests from the surrounding parishes filled the air.

The crowds pressed forward against the heavy iron gates while they waited to enter the doors of the cloister. Seeing the large assembly, the Royal Guard, whose job it was to protect the remains of the venerable friar, began to worry what would happen when the doors were opened.

They asked for the support of the friars of the convent and received it just before the gates opened. The crowd of people, from all castes and corners of the city, rushed into the room.

The friars and the soldiers could not control the multitudes that surged forward to see the holy priest. They came to feel and kiss the feet of the beloved friar who had traveled thousands of miles, through mountains, jungles, deserts, and swamps, to deliver God's word to so many. As they passed, they touched medals, rosaries, and handkerchiefs to his body as a pious memory of his faith.

Members of the Royal Guard were horrified to see the demonstration of the devout rip off pieces of his holy habit to keep as relics. It was not long before the pious pilfering prompted several changes of the sacred shroud. The guards thought the discretion was excessive, but the religious described these acts as indiscreet excesses of piety.

The lines of people were endless. All day and all night, the religious associations, guilds, arch confraternities, congregations and socialites of the city and the surrounding towns filed past to give their respects.

On the morning of the third day, his body was taken from the sacristy by the pall bearers who left the convent by way of the door facing San Juan de Letran Street. The public procession followed as they turned onto the street leading to the front gates of the convent where they entered the main chapel. They placed his corpse, covered with coarse baize, on a wooden platform with lights that were customary in the burial of religious men.

Ministers, nobles, courts, officials of the Royal Treasury, councils, both ecclesiastical and secular, the Royal Audience and the Viceroy Don

Juan de Acuña, Marquis of Casafuerte, were all there with the consolation of witnessing his burial.

Religious communities from far and wide attended the ceremony: the religious Fathers of St. Dominic, St. Augustine, Our Lady of Mount Carmel, Our Lady of Mercy, the school of the Society of Jesus, St. John of God, and students from schools and seminars of the city. The crowd of people who attended the funeral ceremony was so large that the temple and porches of the convent filled quickly and spilled onto the surrounding streets.

The High Mass was sung by Dr. Don Juan Ignacio de Castorena y Ursua, Chaplain of Honor and His Majesty's Preacher, Theologian of the Papal Nuncio in Spain, former President and retired professor of Scripture at the Royal University, Vicar General of the Indian, and Cantor of the Cathedral of México.

In the first of four funeral sermons, the Illustrious and Very Reverend Archbishop of Manila, Don Carlos de Bermudez y Castro said:

> Only do not forgive his great prudence that distinguished his pecularity that all observed in the feet of the religius cadaver, so docile and so tractable, so beautiful without a wrinkle or any mark. Feet that traveled so many thousands of leagues, so barefooted and tired on the journeys, so hardened in the stony ground, so muddy in the swamps, so broken in the mountains, so injured in the brush, so bloodied in the thorns, as we all know, it seems prodigy, more than contingency as many times the Lord is worthy of manifesting his acceptance as Saint Anthony's preaching in the incorruption of his language, the alms of Saint Esteban, the king, in the incorruption of his arm...."

He concluded by saying, "It was these magnificent feet that were the target of the attention of the people of México City the last three days as he lay in his coffin."

The venerable ceremony lasted from ten o'clock in the morning to one o'clock in the afternoon. The beautiful and majestic temple, rebuilt ten years earlier, looked glorious. The church had a splendid history as the headquarters of the first twelve Franciscan monks, headed by Martín de Valencia, who were authorized by the Pope to evangelize New Spain. It replaced the church dedicated to Saint Joseph and now was the home of many relics, among which were: a thorn from the crown of Jesus, a splinter of his Holy Cross, a bone of San Felipe de Jesus, another from Saint Anthony, another from St. Diego, and a tooth of Saint Lorenzo.

But on this day, the beauty of the main chapel of the old church was impossible to appreciate for the large number of faithful who had come to pay their last respects to the venerable father. Even the authorities, both civilian and religious, had difficulty performing their duties. Every step of the procession carrying the simple wooden coffin to its final resting place was incredibly difficult.

It was one o'clock in the afternoon when the procession reached the presbytery and his body was laid to rest in a vault, graciously donated by Don Joseph Hurtado de Mendoza and his wife, both counts of the valley of Orizaba. Here the venerable Father Margil was placed next to the gospel, at the foot of the altar of San Diego beside two small infants who were relatives of the counts. The people felt this was a fitting tribute to a man who lived like an angel to be accompanied in death by two small angels.

The very reverend teacher Juan Antonio de Mora, eyewitness to the funeral, said of the funeral, "*In my judgment, there have been no greater if San Antonio de Padua or San Francisco Javier had died in México with everyone publicly announcing the heroicness of his virtues through voices.*"

In death, the extraordinary life of Father Antonio Margil de Jesús became a legend for future generations to honor his works. During his lifetime, this venerable servant of God was known for his devotion to the teachings of Christ and his zeal for the religious advancement of others, all the time guided by the virtue of humility and considering himself as "*nothing.*" He lived by faith alone.

EPILOGUE

Rome, Italy
July 1836

After Father Margil's death in 1726, information was gathered on his life works and reported miracles. A book was written by his fellow brother and friend Fray Isidro Félix Antonio de Espinosa in the mid-1700s. Since then many other works have been written and dedicated to the friar in hopes of preserving his legend and myth for future canonization to sainthood.

Records show that a decree for introduction of the cause of Father Margil was first issued on July 19, 1769. But due to political unrest in Europe, the push for his beatification to sainthood was interrupted. During this time, México continued to champion his saintly prospects by raising the necessary funds and documentation of miracles needed for the process. It was not until July 31, 1836, that Pope Gregory XVI, through the Sacred Congregation of Rites, issued a decree recognizing his theological, cardinal, and appended virtues by raising him to a heroic degree.

With this act, this Holy Man became Venerable Father Friar Antonio Margil de Jesús and was recognized as a true servant of God, the first breakthrough in the long process of beatification and canonization.

Today in México, where he is already considered a saint by the masses, his saintly prospects for beatification continue through the efforts of the Franciscan Province of Saints Francis and James in México. In the United States, the efforts are through the Margil House of Studies in Houston, Texas.

Three days after his death, he was buried in a wooden coffin at the Church of San Francisco in México City where his tomb became an immediate place of pilgrimage. In 1861 he was exhumed and reburied at the Chapel of La Purísima in the metropolitan Cathedral of México City. From there, his holy remains were exhumed again and finally came to rest at the Guadalupe Friary in Zacatecas, formerly known as the College of Guadalupe de Zacatecas. A place he knew well and a place that remains a site of pilgrimage in his honor to this day.

A simple Latin inscription was engraved on his coffin. Its translation reads:

"Here lies the mortal remains of the Venerable Servant of God, Fray Antonio Margil, founder, missionary, prefect and guardian of the Colleges of Propaganda Fide of Santa Cruz de Querétaro of Cristo Crucificado de Guatemala and of Santa Maria de Guadalupe de Zacatecas, which he erected in the Kingdom of New Spain. He was famous for his virtues and celebrated for his miracles. He died in this Convento Grande de San Francisco in the City of México on August 6, in the year of our Lord, 1726. The memory of him shall not depart away, and his name shall be in request from generation to generation."

ACKNOWLEDGMENTS

Writing a historical novel takes the coordination of many people and institutions, directly and indirectly. For this reason, I give my sincere thanks to all who provided data, reviews, and encouragement for the realization of *Espinas.*

In particular, I thank our Lord for the joy of allowing me to see this work completed and the Blessed Virgin Mary for her many intercessions.

To my wife Elia and our daughter Magali, for their infinite patience during the many months it took to develop this work. Without their loving support, it would not have been possible.

Miraculously, I believe the spirit of Father Margil through God's divine intervention brought this English version of *Espinas* to fruition. On Leap Day, February 29, 2012, I met the Nacogdoches sisters, Peggy Arriola Jasso and Linda Arriola Austin, over the Internet. It was totally by accident as they were researching Father Margil's extraordinary life. It was through this chance encounter and their tireless work editing the book from Spanish to English that this work was made possible. They made important additions to the text, reorganized some chapters, and helped to make it more readable and understandable in English. I am deeply grateful to them.

My greatest gratitude also goes to Franciscan Friar Father Flavio Chavez Garcia O.F.M., Vicar of the Franciscan Province of Saints Peter and Paul of Michoacán and the Rector of the *College of Santa Cruz of Miracles* in Querétaro, México, for allowing me to live the life of a Franciscan missionary at the convent for two months. From this experience the idea for this book was born.

Also, my gratitude goes to Father Fray Octavio de la Cruz O.F.M., the postulator of the cause of Father Antonio Margil, from the Franciscan Province of Saints Francis and James of Jalisco for his support.

Others who helped by reviewing the book are the prominent Catholic journalist Gilberto Hernández García, correspondent of the *El Observador* newspaper; Pilar Meyer, historian from the Anahuac University of Puebla; and Father Fray José Maria Falo Espés, O.F.M., secretary of the Franciscan Province of Valencia, Spain.

My historical research has come from professional thesis, articles and publications of various authors. Three authors are critical when approaching the work. They are *The Exemplary Life of the Venerable Father Friar Antonio Margil de Jesus,* written in the mid-1700s by Father Isidro Félix de Espinosa and translated by Debbie S. Cunningham, and edited by Brian Imhoff, both from Texas A&M University, and made available online by SFASU; *1792 Crónica of Fray Juan Domingo Arricivita*, of the College of Propaganda Fide of Santa Cruz; and *Life of Fray Antonio Margil, O.F.M.,* written in 1959 by Eduardo Enrique Rios and translated by Benedict Leutenegger, O.F.M.

ABOUT THE AUTHOR

Fernando Pérez Valdez is a full time writer with special focus on historical novels based on the lives of Spanish missionaries who lived during the sixteenth and seventeenth centuries. His first novel *Morir en Japón,* To Die in Japan, was about the Franciscan missionary Friar Bartholomew Laurel, who was born in México City and died in 1627 in Nagasaki, Japan when he was thrown into a bonfire. It was published in Spanish in 2011 by the Archdiocese of Acapulco with the seal of approbation from the Archbishop Carlos Garfias Merlos.

He is also the co-author of the art book *Santuario de Nuestra Señora de El Pueblito* published in 2009. It is a collector's edition that showcases the artistic treasures of the holy sanctuary located in Querétaro, México. His second novel, *Espinas,* is about the Franciscan missionary Venerable Friar Antonio Margil de Jesús, was published in Spanish in March 2012 by the Franciscan Province of Saints Peter and Paul of Michoacán, México. The book was reviewed and approved by the postulator of the canonization cause for Venerable Father Antonio Margil de Jesús in Rome, Italy.

He is working on his third novel, *Siempre Alelante, Always Forward,* is about the life of Father Junipero Serra, the Franciscan missionary who was the driving force behind the establishment of the Spanish missions of California during the colonial era.

He has also written several short stories. One of them was awarded with an Honorary Citation by the Ketzakoatl newspaper and the other was included in a compilation of short stories published in Argentina. He serves as executive editor of the *Santa María del Pueblito*, a bimonthly magazine.

He lives in Corregidora, Querétaro, México and is a member of the Historical Novel Society.

www.ingramcontent.com/pod-product-compliance
Lightning Source LLC
Chambersburg PA
CBHW020508120726
47904CB00003B/743